Simon's Choice

by

Charlotte Castle

Comment from Kim Jewell, author of 'Invisible Justice': *Emotionally charged, vivid detail, delivered with a loving touch that makes the reader feel a part of the family and their turmoil.*

Comment by David Loftus, author of 'End Time Gentlemen': *I can hear them setting my table in Hell now because there were parts of this that made me laugh. The fact that it's about something so dark and traumatic gives it a real edge. Powerful rather than bathetic. An excellent book that deserves to do tremendously well.*

Comment by Sly, author of Stonefish: *I couldn't stop reading. It turns from heart warming to heart breaking, with no 'reality Etch a Sketch'. Seldom has a piece of fiction moved me so much. The reader becomes so deeply enmeshed in this entire family and its tragedy.*

Comment from author Garlen Lo: *A great writer. Clear, crisp, with that all important great 'voice.'*

Comment from Patricia Herlevi, author of 'All Saints' Day': *A powerful and transformative novel about battling with an illness, free of clichés and stereotypes and full of humanity.*

ISBN   1453681795

EAN   9781453681794

'Simon's Choice' is published by Taylor Street Publishing LLC, who can be contacted at:

http://www.taylorstreetbooks.com
http://ninwriters.ning.com

Dedication

For those who believed in me

SC, RE, KMcM, AB, PB, DB, HB, GS, TR, SAC & MS.

...and anyone who has ever lost a child.

Chapter 1

"Sarah! Hurry up!"

Sarah thundered down the stairs. Porridge, the yellow Labrador, bounded behind her. The little girl stopped in front of her mother, chin lifted defiantly. "I'm not wearing it, Mum,"

Melissa studied her daughter. Slight for seven years of age, and pale. But Sarah was unmistakably beautiful. "Are you sure?"

"Yup."

"Alright, then. Oh Christ, Sarah – you can't wear that top, it's got a stain. You'll have to go and change it." An insistent car horn sounded from the driveway. "Quickly, please. Porridge, kitchen." She turned toward the door. "We're coming."

* * *

Simon glared at the open front door of the house and bashed the heel of his hand on the car horn again. He flicked a switch, lowering the Jaguar's passenger side window. "Guys! Did I mention we're late?"

Still, the doorway remained infuriatingly empty. His wife's disembodied voice floated toward him from somewhere inside.

Somewhere, Simon noted with weary irritation, that was not nearly close enough to the car.

"I'm just feeding Porridge, Sime." The voice yelled. *"I've sent Sarah up to change her top."*

"Brilliant," Simon muttered. He turned on the radio, resigned to a long wait, and caught his reflection in the rear-view mirror. *Was that more grey in his hair? It was certainly still thick. He wasn't doing badly for forty-two, he supposed.*

"And you're really sure?" His wife's voice through the open window interrupted his thoughts. He glanced up, confused, until he realized she wasn't speaking to him.

"Yeah, don't worry about it, Mum."

The rear car door opened, then slammed shut.

"Come on then, let's go." Melissa slid into the passenger seat. "I swear that dog of yours is unfillable. Next time, we get a goldfish, yeah? You strapped in, Sarah?"

"Yup."

Simon glanced up again at the rear-view mirror. His daughter beamed back at him and he immediately shot a quizzical look at Melissa. A slight frown and shake of the head warned him not to mention it.

Shrugging, he nosed the car out of the drive. "Do you think the Bailey family will ever be on time for church?"

"Probably not," Melissa said, smoothing a blonde hair back into her chignon. "We'll just sneak into a back pew. Are you warm enough, Sarah?"

"Uh huh."

Simon allowed himself another quick look at his daughter. So. She'd decided not to wear it. She'd complained about it itching before. It wasn't that he was uncomfortable seeing Sarah like that, it was just… she looked so different from other kids. So vulnerable.

So bald.

He turned left down their road, heading towards St Matthew's. Now that they were finally in the car, he gleaned a simple enjoyment from the normality of it all. He particularly relished Sundays these days. Family day. Those words meant so much more when their continuity had been threatened. How very different it had all been a year ago.

Sarah was five when she was first diagnosed with acute lymphocytic leukemia. They say General Practitioners, or GP's as they are commonly called, are the most unsympathetic parents. It was true that at first Simon didn't find Sarah's tiredness concerning. She was at a whiny age and really, who *did* want to get up and go to school or work? Simon was strict. She wasn't ill, so she went to school.

Then things began to change. Little signs that dropped in unannounced. Teachers began to report back that her grades had dropped. She wasn't playing with friends. She wasn't taking part anymore.

They decided to move her bedtime to half an hour earlier. She asked to go to bed even earlier. She lost weight. She flinched as if in pain when hugged. She was constantly covered in bruises.

Simon, the GP, finally sent her to *her* GP. Her GP sent her for tests. The results came back. Leukemia.

So they had their answer. An answer as to why the sink was full of blood after she brushed her teeth; why their formerly vibrant little girl missed the cartoons and stayed in bed until 10 a.m. on a Saturday. Their daughter wasn't lazy, she wasn't stupid. She was tired. She was tired because she was ill. Very ill.

The trips to hospital began. Back and forth, sometimes three times a day. Tests, radio, chemo, more tests, more radio. Unlike Melissa, it wasn't the smell that bothered him. That hospital tang: chemicals, latex, cabbage, sick. As a medical student twelve years ago, he had become immune to the institutionalized odor of the wards and corridors. What bothered Simon was the noise. The beeping, the murmuring. The hushed tones of the other parents desperately trying to pretend that *everything was alright*, or the abrasive, too-loud chatter of the nurses. The beeps and bongs, coughs and retches – each sound redolent of private miseries. Miseries that the parents, passing each other in the hallways, sharing the family room, making endless cups of tea, never really discussed – never allowed to crack their carefully crafted veneer of optimism. There was no need of course - *everything was alright.*

Staring at Sarah's tiny little body, pitifully small on a strange, hard bed, it was hard to pretend things would be okay. Cold bed-frames surrounded her. Her only lullaby was the interminable beeping of machines. Usually she had the same bed in a corner of the children's cancer ward. Once, during a particularly harrowing time, it was hers for three long months. On shorter visits the nurses tried to make sure she got *'her bed'*. It was rather like being the best customer of a smart restaurant - *'Your usual bed, Madame?'* - only the food wasn't as good, and you got your drinks through a tube.

The family made friends with the nurses, got to know shift patterns. They knew which coffee machines worked best, which canteen sandwiches were most palatable. Security greeted them by name on arrival. Confused visitors in the foyer would instinctively ask them for directions. They recognized Simon and Melissa as people-in-the-know. As people who *belonged.*

The prognosis remained the same: thirty percent chance of survival. Simon had mulled this terrifying, all-important figure through his mind for nearly two years. He knew every permutation, every manipulation of those numbers so that they sounded best. Three in ten chance. Fifteen in fifty. He massaged the statistic, he summed up. He pushed it further to forty. And hey, eighty seven percent of all statistics are made up, aren't they?

15

And then came the breakthrough three months ago. The cancer was in remission. The blood cells were regrouping. Following the trauma of chemotherapy the granulocytes and monocytes were re-armed, the rebel lymphocytes were retreating and the battle had turned in their favor. Macrophages joined on the Allied side. The consultants reported from the front line with renewed energy – the tide was turning. The numbers changed – sixty percent chance of survival.

And Sarah came home. His beautiful, clever, precious daughter came back. Twice a week she returned to the ward for chemo, but every night he tucked her into her own bed. Not the second home the nurses so wrongly called 'her bed', but her proper bed. It was wooden and traditional with hearts cut out of the headboard. Not wipeable, nor wheelable. It didn't have bars and it didn't raise or lower. It was homely, traditional – normal.

They were becoming a normal family again. Doing normal things. Having normal rows. The house resonated with normal complaints – *"Don't leave your PSP there", "I can't find my trainers", "Straight to bed if you don't eat those sprouts", "It's not fair…"*

Not once over the entire two years, did Sarah ever mention the fairness of having cancer. Having to eat sprouts, brush her teeth, tidy her room, stay away from sweets after 6 p.m., all these were unfair. All these were loudly moaned about. But never, never did she complain about cancer.

Simon smiled a thanks at the elderly lady handing out hymn books at the church entrance. He flinched as her face crumpled with pity as she took in Sarah's head, her skull looking as fragile as a bird's in its pinkly naked state. Simon followed Melissa and Sarah as they walked hand in hand down the aisle, feeling a surge of anger. He hated watching members of the congregation turn to watch the little bald girl. The quick whispers and the sly second glances, followed by apologetic and pitying smiles aimed at him. A woman in an expensive looking Russian fur hat actually pursed her lips in a *moue* of distaste. Simon wanted to hit her.

Just as the family were filing into the pew in front of her, Sarah's head suddenly turned. She piped up with bell-like clarity. "Daddy, why does that woman have a cat on her head?"

Chapter 2

Terry grinned and held out his arms. "Hey, Tiger. How's my beautiful girl?"

"Granddad!" Sarah flew down the garden path to greet Simon's father. Porridge padded along beside her. "We've just got back from church. Grandma and Grandpa Aitch are already here – Grandma says she's gone to look at the veg' patch, but she's not really, she's having a fag and Grandpa's in a mood 'cos Mum won't let him watch Formula One and she says she's made special mash for him without butter in, and gravy without any fat in, and he says the diet will be the death of him, never mind the heart attack, and Dad says we can take Porridge to the Shibden Park Dog Competition and I'm going to…"

"Whoa, let me get in first, Sarah. All in time." The seventy year old man, trim and attractive in his pale pink Pringle jumper, glanced back down the smartly bricked driveway towards his car and his wife. "Help Granny bring the pudding and things in. There's a good girl."

He looked up at his son and daughter-in-law's imposing brick house, admiring it once again and filling with pride at his son's achievements. Modern, but with a nod to the regency style, with large bay windows and a grand portico over the door. Sarah trotted back to his side, carrying a couple of Tupperware boxes.

"You're looking well, Tiger, looking lovely. What a pretty skirt."
Terry Bailey appraised his only Grandchild quickly, hoping his face
didn't reveal his shock. She looked more rounded, less breakable, but
- her head. Her little bare head. It seemed so brutal, so acute. Still,
she was out of bed and clearly well. "Have you put on weight? You
look almost plump. You'll be on mash without butter soon. Get
down, Porridge." He gave the over-excited Labrador a hearty rub
and a pat, then followed Sarah into his son's house for their family's
weekly Sunday get together.

Melissa appeared in the doorway, glass of wine in hand. "Terry!
Barbara! I love your new hair-do. Very Honor Blackman." Melissa
embraced her in-laws. "Dad's in the conservatory. He's in a huff
because I won't let him watch some nasty, noisy cars going round a
track and Mum's having a look at the vegetable patch."

"Still smoking then, is she?" Terry's kind face wrinkled with
laughter.

"Terrance!" Barbara clouted her husband with a glove then turned
to her daughter-in-law. "That crumble needs forty minutes on gas-
mark five, Melissa. You're looking well and let me see. Let's look at
Sarah properly. Say! You *have* put on weight, Sarah. You look great.
Get *down*, Porridge."

The two women walked into the sunshine yellow kitchen, flooded
with light that streamed in through the new conservatory. Melissa
ducked under a large chandelier so she could set the crumble on a

vast pine table that was surrounded by an assortment of mismatched chairs. Beyond the table, the room merged into the conservatory area where Robert, Melissa's father, sat on a sofa, a glass of merlot beside him, frowning as he scanned the TV Times. Beanbags and video games scattered the terracotta-tiled floor. Porridge's basket, overflowing with well-loved and well-chewed toys sat by a wood-burning stove

The back door flew open as Diana, Melissa's mother, swept into the room, bringing with her the frozen January air.

"Barbara, darling, You're here." Diana flung a cashmere-clad arm around her son-in-law's mother, the gesture releasing a waft of Coco Chanel into the room. "I love your new 'do. Terry, you old rogue, let me give you a hug. How's that back?"

Terry grinned. "Not bad. A week on a sun lounger would help it. Did you get the brochures we sent you?"

Melissa smiled to herself as she made her way back into the kitchen to check on the roast chicken and stir the bread sauce. She opened another bottle of wine, half listening to the two sets of grandparents as they amicably discussed the pros and cons of various gîtes in Brittany.

The Bailey Sunday Lunch, attended weekly by both Bailey and Halford grandparents, was a twelve-year old tradition. Despite their different backgrounds, Melissa and Simon's parents had become firm friends from the moment they first met at a BBQ arranged by their courting children.

"Do you remember that watermill we stayed in, when Sarah was about four, Melissa?" Barbara, called from the conservatory end of the kitchen. "There's a lovely gîte very close to there. Just the right size for the lot of us and walking distance from the sea."

"I'll take a look at the brochure after lunch. Red or white, Barbara?"

"Can I be a pain and have a sherry, pet?"

"Course." Melissa poured the sherry and a bitter for her father-in-law. "It would be lovely to all get off together again. Like old times. Like before."

Barbara took the drink. "LBL – that's what Terry and I call it. Life Before Leukemia. A holiday is just what we all need. What will this be? Our sixth all together?"

"Fifth." Simon strolled into the kitchen and poured himself a glass of wine. "Sarah's just putting her Lego away, by the way. Yeah, it's the fifth. Do you know, I feel quite robbed of the opportunity to tell mother-in-law jokes. We all get on far too well." He grinned and joined his family in the conservatory area. "It's all a bit smug really, isn't it?"

Robert, Melissa's father, put his magazine down and took up his glass. "Lucky thing. You need a bit of unity in your life, what you've been through. To the Halfords and Baileys. Long may we be a family unit."

The family raised their glasses together, the toast familiar.

"Halfords and Baileys!"

Diana and Robert Halford, were both retired school teachers. Barbara and Terry Bailey, on the other hand, were respectively a housewife and the supervisor of a bus depot. Both couples were equally thrilled with their children's match. Diana and Robert were just as proud as his own parents when Simon, the shy South Yorkshire medical student, became a fully-fledged GP.

Both sets of grandparents took news of Sarah's leukemia staunchly and with British grit. They had rallied around their terrified children - dog-sitting, tea-making and house-watching whilst staying resolutely cheerful throughout, constantly optimistic. Melissa's freezer was kept well stocked and her floristry business babysat when she needed to be at Leeds General Infirmary eighteen hours a day. Simon's car was washed and the leaking gutter mysteriously fixed whilst he was at work. Individual child-sized portions of homemade favorites were dropped into LGI for Sarah. Barbara's cat got used to having Porridge around.

For a while Sunday lunches had stopped. But the weekly summits between the grandparents had continued at Diana and Robert's house. Diana always provided the main course and Barbara, as ever, brought puddings. It was around Diana's pine refractory table that they shared out dog-sitting duties, agonized over prognoses, and made practical plans for a potentially dark future.

Now the tables were turning. The statistics were looking better. They had quietly discussed emergency measures for so long, planned how best to deal with forthcoming grief. Now it seemed action would never have to be taken. Their clever little granddaughter was beating the odds. The family that they had been so careful to nurture, so horrified to see so damaged, was starting to find happiness again.

* * *

"Am I to be banned pudding as well?" Robert snapped as his daughter handed him a specially prepared, low-cholesterol, non-heart-condition-aggravating version of their meal. Robert's heart attack six months ago had been minor, his weeklong stay in hospital completely over-shadowed by a pivotal week in Sarah's treatment. But his collapse during a weekly bridge game still served as a stark reminder that they needed to look after themselves, as well as Sarah. All three women had leaped into action, promising the doctor to reduce the bon-viveur's waistband from a well-rounded forty-two inches, to the medically preferred thirty-four. The patient was an ungrateful one and Diana was forever finding Fruit & Nut wrappers under his car seat.

23

"Dad, you know you can have the crumble. Just not the cream." Melissa gave the same answer she gave every Sunday. "Sarah, I want to see all those greens gone please, no excuses. Porridge, there's no point sitting there looking like that. Nobody's going to feed you at the table." Simon and his father both whipped their hands back into view as Porridge settled himself down between them.

Terry helped himself to gravy. "So, no more chemo eh, Tiger? I hear you're back at school full time now. Climbed back up to top place yet?"

"Terrance!"

"I'm only asking, Barbara. She's a clever kid. If anyone can catch up she can. Comes from clever stock eh, Simon?"

Sarah looked up from her chicken. "English is okay, but I'm rubbish at math. I hate math. I missed the seven and eight times tables and the whole beginning of fractions. Caitlin Harris is worse than me though. She doesn't even know her two times table and she never misses school. Oh and Jacob Davidson got detention and had his lunch monitor badge taken off him because he said I was a freak with no hair and Mrs. Bainbridge heard him. Did I tell you, Dad says we can take Porridge to the dog show?" Sarah swerved the conversation suddenly, as seven year olds are apt to do.

"You should have thumped him, lass."

"Terrance!"

"What?"

"How's everything at the surgery, Simon? Shall I top you up?" Diana glugged cheap red into her son-in-law's glass and filled her own. "Everyone still off having babies?"

Simon took a sip from his replenished glass. "The Practice Manager is back, thank God, but the Practice Nurse goes on Maternity Leave next week and one of the admin staff has decided she's not coming back. Also, there are talks about the surgery shutting and us moving into a sparkly new Medical Centre in town. The local ladies of leisure have embraced it as a *'cause'* and keep popping up with placards. Add to the mix that every person who's sneezed or coughed in the last month thinks they've got Swine 'Flu, it's been a pretty fun week."

Diana scoffed. "Swine 'Flu. Load of stuff and nonsense. How's the florists, Melissa?"

"Not bad, Mum. Ticking over. Can't expect better in this climate. We're starting floristry courses – glass of wine thrown in, learn how to hand-tie a bouquet, that kind of thing. Got a wedding coming up next Saturday. I'm hoping Swine 'Flu is going to take off – lots of funerals…"

"That's not very nice, Mum." Sarah said quietly.

There was a slight pause. "Your Mum's just kidding, Tiger. Load of sensationalized nonsense anyway. It'll all be over by the end of the week. Now tell your old Granddad about this dog show. What's

Porridge going in for then? Best Fed Dog?" Porridge put his chin in Terry's lap, hoping for another bit of chicken.

Barbara got up. "I'll help you clear, love. Who wants custard and who wants cream?"

* * *

"That was a pretty crass remark you made over lunch."

Simon and Melissa leaned against the counters in the kitchen as Simon poured the last of the wine. The grandparents had gone in the same flurry of kisses as they had arrived, and Sarah was drinking warm milk and watching cartoons in the sitting room.

"I know. I didn't think."

"Didn't think? Christ, Melissa, how can you think of anything else? If our daughter catches a bloody cold it could kill her, never mind Swine 'Flu. What, are you planning to do the flowers for her funeral, too?"

"Simon, that's a disgusting thing to say. You're drunk."

"A little." Simon sighed heavily. "Come on. Let's get her off to bed then we can watch Midsomer Murders."

"Dad, can I watch Midsomer Murders?" Sarah's head popped through the kitchen door. "I'll be very quiet."

"No, darling, you've school tomorrow. You look shattered anyway. Go on, go up and get those teeth brushed and I'll come up and read you a story."

Sarah traipsed off, muttering, Porridge faithfully in tow.

"I'm sorry, Mel. I shouldn't have said that. It's just that with things looking so much better ... you are using the antibacterial wipes, aren't you?"

"Don't worry, Simon. We're going to be fine. She's a fighter, we've been through the worst."

"I know. Come here, give me a hug. That was a cracking roast you did today, honey - my Dad always said - at *least* she can cook." He gathered his wife into his arms but quickly leaped back, laughing as Melissa pretended to clip him around the ear. "Are you ready for me, Sarah?" Simon yelled up the stairs, dodging as Melissa changed tactic and tried to flick him with a tea towel. "I hope those teeth have been cleaned properly…"

* * *

Upstairs, Sarah rinsed out the sink and held her toothbrush under the tap. There was no need for Dad to see all the blood that had streamed from her mouth as she gently brushed. They'd been bleeding again like that for a week now but it didn't hurt.

Dad would only worry.

27

Chapter 3

"No, no, Mr Varley, you did the right thing making an appointment. Always better to err on the side of caution."

Erring on the side of caution was not something Mr Varley actually needed encouragement to do. As one of Simon's most determined hypochondriacs, Ernest Varley visited his doctor at least once a month, and frequently more. The mole that Simon had just inspected, sited as far down Mr Varley's back as is possible before it became an internal examination, was fine. Mr Varley's moles, pains, veins, coughs and aches were always fine.

His previous three patients - a teenage girl dragged in by her mother who wanted her prescribed the pill, a particularly odious four year old with conjunctivitis and a jolly lady with quite the worst fungal nail infection he had ever seen – had all been dealt with quickly and he was, for once, running on time. As long as the Practice Meeting didn't over-run (and without Howard, the Senior Partner, there to meddle it wasn't likely to) he should be away and in his car for 6 p.m.

He saw Mr Varley to the door then pulled at his tie, unbuttoning his top shirt button.

His consulting room was small, but full of light, with an unobstructed view of the small town's scrubby park.

Brighouse was not an attractive town. Any proof of its bustling industrial past was limited to a couple of handsome Edwardian high street bank buildings and a couple of cheaply done mill conversions. The canal and river that ran through the town had been tidied up, and an attempt made at creating 'waterside living'. A number of family delis and bistros had managed to find sufficient business to tick over, but the main shopping street looked tired. The serried ranks of West Riding back to back terraces were largely uncared for. Vast council estates provided housing for legions of impoverished families who kept Simon's practice busy with teenage pregnancies, alcohol and drug related illnesses, and ailments caused by bad nutrition. There had even been a recent case of rickets – an illness supposedly wiped out by 50 years of improved national nourishment.

Simon had grown up in a 1960s two bedroom semi', in the South Yorkshire town of Barnsley. Not poor, but certainly not well off, his working class parents had encouraged him to study hard and believe in himself. His nights were spent furiously scribbling away in his bedroom at a desk made out of bricks and an old door. Terry and Barbara had been so sure of his place at Barnsley Grammar School that they had saved for two years so they could buy him a watch for passing his eleven-plus entrance exam.

His school days were unremarkable. He kept his nose down, largely eschewing the common distractions of girls and stolen cigarettes. He was no 'square'. He managed the occasional school disco grope and he got drunk on cheap cider once or twice – the most memorable occasion being when he was sick in his friend's mother's goldfish bowl. (The fish were still in it).

Still, Simon worked hard, his natural ability greatly enhanced by his determined nature. It came as no surprise when he was given a place at Leeds Medical School. A steady student career followed, in which he adequately met the course requirements but failed to shine by the highly competitive standards of the prestigious medical college.

In the summer term of his final year, his last surviving grandmother died, leaving her house and a small nest egg to his father. For four years, Simon made daily commutes from their small terraced house in Barnsley to Leeds, using the 50 minute train journey to study. Whilst the journey was not arduous, he was largely left out of 'student living' and had only a small circle of friends as a result. His father, deciding his son deserved the full student experience, bequeathed his inherited house to Simon and with this grand gesture bought Simon a social life.

The house, a little red brick, three-bedroom terrace in the Burley Park area, became a Mecca for (what felt like) much of the student population of Leeds. Since it was privately owned and not subject to the rules and regulations of a long-suffering landlord, the parties were frequent and legendary. His flatmates, who paid a small rent to Simon's dad, painted the previously floral sitting room black and installed marshal stacks and disco lights. The house shook to the strains of Guns 'n' Roses and Def Leppard. The neighbors gave up complaining and bought earplugs.

Simon had never met most of the people who passed through his front door, filling the avocado colored bath with bottles of beer and throwing up spectacularly in his toilet.

During one such night, he staggered into his room, intending to sleep before an important ward round the next day. In the gloom he tripped over a body on the floor. Irritated at this intrusion of his personal space, he woke her up, and then spent half an hour holding her hair back whilst she vomited cheap red wine and cheesy puffs into his basin. For the rest of the night they sat on his bed, talking about everything and anything.

By the time dawn broke, he had fallen in love.

He lent her a Motorhead t-shirt since her Lurex boob tube was unsuitable for the early morning walk home. It also provided a perfect excuse to see her again. Melissa was an art student. Her moderately wealthy parents had set her up with digs near the School of Art and they began to meet each day to drink coffee in her pretty little kitchenette, talking about everything from politics to George Michael to Rubens and surgical procedures.

They didn't kiss for three weeks. When they did, it felt right. A Liebfraumilch-fuelled mutual loss of their virginity sealed their couple status. Melissa moved into the Burley Park terrace, sent

Simon's tenants packing and started saving for Laura Ashley wallpaper. Anxious to start her life as a grown-up, and realizing that she had expensive taste in soft furnishings, she dropped out of her art degree and took a part-time job in the glove department of Marshall & Snelgrove's Department Store.

Even now, twelve years later, it still felt right. Mostly. The last two years had been hard. The worry, the overnight vigils at the hospital and the constant fear for Sarah had an impact on their relationship. Simon felt they had drifted apart a little. Sometimes it felt as if they were little more than friends. Friends who happened to sleep in the same bed and share a bank account. But, after all he assured himself, it had been twelve years. Of course some of the passion had gone.

He put the photo of Melissa back on his desk, next to one of Sarah and Porridge. He'd nip over to Sainsbury's later and grab a bottle of wine before the practice meeting. He knew better than to buy Melissa supermarket flowers, but perhaps he'd get her a box of chocolates or a special bubble bath as a treat. Things were so much better at home now. It was time to spend some time on his marriage.

* * *

"Wine and bubble bath. I am a lucky girl. What's the occasion?" Melissa stretched luxuriantly in the gardenia-scented bath water and took the glass of Gewürztraminer Simon held out to her.

"Being married to you. Getting home on time for once. Loving my family and thinking perhaps I ought to say it more often. Want me to do your back?"

"Ooh, yes please. God, it must be two years since you washed my back for me, Simon. Do you remember that hotel? We did two bottles of champagne in the bath. It seems so very long ago now. Like we hadn't grown up yet then."

"A lot's happened since then." Simon unclipped his cufflinks and laid them on the edge of the bath, then rolled up his sleeves. "Anyway, we have grown up. You're getting to the wrong end of your thirties. What do you want for your fortieth, old lady?"

"I'd like to be 21 again, please."

"Not possible. How about a tumble dryer?"

"Done."

* * *

"... David Cameron threw down the gauntlet last night, when he told Jeremy Paxman that Labour were out..." Simon switched off the morning news and slipped his hands around Melissa's waist.

Melissa jabbed one elbow into his ribs and he grunted. "Oi! I was listening to that. Give Sarah a shout will you? She's still not surfaced. Do you want a bacon sandwich as well?"

"Yes, and I'll pretend you said muesli. I'll go get lazy bones." Simon gave his wife a lingering kiss on the neck. "Last night was fun. I should bring you goodies home more often."

"Yes, you should."

Simon patted his wife fondly on the bottom and went off in search of Sarah. Her door was plastered with colorful 'Girls Rool' and 'Kids only - *keep out!*' stickers, and it was closed. He was surprised to find the room still dark, Sarah's hunched shape still curled under the covers. "Sarah! It's ten past eight." Simon pulled open the High School Musical curtains. "Sarah?"

"I'm sleepy. Leave me alone."

"Sarah, honey, are you ill?"

"No, Dad, I'm just tired. Can I stay at home today?"

"Sarah, sit up. I want to look at you. Do you think we should take you in? How long have you been feeling tired? Do you have any pain? Headache?" Simon sat down on the bed and pressed his fingers against his daughter's neck. "Does this hurt? You don't feel swollen."

Sarah groaned and turned over to face him. "I'm just tired, Dad. That's all. I'm OK, I'll get up now."

"Okay, but you're sure you're alright? Just tired? You can stay home if you want. I'll call Grandma Aitch, have her take you back to her house…"

"I'm fine, Dad. Really."

"Alright. But call me at lunchtime if you want picking up, okay? Now hurry up, you've got ten minutes and I want you downstairs. Mum's made you a bacon sandwich. Hey! Last monthly check-up session next week, isn't it? Shall we do something to celebrate? How about Pizza Hut and a film?"

"Yeah, I'd like that. Can I bring a friend? Can Izzy come?"

"Yes, tell her to ask her mum today. You can invite someone else as well if you like. Come on now, up and at 'em."

Simon grabbed a tie from his wardrobe and headed back to the kitchen. "Have you noticed any changes in Sarah recently? Is she more tired at the moment?"

"No, I don't think so. I certainly struggle to get her to bed at night. I think it's just that she's back at school full time; she's got a lot on, keeping up with the rest of them. Who does want to get up at this time of year? I hate getting up in the dark."

"Alright. Well, keep an eye on it, yeah? Last monthly check up's next week, yes?

"Yup."

"Good. We'll take her and her friends out for pizza to celebrate." He peered at the sandwiches that Melissa had prepared and left on

35

the side." Has this one got brown sauce in it? Can I grab it and go? I'm running behind. Thanks, love. See you tonight – I'll be a bit late, I'm going down to St Matthew's to help move the stacks of chairs out of the small hall. Have a good day. Get *down*, Porridge."

Simon kissed his wife and dashed out of the door, bacon butty in hand, briefcase in the other. It was barely light outside, the street lamps shining orange dapples on the wet tarmac. He swung open his car door and tossed in his briefcase, then lowered himself into the driver's seat. Inside the car, he balanced his breakfast on one leg while brushing off blonde Labrador hairs from his suit. He wondered if eight years old was too late to send a dog for training, then slid his key in the ignition and steered his Jaguar out of the drive.

* * *

The Scouts were already helping the Rev Duncan Hughes when Simon turned up a little past seven that evening.

"Sorry, sorry – I got held up. I see you found some helpers, though." Simon watched a small boy attempt to lift a stack of eight chairs before coming to his senses and splitting the tower into more manageable twos. Trying not to sound like an overbearing grown up, he stepped toward the next stack of chairs. "Here, let me give you a hand."

"Simon, it was good of you to offer at all. I do have some excellent helpers. I think Mrs. Hughes is planning to reward them all with squash and biscuits in the vicarage. We may be able to find something a little more fortifying for ourselves, if you take my meaning. Harry, ask Akela to bring you all over when you've finished, will you? Come on, Simon. There's not much more to do here and I want to show you my new bantams."

Simon followed the amiable vicar out of a side door of the church and across the road to the small house that served as a vicarage. The original Victorian vicarage had been sold off long before. It was considered too grand for a modern vicar with his small family, and too big an asset to be wasted on the vicar of a minute and shrinking congregation in the backwaters of West Yorkshire. The 1960s dormer bungalow opposite St Matthew's now served as accommodation for the Rev Duncan Hughes and his wife.

Having no children to fill the four-bedroom property, Rev and Mrs. Hughes had fulfilled their parental instincts by acquiring a bewildering number of animals. Two Jack Russells yapped at the window, their claws tappetty-tapping on the wide windowsills. When Simon stepped inside, he was immediately nearly bowled over by an enormous husky.

"Rasputin, leave him alone."

"It's alright. He can smell Porridge. You're a handsome boy, aren't you? Hullo, Mrs. Hughes. I hear you're expecting the entire Brighouse West Scout Brigade for tea."

"Simon, how lovely to see you. I am. I'm just getting some biscuits out. Would you like a cup of tea, or is Duncan going to sort you out with a whisky?" Mrs. Hughes, a tiny lady, with exquisite bone structure who habitually wore her hair in an elegant grey bob, looked up from the kitchen table, at which she was pouring twenty cups of orange squash. "Have you come to see my new girls?"

"I'm just taking him to see the harem now, Muriel. We'll get a drink in my study. Call us if you want help feeding the five thousand, won't you?"

"Oh, I'm sure I'll manage." Muriel said breezily, removing a cat that was winding its way around the plastic cups.

Simon trailed after Duncan through the back door and into the garden, followed by a motley assortment of dogs and cats. "Is it appropriate for a Church of England vicar to be keeping a harem in his back garden, Duncan?"

"Absolutely not, which is why I wanted one. Look. What do you think, aren't they beauties?"

No. They were not. Simon took in the appalling cluster of hens that stood with a rigid, un-chicken like stance in a large coop in a corner of the garden. Largely without feathers, they were the ugliest

38

birds Simon had ever seen. "Aren't they missing something, Duncan? Feathers for instance?"

"Don't worry about that, they'll be back in no time. They're battery chickens. Rescued them from a charity. They're all a bit shell-shocked at the moment, if you'll pardon the pun, but I'm assured they'll perk up in no time. We've got a cockerel coming as well. Caligula. It's his harem really, not mine."

"So will they lay?"

"Oh yes. They just need a few days to get comfortable with their surroundings. Leonidas! Come away from there." Duncan shooed away an enormous longhaired ginger cat, which was taking more than a passing interest in the hens. "It's alright, he won't get at them. Let's get a drink, shall we? Tell me how everything's going."

They went back into the house and into the dining room, which now served as Duncan's study. Theology books lined the walls whilst more books quivered in unwieldy towers around the corners of the room. A glass vivarium housed a slow worm. Duncan had found the little legless lizard, so often confused with a snake, during a walk and had valiently rescued it from an attacking crow. The Reverend poured two generous whiskies from a cut glass decanter and gestured to a scruffy armchair covered in dog-haired blankets.

"So, Simon. How is Sarah? How are you and Melissa? It's been a rough ride."

"We seem to be coming to the end of the ride. Sarah comes out of monthly supervision next week. Chemo was stopped three months ago. Things are looking up. I admit there were some very bleak days. Overwhelming. You know, I don't think I would have got through it all without you. Thanks for all your help, Duncan."

Duncan had supported Simon through some of the darker days. When they first got the diagnosis, Simon had raged against the Church and against God. Brought up by mildly religious parents and sent to a Church of England primary school, Simon had always kept a quiet faith. Neither pious nor devout, there had been periods in his life when he had not gone to church, when he had questioned the existence of God. Certainly as a medical student there were many times when he doubted the traditional idea of a pre-organized world, a universe in which he was merely a puppet to a grand puppeteer.

Then, a couple of years into Simon's career, Melissa and he had married. A year later, when Sarah was about a year old, they had started going to church weekly, believing an understanding of religious culture and tradition to be an important part of education. Simon enjoyed the simple comfort that came from being a member of a congregation, cushioned from the worries of life for just one hour each week. He enjoyed the ritual, the words and the music. He began to reclaim his faith and to trust there was a good and evil, an afterlife, a heaven. He offered his services for the occasional fête or community clear up and struck up a close friendship with the charming vicar and his elegant, generous wife.

Then Sarah got ill.

Two words: "It's Leukemia", and Simon's whole world, his happy life, came crashing down around him, his ordered existence immeasurably damaged, and it became clear to him that there was no higher being making great spiritual decisions. No Grand Master, looking over us and guiding us through life. How could he believe in a God that could torture a child? How could there be a deity that necessitated the need for Bone Marrow Aspiration from a terrified seven year old? That needle – so big, so brutal, plunging through skin, flesh, fat and finally into the child's actual skeleton, was not the product of a celestial being. It was a man-made instrument made to deal with man's own weaknesses. There was no supreme Father orchestrating a pre-formed plan that day. Only a biological father, scared, shaking and trying to be strong for the weeping little girl in his arms.

So he had stopped going to church. Couldn't face the blind optimism, the promise that we were all loved and would eventually be happy. How could God love his daughter and yet subject her to all this? How could God possibly love him? How was Simon supposed to love a God that had cursed his daughter?

His parents tried to get him to go with them. He refused. Melissa attended when she wasn't required at the hospital. She lit candles and prayed. She read books on theology and spent hours on the Internet reading studies on the power of prayer, trying to find a spiritual solution, an explanation of what was happening.

She brought Duncan home with her one Sunday. Over roast chicken and Chablis, the Reverend reached out to his troubled friend. Simon, having reached a point of mental exhaustion needed a buoy in his emotional storm and trusting his friend and wanting a sense of belonging again, returned to the flock.

Now, sitting in Duncan's cramped little study, Famous Grouse in hand, Simon felt a great sense of calm. The separate components of his life were dropping back into place and the anxieties that had plagued him for two years were slowly seeping away.

"You don't need to thank me, Simon. You always had the strength. You just couldn't remember how to channel it. We all lose faith from time to time."

"Even you?"

"Even me."

"I should have thought you would need an unswerving faith to think those bloody hens are going to lay."

"You watch. You'll be enjoying *Oeuf à la Hughes* by next week. Ah. That sounds like the troops." A flurry of activity in the hallway commenced, as twenty thirsty scouts poured into Mrs. Hughes's kitchen.

"Should we go and help?"

"No, we'll only be in the way. Mrs. Hughes will deal with them. She rules the Foxes Biscuits tin with a rod of iron. I'm too soft and we run out before half of them have had one. Have to keep your eye on the little blighters."

* * *

Twenty minutes later, warmed by the welcome finger of whisky, Simon fought his way through the battalion of differing sized dogs in the hall. He climbed back into the Jaguar, glad to be sheltered from the heavy rain that had begun to fall during his time inside the vicarage. Feeling pleasantly satisfied after his catch-up with Duncan, Simon was looking forward to supper with his family.

As he nosed his car down the familiar street, he was mildly surprised to see his mother-in-law's car on the drive. Whilst the little red Honda was hardly a rare sight by his garage, it was nearing 8 p.m. and Diana, dedicated to her TV Times, would usually be happily ensconced in her sitting room by this time, snuggled up with her husband, dachshund and tray of Turkish Delight.

He waved to her as she popped open the car door and stepped out, seemingly unbothered by the heavy rain. Simon parked the Jag in its usual spot, trying to ignore the slight feeling of unease creeping over him. "Hello, you" he said, grinning. He pressed the button to lower his car window. "Just can't keep away can you?"

Diana's face remained neutral. No smile or amiable riposte was forthcoming. Simon immediately felt a charge in the air, the hairs on his neck rising with fear. "What is it?"

Diana leaned down and peered through the car window. Her face showed the strains of a person who has been rehearsing the delivery of bad news. "Simon, I'm sorry. It's Sarah. We've been trying to call you, but we couldn't get through. Your phone ... Why didn't you have it on? Sarah, she - she collapsed. When she came back from school. They've gone to the hospital. She's very unwell. Your phone was off ..."

"Get in."

Simon wrenched the car into reverse, his expression sharp and cold. Any warmth left from the whisky was gone.

"Which hospital?"

"Huddersfield Royal Infirmary, the ambulance man said ..."

Diana broke off, instinctively grabbing the handle above the passenger door as Simon screeched the Jaguar back down the street-lamp lit road. Back past St Matthew's, back to the hospital.

Back in the direction from which he had only so recently come.

Chapter 4

The car park was beginning to empty at the hospital, visitors reluctantly leaving for the evening. Simon, retaining a doctor's parking permit, nudged his car at the barriers to the staff car park, impatient for the achingly slow hydraulic arm to raise and let him through. The large car splashed through puddles in the badly surfaced car park, the sheets of rain backlit by the neon hospital sign. Diana and Simon leaped out, oblivious to the rain, and ran towards the main hospital entrance.

Inside, the vast four-story atrium was quiet, the only sound a squeaking of rubber shoes as porters scurried between lifts. A woman was packing up a second-hand bookstall for the day. She glanced up at the pair, then looked away quickly, embarrassed by the trauma she instinctively knew she was witnessing. At reception, the man in charge nodded a cool greeting. Simon snapped out his question, demanding the whereabouts of his daughter, and the man calmly checked the records.

"Intensive Therapy Unit, 2nd floor, yellow lift." Diana and Simon ran off in the direction of the lifts, their wet feet slipping on the smooth hospital floor.

* * *

45

"Why the fuck was your phone off?" Melissa rounded on them in the lobby of ITU, too anxious for preliminaries.

"I forgot to turn it back on after surgery. I went to see Duncan. I told you." Simon combed his fingers through his wet hair. "Where is she?"

Melissa brusquely brought him up to speed. "She's in there. She has an infection. Her temperature has been up to 106 and her organs were at risk of failing. They've got her hooked up to all manner of things and she's stable. They're carrying out another Bone Marrow Biopsy now. She's under anesthetic this time." She stopped and swallowed. "Simon, she was covered in bruises. All over her legs. I missed it. *I fucking missed it.*"

Diana stepped forward and folded her distraught daughter into her arms, nodding at Simon over Melissa's shoulder. Simon glanced at a set of swinging doors to his right, labeled 'ITU Bay 4'. A nurse in scrubs shoved through, carrying a kidney dish containing blood-filled vials and assorted clinical detritus. He headed straight for the room, knowing instinctively that his daughter was inside.

A doctor looked up from the bed where his little girl lay prone, attached to tubes, bags, lines, pumps and monitors. Her bare white hip protruded from under the cover, her skin almost as white as the starched sheet.

The consultant looked up. "Dr Bailey? We've just finished the biopsy. Your little girl is very ill. We're doing everything we can."

Simon stared numbly at the seven-year old, barely recognizable through the clutter of apparatus attached to her face and arms. "We missed it. It's back and I missed it." He moved towards the bed, wanting desperately to touch her, but terrified of hurting her, of contaminating her.

"I'm afraid it looks that way. We'll have the results of the biopsy as soon as we can. She has an infection that caused her collapse and we're fighting it successfully at the moment, but it does seem the leukemia has returned. If it has, we'll need to do a spinal tap to ascertain whether the cerebral spine fluid is under attack. If it is, then aggressive treatment will begin immediately. I'm terribly sorry." The consultant covered Sarah's hip back over with the sheet and made a note on a clipboard. "You mustn't blame yourself, Dr Bailey. Relapses at this point can be hard to spot. Your daughter is still weakened by the months of chemotherapy. Parents get used to their child being frail. The parameters are different. The signs that originally rang alarm bells have become normal. The child often doesn't report symptoms, unwilling to cause alarm and accustomed to a different level of wellness than other children. This is not your fault."

Simon stared right through him. "But I'm a doctor." He sank into the institutional blue armchair in the corner of the room.

"But you are a father first, Dr Bailey." The consultant put his pen back in his suit breast pocket. "Sometimes we don't see things that are too close to our eyes."

Simon sat back against the familiar faux leather of the chair, ignoring the clammy stickiness as it pressed against his sopping wet shirt. Those plastic chair backs. He had sat in so many of them. The familiarity was matched by the fears and terrors as they rose to the surface. A machine bleeped, regurgitating dot matrix paper lined by violent peaks and valleys. A respirator wheezed and clunked, breathing for the troubled little girl as her lungs struggled under the attack of infection.

As he watched her, statistics began to whirl once again in Simon's mind, his medical knowledge as both a doctor and a parent of a seriously ill child spinning into action, computing data he had safely filed away. A figure popped up, an unwanted one. Relapse. Twenty five percent.

A one in four chance of survival.

Chapter 5

January passed and with February came snow. Not the attractive white drifts that drive even the most mature of men to   manically to turn out the garage in search of the family sledge – it was the dirty grey slush that coats every pavement and road, melting into dog muck, causing accidents and delays, soaking through shoes and making the whole country irritable.

The Baileys and the Halfords convened once again around Simon and Melissa's kitchen table. The easy companionship of the previous months had been replaced again by the hushed conversations of a family on the edge.

Barbara fiddled with her napkin. "But at least she's coming out of ITU. That's got to be good news hasn't it?"

Simon nodded vaguely. "She's going back onto the Cancer Ward. The infection has passed and she's stable but that doesn't mean she isn't a very poorly girl. The biopsy showed up blasts…."

"What's a blast?" Robert interrupted.

"New cells, presumably leukemic. The spinal tap showed the cancer has been found in the brain lining. She's on the strongest course of chemo they dare give her."

Porridge sighed heavily in his dog basket, aware of the heavy atmosphere. He missed his friend.

"What happens after the chemo - radiation therapy? How about the bone marrow transplant? They can do that, can't they?" Terry stared intently at his son. Of course they would do something for his only granddaughter. It was 2009, for God's Sake. They could cure everything now.

"The transplant is better carried out during a remission. The state of a patient's disease at the time of the transplant can affect the likelihood of a good outcome. Sarah isn't in remission anymore. Allogeneic transplant was discussed during her remission, but the prognosis was so good a chemotherapy course was considered the least dangerous option. Also, her best chance would be a matched sibling transplant. Sarah's an only child."

Terry sighed. "But she'll get through it. She's fought it off before. She'll do it again this time."

"*It's not so bloody simple, Terry!*" Melissa threw the saucepan she was washing to the ground, sending splatters of water across the floor. "You're as bad as your son. Everything is not going to just *go away*. She hasn't got mumps. It's not a bout of fucking chicken pox. *Jesus*." Melissa tore past the kitchen table, wrenching open the kitchen door and barging into her mother, Diana, who had been outside. A crunch of gears and Melissa's car disappeared down the slushy street, leaving behind an astonished Diana, fag in hand.

* * *

Melissa was relieved to find nobody else in the 'Family Room', the cramped common room-cum-kitchenette provided for parents just off the Pediatric ward.

She slumped onto a brown foam sofa, staring unseeing at the notice board in front of her which displayed a mix of taxi numbers, MMR jab reminders and pizza delivery flyers. When they had begun their long hospital stints two years before, the take-away menus scattered across the coffee tables had alarmed her. The cheerful leaflets, advertising *'kebab meat and cheese'* and *'super-sized, stuffed-crust Hawaiians'* appeared incongruous in the dour environment.

For the first forty-eight hours, Simon and Melissa had survived on black coffee, dutifully flicking donations into the Tupperware container provided. Neither wished to admit to the selfish state of hunger, both embarrassed by their own petty requirements in the face of their daughter's far greater need. Their fast was broken when another couple wandered into the little common room and calmly ordered a large pizza. The delivery boy had arrived quickly, obviously familiar with the route through the hospital. The other couple were old hands, parents of a boy with cystic fibrosis, and they shared the pizza with the grateful Baileys. Melissa remembered how the smell had seemed somehow sacrilegious in that temple to good hygiene and health. She had no such concerns anymore. She had probably shared fifty pizzas in that room over the years, though she had not tasted a single one.

A twitch of a smile flickered at the corner of Melissa's mouth. She had once gotten into an awful lot of trouble over a pizza at school. In fact, Melissa had gotten into a lot of trouble over a lot of things at school. 'Pizzagate' as her mother still referred to it, was merely one battle of many at the minor girls boarding school at which she had spent her formative years.

Beecham House Independent Girl's School was set in unremarkable grounds and produced largely unremarkable results. The girls did reasonably in their exams, and acquitted themselves moderately on the sports pitch. The fees were low and the parents, mostly middle to upper-middle-class professionals, put up with the lack of facilities and prestige in return for termly bills that didn't bankrupt them.

As is required of any budget manager, corners had to be cut in order to provide the low cost service. The sports equipment was circa 1951. The 'Theatre Department' was an old wicker basket filled with hats. The food was abysmal. Melissa, athletic and tall, was constantly hungry.

The Victorian red-bricked manor which housed the school was fifteen miles from the nearest small Yorkshire market town and surrounded largely by cornfields. Once handed over at the beginning of term along with their tuck boxes and lacrosse sticks, girls had contact with the outside world only through the medium of television, telephone (Upper fifth and Sixth Form only, younger pupils permitted a ten minute call home on Saturday), or acceptance onto a sports team. Away games created much excitement, particularly when they were to be played at a co-ed school. The brief glimmer of the opposite sex was enough to inspire a month's worth of crushes and romantic scheming.

In summer, there was a weekly Saturday trip to Ripon for the older girls when they would shrink down in their seats as the ancient minibus, emblazoned with the name of the school and therefore proclaiming their shameful middle-class status to the 'townies', spluttered and backfired into the town square. Scuttling away from the Beecham House bus, the girls had two hours in which to acquire as much contraband as possible. Melissa, looking old for her age in purple crushed velvet and heavy eyeliner, was particularly successful. She took a number of orders for Marlboro lights and cheap perry. After purchasing and stashing their haul and having a quick smoke amongst the gravestones of the Minster, they had sufficient time to traipse into the nearby takeaway to purchase 'chips 'n' scraps' and flirt with the greasy boys who worked there.

One particularly unlikely love affair involved Melissa's best friend, the daughter of a local solicitor, and Kyle a member of *'The Happy Cod's'* staff and son of a local car thief.

On one occasion they took a menu back to the school, promising to call during the week. The following Tuesday, after a particularly small and inedible supper, Melissa and Laetitia grabbed the excuse to talk to the monosyllabic Kyle and ordered a pizza to be delivered to the school for 7.30 p.m.. It was unfortunate that Mrs. Metcalf, the Headmistress, happened upon them, waiting at the top of the school drive just as Kyle's moped whined into sight. The Headmistress encouraged them to pay for their goods, politely dismissed the slack-jawed Kyle, then promptly informed the stricken girls that the pizza was to be confiscated, shoving it unceremoniously into a large bin outside the kitchens.

Hauled into Mrs. Metcalf's study the two girls explained, in part truth, that the takeaway had been purchased simply because they were hungry, but the headmistress wasn't interested in excuses.

"Ladies do not eat pizza. Ladies from *this* school certainly do not eat from boxes," Mrs. Metcalf announced grandly, a plate of unfinished macaroons on her desk, undoubtedly the product of Fourth Year's domestic science class that morning.

"Ladies," Melissa replied calmly, "do not knowingly starve children in their care, whilst using the savings they make on the catering budget to provide higher quality food for themselves and their staff."

Mrs. Metcalf eyed Melissa. Melissa eyed Mrs. Metcalf. Laetitia stared intently at a smudge on the corner of the desk. "Go back to your dorm, Laetitia. I shall deal with you in the morning."

Melissa chewed the inside of her cheek as her friend scuttled out of the room. She had gone too far.

Mrs. Metcalf sat down at her desk. "Never in thirty years of being a headmistress have any of my charges ever spoken to me like that, Melissa. We have met in this office many times now and there is really very little left to say. I think it high time that your parents took you away. In fact, I think it prudent that you be removed from this school tonight. Now, to save my getting your file out, you will kindly provide me with your mother's telephone number."

Melissa blanched. Her mother generally fought her corner, but even her mother would consider speaking to her headmistress like that unacceptable. Being expelled with immediate effect at 8:00 in the evening was even worse. Nevertheless, lifting her chin just a little and determinedly looking the older woman in the eye, she gave her home telephone number.

Melissa was dismissed to her dorm with orders that she pack. She traipsed upstairs and tried to speak while her friends fell on her, talking all at once, eager to hear the news. She started to gather her things, gloomily imagining her mother receiving the call in the hallway of their house, a twenty minute drive away. Her father would be standing in the doorway, listening to one half of the conversation, his evening whisky in hand. *Oh God, she was going to be in trouble with her father.*

The girls assembled around the dorm window, which looked out over the drive, and waited for Melissa's mother's dreadful Rover Metro, pockmarked with rust, to roar down the drive for a final time.

Eventually, it did and, as ever, Diana's graceful legs appeared out of the battered old car, followed by her slender body, a cigarette held dramatically between her beautifully manicured fingers.

She finished her cigarette, dropped the butt onto the driveway and ground it under her elegant heel. Then, with her chin raised in an expression that looked remarkably like her daughter's earlier regal pose, she slammed the tinny little car door shut and sashayed into the school.

Fifteen excruciating minutes later, the girls watched in astonishment as Diana glided back out of the school, got into the car and disappeared. The dorm exploded in cheers and Melissa began a tense wait to be recalled downstairs.

After another twenty minutes, Melissa had yet to be de-briefed. Instead, the girls heard the familiar tappety chunter of Diana's metro coming back down the drive. They re-congregated in the window and watched in amazement as, once again, Diana unfolded herself out of the car and walked briskly back into the school, pizza box in hand.

Melissa smiled at the memory. Her mother, and by association she, had been a school hero for a month. The pizza had been delivered to her dorm by a junior member of staff. The matter had not been mentioned again. The girls did not, however, order takeaway again.

* * *

She dropped the pizza flyer back onto the Formica coffee table as her thoughts returned to her present situation. She had been rude to Terry. Her father-in-law had certainly not deserved that.

She had always had a problem with her temper – words tumbled out of her before she had time to stop them. There had been countless instances where she had said things that she had regretted. She supposed she had better apologize, though it was coming up to 6 p.m. now and she would need to go and settle down for the night with Sarah. They were reading 'Harry Potter and the Half Blood Prince', the sixth book of the wildly popular series of seven, and she had come to the Family Room only to make a coffee. An apology could wait until morning. Everyone would understand the pressure she was under.

Chapter 6

Simon nodded at the nurses milling around their station as he took a well-worn path through the ward, to the bay that held Sarah's bed. Giant, brightly colored stickers of jolly children's characters decorated the glass partition windows and walls, in sharp contrast to the wheelchairs, drip stands and monitors that were parked along the corridors. Food trolleys designed to look like trains lined the passage-way outside Sarah's bay, stacked with the remnants of the evening meal. The familiar stink of overcooked cabbage hung in the air.

"Hullo, Princess." Simon kissed Sarah's smooth, hairless head and glanced up at Melissa who sat nearby, Harry Potter in hand. "More quidditch matches? Here, let me help ..."

Simon grabbed the plastic beaker Sarah was reaching for and positioned the straw so she could drink. She remained still, propped up with pillows, her pallor clashing with the green hospital blanket. She sipped the drink and then squinted to indicate she had had enough. Her voice was hushed, labored. "Potions lesson. Harry just won a bottle of lucky potion. That would be good, Dad, wouldn't it? If you could have pure luck for a whole day?"

"It would." Simon sat on the edge of the bed. "How are you feeling, Princess?"

"Sick."

Melissa cut in. "Sarah's having a bad evening. the chemo's really got to her today. Oh shit …"

Melissa leaped up as Simon grabbed a grey cardboard bowl from by the bed. He thrust it towards Sarah's chest as she began to retch. The tiny amount of water she had ingested returned violently, tinged with green bile. Her body was trying to eject the poison of the chemotherapy, but there was nothing inside for her grasping stomach muscles to bring up. Tears coursed down the child's face.

A nurse in cartoon character printed scrubs appeared, a sympathetic smile on her face. "Oh, Sarah. It should calm down a bit soon. We'll give you more anti-emetics in half an hour if it hasn't, but we don't really want to give you any more drugs at the moment if we can help it. Would you like an iced lolly to suck, sweetheart?"

Sarah nodded, the tears still streaming down her little cheeks, her whole body undulating with each muscular contraction.

"Orange or blackcurrant love?" The kindly nurse asked, removing her water jug to refresh.

Sarah didn't respond.

"I'll choose then shall I, pet?" The nurse wandered off as Sarah gave a little groan.

"I'll stay tonight." Simon looked up at Melissa. "You slept here last night."

"No, I want to stay. You go home, I'm fine."

Simon wanted to argue. He wanted to stay on the little pull-out bed the hospital provided for one parent by the bed of their child. But rows were the last thing his daughter needed now. Besides, it was near impossible to get a decent night's sleep on the ward, the children regularly being woken for temperature checks and drip changes. He had to work, therefore he had to sleep.

The nurse returned, ice-pop in hand, a re-constituted grey cardboard bowl in the other. "Here you are, sweetheart. I got you orange. Let's just change your hydration bag shall we?" She proceeded to unhook an empty bag from above Sarah, replacing it with another, chatting to Simon and Melissa as she worked. "Mr. Abnam would like to talk with you both in the morning. He'll be doing his rounds around 9 a.m., so if you could be here for 9.30 a.m. that would be great. There now, flower. That's all done. Try to get some sleep. Mrs. Bailey, will you be sleeping here tonight?"

Melissa nodded.

"Okay, well you know how to make the bed work. It's quiet at the moment, so I'll get you both a cup of tea if you'd like? No? I'll see you tomorrow, then." The nurse sidled off, waving at other parents as she left.

"Can you get off work?" Melissa sounded tired.

"I'll have to. It's no problem, I'll call in first thing. They know what's going on. Are you sure you don't want me to stay?"

"No. Thanks. I …" Melissa gave a false little smile. " … I have to be here."

"I understand. Sarah, darling? Are you awake?"

The little girl had rolled into a ball on her side. Now she mewed a quiet affirmative.

"Here, shall I open your ice-lolly? It'll help settle your tummy." Simon helped Sarah sit up again, then tore the wrapper with his teeth, and handed her the cool, soothing ice-pop. "Should Daddy get off then?" Simon asked, unwilling to leave them, not wishing to tear himself away but knowing both his girls needed to settle down for the night. Sarah nodded her head once in agreement.

"I love you Daddy."

"I love you too. I'll be back in the morning."

* * *

When Simon arrived back at the hospital the next day, the ward was alive with activity. It was a stark contrast to the strained, half-lit, whispering world of the evening before.

Porters criss-crossed the ward, wheeling children to other parts of the hospital for tests and scans. Nurses called greetings to each other as the night-shift handed over to the incoming team. Crockery clattered as health care assistants retrieved the children's breakfast cereal bowls and teacups and loaded them onto the little train

61

trolleys, ready to be returned to the kitchens in the bowels of the building.

The parents who had stayed with their children were packing up their beds, bringing order to their individual campsites. Mothers struggled into day clothes, pushing overnight bags out of the way, throwing down cups of weak, milky tea and munching on cold toast. Televisions, swinging on arms above each bed, blared out a selection of cartoons.

The Ward Sister, newly arrived on the day shift, went from bed to bed, familiarizing herself with each patient's night time notes, greeting children and soothing fraught parents. Two volunteers made their way up the ward with a trolley, the bottom loaded with tired looking paperbacks, the top with sweets, crisps and tabloids. Simon passed them all as he returned to Sarah's ward.

"I'll take a Daily Mail, please." Simon counted out some money and handed it to one of the ladies. "And some polo mints as well. Thanks." He pocketed his change and headed towards Sarah's bed, relieved to see her sitting up and watching TV while her mum folded clothes into the nightstand.

"How are my girls?"

"Better. Daddy! It's Ben Ten! Look!" Sarah grinned, pointing at her television. He glanced up at the small cartoon boy fighting an enormous green alien. "Are those for me?" She pointed at the polo mints in his hand. The ravaging effects of yesterday's chemo had obviously lessened overnight and Sarah's indomitable spirit had made a welcome return.

"Yup. You had some breakfast?" Simon pulled up another of the shiny armchairs. The wooden arms and high back were so familiar now.

"I had a bit of cereal. I wish they had oranges. I'd really like oranges right now." Sarah continued to stare, rapt, at the screen. On the television, drool poured from the alien creature's mouth.

"Oranges, eh? I think we can provide those." The cravings, Simon knew, were similar to those of a pregnant woman. Chemotherapy affected patients in different ways. The nausea was standard, but controllable to some extent by anti-nausea drugs. Patients often didn't want to eat, but equally would crave certain foods. It was important to help Sarah eat as much as possible on good days.

"Hey, Babe." Melissa leaned forward and kissed Simon on the cheek. "You're here early."

Simon gave an inward sigh of relief. Melissa, though looking dog-tired, seemed to have thrown off the anger of the day before. He pointed at a Starbucks bag he was carrying. "Thought you might like some proper breakfast."

He pulled up the sliding hospital bed table and unpacked two large lattes and a small hot chocolate, along with assorted Danish pastries, paper napkins and plastic stirrers. "Better than cheapo cornflakes and cold tea, hmm?"

"Hell, yes." Melissa fell on the Danish pastries. "Can I have the pecan one, please?"

Sarah nodded, grabbing the cinnamon swirl, leaving Simon with his usual apricot. He grinned. "Did I do good?"

"You did good." Both Melissa and Sarah mumbled affirmatives, their mouths full of pastry.

Simon settled back in the chair with his coffee. "Has anyone been round yet?" It was only 8 a.m., but ward life started early, as Simon knew only too well.

"The SHO came round half an hour ago. She was pleased to see Sarah is feeling stronger today. We go onto bag three of six – high dose Ara-C, through the chest catheter. They're pumping her full of saline solution to keep her kidneys and bladder happy, which is making her pretty uncomfortable. Mr. Abnam is coming later and we'll hear more. Is there any sugar?" Melissa scouted through the contents of the Starbucks' bag.

"I don't think I grabbed any. Sorry. Listen, Mel, Dad's a bit upset. He didn't mean to …"

"I know. I know. And I'm sorry. I was tired and … well, I'm sorry. I'll give him a call this afternoon. It's just all so …"

"He'll be fine. He takes everything on the chin, my dad."

"I know. Aha!" Mel victoriously brandished a small packet of Sweet and Lo, which she had dug from her handbag. "These will do."

"All meals free! Look, Dad! All meals free!"

Melissa and Simon turned to look at the television screen. The final frame of an advert stared at them: a telephone number surrounded by fireworks and a familiar pink fairytale castle in the background.

"You said the meals were astronaughtily expensive. No, they're not. They're *free*, so we can go, right?" Sarah beamed up at her dad, her face arranged in a well-practiced cherubic expression. The same eyelash-batting look that little girls learn from the age of two and which mothers are largely immune to. *"Pleease ..."*

Disneyland. It was a well-worn argument. Sarah desperately wanted to visit the theme park in Paris. Her parents considered it anathema.

To an outsider it might have seemed odd, even cruel, that Sarah's parents, who could easily afford such a trip, had so far refused to grant the child's wish. However, it is important to remember that there are many things that little girls urgently crave. Puppies. Ponies. Ten foot teddy bears. Candy-floss factories. Most longed-for desires are forgotten after six months, replaced with newer, better fantasy objects. Some remain, but remain impractical.

On Sarah's diagnosis, her parents had determined not to spoil her. They had to believe that she had a future, and therefore they had to continue to shape the personality and attitude of their daughter in the same manner they would have had she not been diagnosed with such a ravaging illness. It was hard, seeing her little frame clothed in open-backed hospital gowns, not to promise her the world. She was, of course, fussed over. She was given teddies and game consoles, board games and craft kits. But all these were practical. The child needed entertaining. Riding lessons were promised for when she was better. Theatre trips were booked when she was well enough. But still they held out on Disneyland.

Simon felt strongly about Disneyland, in particular the European park, situated outside Paris. What possible motivation, he wondered, could people have for travelling to France to see a fake plastic palace in a land scattered with real-life fairytale castles? In America, where there was no such thing and popular culture had its foundations in pretence, the cinematic, the futuristic, the 'stars', then yes, he supposed there was a place for giant mice, burgers and saccharine sentiments. But in France? The land of chateaux, musketeers, Marie Antoinette and Monet? How could anyone want to visit a fiberglass fabricated kingdom dedicated to capitalism and commercialism? Where the request for a glass of wine and a chunk of Camembert would be met with blank-eyed contempt. It was France for God's sake.

And the money! Simon was not a cheap man, but he was cautious. His formative years had been spent not in poverty but certainly on the strictest of budgets. His parents' careful planning and saving had been handed down in his psyche. Friends reported back that burger meals in bog-standard, well-known burger joints had set them back £60 for a family of four. For a burger! Not only that – it was a burger which you collected yourself and which you would be expected to clear away. For £60, Simon calculated, he could take his family to a fabulous French restaurant, perhaps by a river, perhaps on the coast where he could introduce them to the gastronomic delights of France. Oysters, lobsters, cheeses, cassoulets … but a burger?

No. Simon had remained adamant. Melissa was largely in agreement. There was no reason to buy passage to France, only to immerse themselves in what they saw as an oversized shopping mall with roller coasters. Their parental gift to Sarah was to feed and stimulate her mind. They wanted to show her wondrous sights that were not experienced by everybody. They wanted to immerse her in the histories and cultures that had created the world in which she lived. To bequeath an appreciation of the foundation on which her society was built. If they truly loved their daughter, they felt, then they would deny her the tawdry falsehood of a theme-park holiday and lavish the gift of knowledge on her instead. Disney could be experienced on television. Versailles could not.

Leukemia or no leukemia.

"Free meals, Daddy. So it won't be thirty pounds for a burger. It will be free. That's good isn't it, Daddy?" Sarah continued to chirrup, patting her daddy on the knee. Simon and Melissa looked at each other with unspoken defeat. Sarah sensed impending victory and moved in for the kill. "So we can go then, can't we, Daddy? We can go to Disneyland. When I'm better. When I'm in remission again?"

"*Dr. Bailey, Mrs. Bailey, Miss Bailey.*" Mr. Abnam, a charming and good-looking Brahmin, in a beautifully tailored suit, approached the bed. "Miss Bailey, you are looking, ah, how do you say … perky today. Not giving my nurses too much trouble, I hope?" He looked kindly at Sarah, who forced a smile. She was pleased with the consultant's manner of addressing her, but irritated to have her Disneyland plea interrupted. "If you are quite happy with, ah, let's see, oh yes, Ben Ten, then I think I should like to take your parents off for a little chat. Would that be okay, Sarah?" Sarah nodded. "Good. Then Dr. and Mrs. Bailey, would you please be following me?"

As she rose, Melissa kissed her daughter on the head. She dropped the empty coffee cups back into the paper bag and checked that Sarah's jug of squash, as well as paper and pencil case were all in easy reach. Sarah gave a small smile, her disappointment at being left alone again obvious. Simon felt a stab of sympathy as he turned to follow the consultant.

"Hey, Sarah." Simon turned back to his daughter. "You'd better decide which of the hellish hotels you want in Disneyland. I'll pick up a brochure for you later." With a wink he was gone, leaving an ecstatic Sarah sitting up in bed, clapping her hands.

Chapter 7

"I know this is a terrible shock."

The consultant assessed the silent couple sitting before him. They had not responded as he had expected. In ten years' experience as a Consultant Pediatric Oncologist, Mr. Abnam was uncomfortably used to giving bad news. Colleagues in adult cancer wards had the onerous task of informing patients that their battle was unwinnable and that they were going to die. Mr. Abnam had the far harder task of informing parents that their child was going to die.

He was used to anger and demands for further treatment. Men often paced the room. Some even punched walls or kicked his waste paper bin. The women tended to cry. A few had been physically sick. Many had walked out of the room. Most blamed him.

It was natural. He was acquainted with the Kubler-Ross model, commonly known as the five stages of grief. He was forced to give the worst possible news to parents. Each differed in their starting position on the arduous journey to acceptance. Many had lived in fear of this conversation for months, perhaps years, knowing deep down that they would outlive their child.

Some parents held onto their optimism so firmly that the news pulled the rug from under their emotional feet, plunging them straight into the first stage of denial. These parents would demand second opinions, accuse him of misdiagnosis, campaign for further bouts of treatment. Normally quite calm, they would remain seated while their minds searched desperately for a way to stop the thing they had been told from being true.

The second stage was anger. These were the bin kickers. Sometimes they moved into anger from denial within the short time they were in his office. Often they had already been in denial for months and the confirmation their child was dying simply jolted them onto this next step on the stairway of grief. They raged and ranted. They accused Mr. Abnam of malpractice, of not caring, of withholding drugs, of not holding a proper degree. He was Asian. Where had he learnt medicine? What did he know anyway, with a tin-pot degree from Karachi?

Mr. Abnam glanced at his University of Cambridge medical degree, framed and displayed on the wall.

Bargaining was the third stage. A uniquely personal experience, this stage usually happened sometime after the conversation in his office. Often the negotiation for an extension to the life of their child was made with a higher power, pleas to God or Gods for their child to be spared. Parents promised to lead better lives, to go to church, to give up drinking and occasionally begged their God to take them in their child's place.

Depression and then acceptance, the final stops on the exhausting emotional expedition, came later.

Right now, he would likely be dealing with either denial or anger.

He surveyed the mute couple again, assessing their body language, unsure as to which well-rehearsed line to use next. The man, the GP, Dr. Bailey, stared at the floor, his teeth clenched. His wife sat next to him, gazing out of the window, occasionally closing her eyes for a few seconds as if, by closing her eyes and re-opening them, she would wipe away the image in front of her. Like a reality Etch-a-Sketch.

He interrupted the silence cautiously. "Sarah may be quite well for a few weeks. Two months, perhaps three. There will be a quality of life there, and you will have the opportunity to enjoy time with her. As I have already explained, there really is no point in giving her any more treatment. It will only make her feel unwell with no discernible remedial effect. The downturn will be rapid, the leukemia is aggressive. When, and I am afraid it will be soon, she takes a marked turn for the worse, she can be swiftly moved into a hospice specially for children, where she can be made comfortable. Palliative care will be carried out in a specially designed environment. In her last few weeks, we will largely be concerned with pain relief. I have here," Mr. Abnam reached for a folder by his desk, "a brochure for Madron House. You can go and look around. It is a truly inspiring place, I'm sure that you will find the work of the staff there a comfort."

Neither parent looked up. Both stared determinedly at their chosen spot.

The consultant broke the silence again. "Sarah is keen on animals, I think. They have rabbits…"

Mrs. Bailey shifted slightly, tears beginning to course down her face, though her expression remained impenetrable. She continued to look out of the window, her hand over her mouth, her head tilted slightly to one side.

"I don't want her to be scared." Dr. Bailey's whisper brought Mr. Abnam's attention back to the man. The GP shifted in his chair, lifting his eyes for the first time and holding the consultant's in his gaze.

"I'm scared," said Mrs. Bailey, and silence resumed.

Chapter 8

The wailing increased in volume, as a woman, her sari the most vivid red Simon had ever seen, began to walk calmly out of the crowd towards the funeral pyre.

Other women stepped forward, clawing at her clothes, imploring her to step back from the inferno. But still she glided, emotionless towards the intense heat. Within the hungry flames, her husband's flesh melted, his fat causing the fire to flare and pop.

Covering his mouth and nose in an attempt to block out the stench, Simon strode out with her. The fire roared and the howls of the women grew in a desperate crescendo. The woman looked back, shaking her head, angrily gesticulating her wish to carry out her self-immolation alone. Simon paused, his desire to join her *anumarana*, to be ravaged by fire, to step over the boundary of life and death, overwhelming.

The keening of the mourners heightened in pitch as another of the women, incongruously dressed in western clothes, flung herself at Simon, her imploring face known to him, though her blonde hair was stained with the black smuts which floated down from the azure blue sky.

Don't, her voice sounded in his head, though her lips did not move. *Don't*.

* * *

Simon woke with a jolt, confused and disorientated. He didn't recognize the room he was in. The bed felt alien, too hard. He sat up. Melissa mumbled something and stirred.

"This is real, isn't it?" Simon swung his legs out of the hotel bed and rubbed his hands over his face. "I had a nightmare. This is worse."

Melissa propped herself on her elbows. "Shit."

Simon filled the tiny electric kettle and plugged it in. Tea bag. Plastic milk pot. Packet of sugar. Going through the motions. Keep going. Keep moving forward. Wade through the mental glue. He turned the television on, letting the chirpy presenters' vacuous banter relieve the silence.

"Rombouts coffee biscuits, Mel. Didn't think they did these anymore."

"What?"

"Rombouts. Remember? You used to love them. You nicked a handbag full from that hotel we stayed in just before you had Sarah. Remember? Here." Simon passed Melissa a cup of weak, warm tea and a familiarly wrapped biscuit. "Rombouts, Mel. You love them."

Melissa sat up again and took the little biscuit. She had developed her taste for them while at Marshal & Snelgrove's, the old-fashioned department store in Leeds, where she had first worked supporting

74

herself and Simon through his medical degree. She and the girls from Handbags, along with the lasses from Lingerie, would meet for coffee at 11 each morning, in the austere cafeteria of the store. Its décor, atmosphere and etiquette had gone unchanged since the 1950s. There they played at being grown-ups, taking turns to pour the tea, sharing the tiny cinnamon biscuits and discussing the more amusing customers of the day. They gossiped and bitched, consoled and comforted. *"Of course he likes you. It wasn't just a one-night stand. I'm sure he'll call tonight ... Of course Melissa is so lucky, settled down already with a soon-to-be doctor!"*

Melissa would glow, so proud of her senior marital status, so proud of growing up so quickly. Sitting in the time-warped cafeteria, the career-driven world of the early nineties existing only outside its flock-papered walls, Melissa's old-fashioned goals focused merely on being a 'Mrs.' and becoming a mother.

Her future stretched out luxuriantly before her. She was to be married to a doctor. They would fill their house with laughing children, dogs and Laura Ashley cushions. There would be wickedly witty guests for dinner and committee ladies in hats for lunch. She would have an Aga, and a dog to sleep before it.

And her dreams had been fulfilled. She had the doctor already. The house came a few years later, and the baby shortly after that. Laura Ashley being momentarily unfashionable, the curtains were instead from Habitat and her range cooker was a Rayburn, but the sparkling dinner parties and charitable luncheons went ahead. Porridge, the puppy, chewed everything and enchanted everyone. Melissa was content.

Now it was as though, in a moment of spite, someone had fed Melissa's contentment into a shredder. The macerated strips of her life had been reduced to a pile of incomprehensible remnants, carelessly heaped on a hotel bed.

They had checked into the St George's Hotel the night before, having spent the day with Sarah. After leaving Mr. Abnam's office, they stood in the lift lobby for a while, steadying themselves, checking their emotions. Without discussion they headed back to Sarah, united in their overwhelming desire to be with their little girl.

"Did you get my brochure, Dad?" No preliminaries. Sarah could pick up a conversation three weeks after it was interrupted and expect her conversant to keep up. "When will you be getting the brochure? They'll have them at Thomas Cook, Daddy. There's one in Huddersfield."

Simon paused, confused. His mind seemed to be struggling to compute basic information. Brochure. Brochure? Disneyland. *"Sarah may be quite well for a few weeks, two months, perhaps three."* Disneyland. Simon attempted a smile, though his mouth refused to contort upwards. He gave up.

"Do you know what, darling? I think I'll go and get that brochure now. I suppose if we're going to see Mickey, we had better get planning. Don't you think, Mummy?" Simon turned to Melissa. She was startlingly white, her expression unfathomable. Shock. "Mummy? Would you like to come with me? We'll only be half an hour. Melissa?"

"No, you go ahead." Melissa turned to him, a blank-eyed rictus passing as her smile. "I want to hear what happens next to Harry Potter."

"Yey! Me too!" Sarah grinned, grabbing the book and holding it out towards her mother.

"Okay. I'll, erm … I'll be back soon. You okay, darling?" Simon asked his wife.

"Yes, fine," she snapped brightly, the unnerving faux-smile flashing once again.

Simon headed out of the ward, stopping briefly at the nurses' station. "Hi. My wife, she's had a shock. Could someone …" His brain once again stalled, its basic mechanism apparently seized up.

"Of course, Dr. Bailey. She's had a terrible shock. I'll get her strong tea and something to eat and we'll keep an eye on her." A young nurse smiled sympathetically, completely unaware of the rage that she had stirred within the handsome GP. 'Of course?' Of *course*? Did they all *know*? How long had they known? Had they all been muttering and pitying them as they had sat watching television with their daughter that morning? Had they known last night? Had these, these *women* all known the fate of his daughter before he had?

"Do that." Simon spat out the words, then turned on his heel, unable to hide his hostility towards this ... *nobody*, who knew more about his daughter than he did.

* * *

"I've still got a couple of those biscuits, you know." Melissa spoke in a dull monotone. "I must have eaten about twenty but I kept the rest in my dressing case. They're still there, tucked into the little pocket at the back. They even went into hospital with me. I had one with the cup of tea the nurse gave us after the birth. Do you remember? That horrible nagging midwife had just been lecturing us about cot death."

Simon did remember. The midwives had left the newly formed family to get to know one another. As Melissa and the baby sat up in bed, Simon took his shoes off and climbed onto the bed beside them. The urge to hold both his wife and his new daughter outweighed the discomfort of three in a bed made for one. For a blissful few minutes they had lain together, his arm around his wife, hers around the child. All linked. Team Bailey. A familial triumvirate.

An unpleasant midwife with an abrasive personality looked in and scolded them for 'unsafe practices' around a baby. With a strong Glaswegian accent, the stout red-haired woman ranted incomprehensibly about *'the bairn'* and *'the beed'*. Simon and

Melissa caught each other's eye and then failed desperately as they both tried not to giggle. Hysteria welled up in both of them in the manner of naughty children. When they could hold on no longer they both exploded, tears of laughter coursing down their cheeks. The midwife strode out in a huff. A member of the nursing staff, one blessed with a sense of humor, made them a cup of tea and Melissa, remembering the pilfered biscuits, shared one with the father of her new child.

"Simon?"

"Yes." Simon's voice was little more than a whisper as he sat down next to his wife on the king-sized hotel bed. The decision to book into the hotel had been mutual. Somehow an unspoken agreement had been made and after settling Sarah down for the evening and checking that she was happy on her own for a night, they got in the car and drove wordlessly to the town centre hotel, past laughing students falling drunkenly out of university bars in a ritual of bad behavior for which Simon and Melissa would never have the privilege of scolding Sarah.

Home had become a hostile place. No comfort could be drawn from a building so reverberant with memories and stuffed with objects that were now so sacred. They didn't want to see the crayon and felt tip scrawls stuck to the fridge door. They could not cope with the pile of shoes and skipping ropes entangled by the door.

They were incapable of facing the closed door to Sarah's room, its *'Kids Rool!'* sign somehow mocking them.

Far better the impersonal sanctuary of a hotel bedroom, with its bland yet tasteful furnishings, and none of the painfully familiar *accoutrements* of domestic life.

Thank God for text messages. Unable to face speaking to either of their parents, they had sent a short message to Diana, who had been both watching the florists that day as well as dog-sitting the indefatigable Porridge: CAN U PLEASE LOOK AFTER P TONIGHT? Diana, intuitive and wise, responded with a mere YES. Explanations would be given later. She allowed herself the fragile fantasy that Melissa and Simon had gone to the cinema, or perhaps the new tapas bar they had talked about.

But a merry trip to a restaurant it was not. They ordered room service, the food lying largely uneaten as Melissa and Simon, two thirds of Team Bailey, had cried with a ferocity neither would have thought possible, until finally falling asleep, their pillows sodden.

Now, the ethereality of night had passed and dawn's raw reality had broken.

"Simon." Melissa looked up at her husband, repeating his name as if for strength. "How do we tell Sarah?"

Chapter 9

Discharged and told only that she had finished her chemo session, Sarah returned home, a little weak, but upbeat and wildly excited about her longed-for trip to Disneyland. Her grandparents, now fully informed of the situation, defiantly threw off the 'no spoiling Sarah' rule and deluged the delighted child in sweets, DVDs and extravagant gifts.

Porridge abandoned his lovingly chewed basket to sleep by Sarah's bed each night. The normally docile dog had surprised everybody by baring his fangs like a hellhound one evening when Melissa had tried to remove him from the room, having finished their evening installment of Harry Potter. Porridge remained, the Tinkerbell rug becoming unarguably his.

* * *

Simon heaved the last bag into the back of Robert's old Audi Estate. "That's the lot, Robert. I'll do a quick run around the house, check the TVs are unplugged and then we can get off. You set, Sarah?"

Sarah, who had been voluntarily sitting in the car since teatime, now almost two hours ago, cheered. She was dressed in a replica Cinderella costume, complete with matching princess head-scarf (cannibalized from a Disney pillowcase) topped with a jauntily balanced tiara. Her hand luggage, a miniature airhostess style trolley emblazoned with Disney princesses, had been packed around ten times, before she had finally decided on the toys, books and 'essentials' she deemed necessary for the one-hour flight to Paris. One Nintendo DS, one Nintendo DS Dogz game, one notepad, one pencil-case, one Disneyland map, one tube of fruit pastilles. "Bye, Porridge! Bye, Grandma Aitch! Don't forget, Porridge likes to watch Ben Ten in the mornings and he doesn't like Pedigree Chum in gravy …" Porridge, fully aware that he was being excluded from some pleasant excursion, huffed and turned back into the house.

Inside, Simon did last minute checks, pulling out plugs and checking windows were shut. He mentally ticked off the list of required documents and felt his inside pocket, reassuring himself that his Euros were where he had put them. In their bedroom, he found Melissa frantically scrabbling in one of her dressing table drawers. "You ready for off then, Mel? Want to go through the checklist?"

"I can't find my bloody passport anywhere. I swear I put it in here. I separated it from the others when I used it for ID the other day. Oh, where is it?" Mel dragged open another drawer, randomly flinging bottles and make-up stained scrunchies onto the bed.

"I've got it here, Mel. I put them all together this morning."

"Oh great! Oh, that's just fantastic, Simon. So you've let me spend the entire morning searching for it, when you had it all the time? Oh marvelous, that's just wonderful. Thanks ever so much." Melissa's eyes narrowed, a sneer contorting her usually attractive mouth.

"Hang on, Mel. I thought I was helping. I didn't know that you were looking for it."

"No, because you don't notice anything do you, Simon? Did it not cross your mind to ask why every conversation we have had today has been conducted while I turn out the contents of a drawer?"

"Well why didn't you ask me? I would have…"

"Because!" Melissa exploded, "I didn't know you had been rifling through my dressing table. How was I supposed to know that you were dealing with the documents? I normally do that."

"Melissa. It's not a problem. You've got it, your Dad's waiting, let's go." Simon backed away from his wife and made his way back down the stairs, chewing the insides of his mouth, a habit that had recently left them ridged and sore.

For the past fortnight, living with Melissa had been like living with a spitting cobra. Whilst she managed to keep from striking in Sarah's presence, venom poured forth regularly and always in Simon's direction. It was exhausting and hurtful. He understood that this was part of Melissa's grieving process and as such, desperately tried to let the shockwaves of anger bounce off him, but it was hard not to absorb some of Mel's ire.

With the exception of his wife's vitriol, for Simon the last month had been a period of strange calm. Granted an indeterminate length of compassionate leave from the surgery, Simon had enjoyed three precious weeks with his daughter, who, though clearly slowing down, remained her usual, bright, funny self. From time to time thoughts of the future crept up on him and, when they did, he simply pushed them away.

Sarah's voice broke his thoughts. "Come on! Honk the horn, Granddad Aitch. Daddy!" Simon gallantly held the door open for Melissa, locked up, kissed his mother-in-law, shouted a farewell to the sulking Porridge and joined his family in the car, ready for Robert to drive them to the airport.

The Audi pulled out of the drive, Simon and Melissa waving back at Diana, who waved them off from their front door.

"Now, everyone." An authoritative little voice piped up from the back. "I thought we could start with *Ten Green Bottles*."

* * *

Mercifully, the trip to Leeds Bradford Airport was short, allowing for only two rounds of *'Ging Gang Goolie'*.

On landing at Charles de Gaulle, an executive car took them straight from Arrivals to The Disney Hotel. The expensive transfer meant that Sarah would need only to walk from the luggage carousels to the exit, from whence they would be taken directly and in comfort to their hotel.

The airport was situated in the industrial part of town, and the Mercedes S Class crawled through the heavy Parisian traffic. The car was large enough to allow all three of the Baileys to sit together in the back and Sarah, exhausted by the short journey, slept soundly between her parents, her mouth open and her breathing shallow.

"Putin!" The driver gesticulated out of his window, a Gallic display of road-rage erupting between three or four cars.

"Sorry I was a bitch." Melissa gave Simon a little smile.

Simon shared a reciprocal grin. "Forget it."

"So, are you dreading your descent into a cartoon character nightmare?"

"Actually, I'm almost beginning to look forward to it, though I do suspect it may be the outer ring of Hell. I'm Dante and our driver friend here is Virgil."

"Surely he is Charon, the ferryman?"

"And this bloody traffic jam the river Acheron." Simon looked at his sleeping child between them. "Then Sarah must be Virgil. Sarah is our guide."

* * *

Sarah, unaware of her promotion to tour-guide of the underworld, slept soundly. She woke an hour later as the car turned into the entrance to the park. Simon had chosen The Disney Hotel, grandest and most traditional of the numerous hostelries serving the parks. The imposing building dominated the entrance, negating the need for shuttle buses or long walks. In the early dusk, lights sparkled from the roof, giving it the appearance of a lit up wedding cake. Its profile was somehow reminiscent of a great Indian palace.

Sarah scooted over onto her father's knee and pressed her face against the car window. Simon kissed the back of her scarf-wrapped head, inhaling deeply, enjoying the little girl smell of Sailor Matey bubble bath and dressing-up box musk.

The Mercedes pulled up to the grand porticoed entrance of the hotel and an American-styled busboy immediately appeared, greeting the driver as he climbed out of the car. "Mademoiselle." The chauffeur opened the door next to Sarah and, as he did so, made a little bow, an indulgent smile flicking across his face.

"Wow." Sarah stared wide-eyed at the chauffeur. "Oh, wow!"

Simon tipped the driver who signaled to two other busboys. There was a rapid exchange of French leading the young men to look at Sarah quizzically. Simon bristled, his protective instincts rearing up irrationally. Sarah, resplendent in her pale blue satin dress, her tiara only slightly off kilter; stared up rapturously at the neon palace. One of the busboys retreated back into the hotel as the other loaded the luggage onto a brass-domed trolley, the type seen in Hollywood movies.

Everything about the moment was, in fact, like stepping into a film. As the bellboys scurried to and fro, their burgundy livery immaculate, the hotel gleamed before them, its windows glowing with welcome. The giant illuminated clock on the façade suggested somehow that here in this magical place, time could be distorted.

A gasp of pleasure from Sarah alerted Simon's attention and he groaned inwardly as a giant Minnie Mouse, with ears the size of dinner plates, appeared in the door of the hotel, greeting guests returning from a day's fun-making. The costumed actors were a key part of the experience and an aspect the shy and serious Simon had been dreading.

"Monsieur, celui-ci est pour la petite." Simon turned toward the quiet voice.

The busboy addressing him pushed a wheelchair, the footrests cumbersome and mechanical, a high head support and drip stand attached to the backrest. It was, Simon realized, a wheelchair used more commonly for those requiring neck support. A leather strap hung down from one side.

"No, Daddy." Sarah looked aghast, Minnie Mouse forgotten as she backed instinctively behind her father's legs. "I don't want it."

A large family in German football tops, making their way into the hotel, paused. Their sticky, junk food fuelled children stared unabashedly at Sarah over the top of their Augustus Gloop style lollypops.

"Daddy. They're looking at me."

Simon eyed the clinical contraption, its ugliness exaggerated by the shiny, cinematic backdrop of the hotel. He put a hand on Sarah's shoulder, drawing her in close, no words available to him. Melissa moved forward seamlessly, crouching to Sarah's height and taking her hand. She grinned at her daughter and gave her a conspiratorial wink. "They are looking, Sarah, because you look so beautiful in that dress. Shall we go in?" She pulled her child towards the door, steadfastly ignoring the gawping group of guests and the ten-foot mouse. "Chin up, Sarah. Princesses always keep their chins up."

Simon watched with relief and fierce pride as his wife, more regal than any Disney royal creation, led Sarah up the steps and into the hotel. A bellboy approached him, gesturing at the chair, irritation belying his pretence of servitude.

"My daughter," Simon said, speaking clearly but quietly, "is not ill."

Chapter 10

When Simon was eight, his pet terrapin, George, died. An inhabitant of 31 Primrose Close for only months, George had succumbed (despite Simon's care and attention) to a respiratory infection. No amount of tank cleaning or freshly dug earth worms could save the little amphibian.

One day Simon returned from school lugging with him a beach bucket full of worms, pilfered from his father's compost heap. He peered through the glass, noting with interest that the dandelion greens he had provided the day before were untouched. Simon pushed his NHS spectacles back up his nose, and tapped the side of the glass. George lay on the raised, dry area of his tank. Simon stared at the tiny turtle, willing it to respond. Still, George remained motionless, his flippers ominously facing upwards.

Simon bit the inside of his mouth, a tic he habitually performed when concentrating or concerned. He thought methodically through the available options.

One, his pet was dead.

Two, George had got even poorlier than yesterday and was having a very long nap.

Three, George was better and was having a very long nap.

Pushing possibility number one to the back of his mind, Simon plumped for option two.

He lifted George gently out of the tank and placed him in a shoebox lined with cotton wool and loo-roll. He cleaned out the tank meticulously, removing the uneaten food and replacing it with fresh. Dropping one of the pilfered earthworms into the tank, he stowed the rest in an old ice-cream box in his wardrobe. Then he carefully replaced George back on the rock on which he had found him.

Three days later, George had yet to stir. Simon's research in the library of Shelton Park Primary had produced limited information. A tatty collection of out-of-date encyclopedias had finally provided some data - terrapins did not hibernate. Terrapins were not supposed to smell - George stank.

Returning from school that day with a heavy heart and an even heavier book-laden bag, he was mildly surprised to find Barbara and Terry waiting for him at the kitchen table. A large plastic margarine container took centre place on the table, and nestled amongst strips of newspaper and tissue lay George.

His mother sniffed. "Simon, sit down, lovey. We've got something to tell you."

Simon wrinkled his nose. George really did pong. "I know," he said simply.

"Simon, lad." His father began, disconcerted by Simon's calm. "Your mother found George today. She smelt something funny in your room and when she took a look at George, well, I'm sorry to tell you lad, but George is dead."

"I know," repeated Simon.

Terry cleared his throat, briefly catching the eye of his wife. "Well, what the devil were you keeping him for, lad? He must have been gone a week."

Simon shrugged, uncomfortable under his parents' perplexed gaze. He chewed his cheek and stared at his shoes. "I thought he might wake up if I gave him long enough. I thought I might make it better."

Terry sighed. "You should have told us, lad. That was a right stink your mother's had to clear. Now, we've made him a coffin and I've dug a hole. I thought you might like to be the man to put the lid on it. He was your terrapin and that. Then we'll pop him in his grave in the garden and you can say a few words if you like. Your mum's taken some cuttings. You can lay some flowers on the grave, right proper like."

"No." Simon looked at his father staunchly.

"No? Well, I can do it alone if you'd like. If you think you'd find it too upsetting, like. Perhaps that's a better idea."

"No. I don't want him to be buried. He won't like it out there."

Terry looked at Barbara again, the well-rehearsed scenario not playing as it was meant to. "He's dead, laddie. He doesn't know anything."

"I don't care. He's not going in a hole. He'll be lonely." Simon held his father's gaze steadily, chewing his inside cheek furiously until he tasted the tang of blood. He knew his pet was dead. He was not stupid. But he was not going to let George be alone in the dark and in the cold. George would not like it, dead or not.

"Simon," his mother began tentatively, "Simon, lovey. George is in heaven now. It's only his little body that's left here. Think of it more as an overcoat. Just a big old overcoat he's taken off. It's just a shell."

"He's not going in the ground."

Terry let out an exasperated sigh. "Simon, be reasonable now. You can't keep him. He's stinks to high heaven. Now I know you're upset, lad, but it can't be helped. I'm sorry you lost your pet, he was a nice little terrapin and you looked after him ever so well, but sometimes our pets die and when they do it is just as important that we behave responsibly about their burial as we did when we were caring for them."

"I want him to be buried at sea." Simon said simply. "He'll like that, will George. Much better. It has to be a burial at sea."

"Simon!" Barbara exclaimed, both relieved and perturbed. "We live seventy miles away from the sea."

"He has to be buried at sea," Simon said evenly, and taking the Stork tub in which his reeking terrapin lay, walked back up to his room to do his homework.

It was nearing midday the next day when Simon, Terry, Barbara and George The Putrid Terrapin, arrived at Cleethorpes. Terry, purple with rage, having followed a caravan at thirty miles an hour for the entire four-hour journey, parked their Austin Allegro on the sea front. Negotiations the previous evening had gone in the seven-year old Simon's favor and eventually, exhausted, Terry had agreed to make the one hundred and forty mile round trip to the seaside, to bury his son's pet terrapin at sea.

Cleethorpes, whilst commonly referred to as a seaside resort, was actually situated on the mouth of the Humber River, the vast and filthy expanse of water that served the industrial port town of Hull. Had Simon been aware of this geographical quirk, he would almost certainly have insisted they travel on to the sea proper, but as it were, he was blissfully unaware of the geography of his country. Water was water.

"Right then, lad," said Terry, looking out over the horizon, "let's say goodbye to George."

The tide was out. The initial sandy beach giving out after a hundred yards, there then sprawled black polluted sludge for the next four hundred yards. Terry sighed and looked down at his suede loafers. Then, taking his son's hand, he started the long walk out to the water.

* * *

"My daughter," Simon repeated to himself, "is not ill." And ignoring, the bellboy and his wheelchair, headed into the lobby of the hotel.

Chapter 11

Simon pushed three postcards into the Disney post box and turned in the direction of the restaurant where he had agreed to meet Melissa and Sarah.

29th March 2009

Dear Mum & Dad,

Well, tomorrow is the last day and we've actually had a great time.

I'm writing this in a café with a beer (7 Euros!!!!). Mel and Sarah have gone for a well-earned nap and I'm meeting them for tea later. Sarah's had an amazing time and even I have to say it's been fun.

See you on Saturday, Sime.

The Mexican restaurant was packed with early diners, the sombrero-wearing waiters irritable. Simon settled in a corner table, ordered a beer, winced at the price, and took out his holiday paperback.

Tomorrow afternoon they would return to Yorkshire. Despite his discomfort with all things Disney, Simon had genuinely enjoyed his week away. The weather had stayed good for them and Sarah's quiet but unabashed joy was infectious. He opened a paper-wrapped breadstick, leaving his spy novel unopened on the table. He supposed it was time to start thinking of going back to work. There was a pane of glass in the greenhouse that needed re-glazing. Porridge was due for a check-up at the vets. He mulled over a number of domestic duties that awaited him in England, enjoying the cold beer and the ambience of the crowded eatery.

His mobile buzzed in his pocket and retrieving it, he pressed it to his ear. "Hi, Mel. It's packed already, but I've got us a nice table. There's a lot of very grumpy Parisians in Mexican hats serving. It's hysterical. There's plenty on the menu that Sarah will like. If nothing else, she'll have nachos, won't she? Do you want me to order your drinks?" Simon's free hand fiddled with his beer mat.

"Simon, Sarah isn't going to make it down there for tea. She's not well enough. She was very weak by the time we made it back to the room, near collapse. She slept for two hours but she's no better. I've made her comfy in bed and I'm going to get room service, but she's pretty adamant that she doesn't want to eat. Her headache's got worse and she's nauseous. I'm checking her temperature now. Should I give her more Calpol? I gave her some a couple of hours ago but it's only kiddy stuff … Simon? Hello? Are you there?"

Simon closed his eyes and tightened his fingers around his beer bottle. "Yeah, I'm here. Give her the Calpol. I'll be right there." Simon threw a couple of notes on the table and, forgetting his novel, edged his way through the packed tables and waiters, back to the hotel.

* * *

"So, what do you think?" Melissa clicked the bedroom door shut, moving into their slightly larger adjoining bedroom and speaking quietly. "Her temperature was 38 degrees. She's lethargic with no appetite. She's complaining that her mouth is full of ulcers – actually she's been complaining about those for a couple of days. Do you think it's another infection? Do you think we should take her into hospital? It's ten kilometers from here, we can get a taxi. Lagny-sur-Marne, I think it's called. Shall I call reception?" Melissa moved towards the phone by the bed.

Simon stayed her hand gently, removing the telephone from her. "No, no hospitals. I think we should just get her home. She's responsive and she can walk. I'll make arrangements for a car and a flight. It's only 5 p.m.. We can have her home by midnight."

Melissa exhaled slowly and deliberately. "No hospitals. Simon, are you sure that you're in a position to make a judgment call on this?"

"What do you mean?" Simon glanced sharply at his wife.

"I mean, are you thinking this through and making the correct decision for the welfare of the patient, Simon? Or are you thinking this through and making the best decision for yourself?"

"How dare you?" Simon spoke quietly through his teeth, his anger palpable.

"I'm not trying to hurt you, Simon, but you know you're not dealing with this. Jesus, Sime – I have been sick with worry, watching Sarah get more and more tired over the week, while you, *you, the fucking doctor*, have carried on as if this is just a normal family holiday."

"Keep your voice down, and stop swearing," Simon hissed.

"You see?" Melissa sprang towards him, her voice lower. "Is this really the moment to argue about how much I swear? You're ostriching, Simon. You're burying your head in the sand and you're leaving me to deal with all this." She moved towards the window, looking out over the panorama of the park and the iconic Sleeping Beauty's Castle at its centre.

"We're not Sleeping Beauty's parents, Simon. We can't hide all the spinning wheels."

"Don't do this, Mel. Not now."

"Then when, Simon? When *are* you going to talk about it?"

"Hiding the spinning wheels didn't work anyway."

"No. It didn't, Simon. You're right." Melissa turned to Simon and lowered her voice further. "I can't go through this on my own. I can't nurse her and worry and make medical decisions and try to guess what is going on inside her. I can't cope with the worry alone, each time I see a bruise, or blood in the sink, or Sarah doesn't feel like ice-cream. I can't struggle with the knowledge that our little girl, who right now is lying in bed in the next room, is going to *die*, while my husband carries on as if nothing is happening. You have to talk about this, Simon. Shit, we have to talk to *Sarah*. How *long* are we going to keep this up?"

"Keep what up?"

"*Pretending*, Simon. Behaving as if nothing is wrong. It's been almost a month since she came out of hospital. Don't you realize that time is slipping away? You haven't mentioned the future once, not once in all these weeks. Do you know what Sarah said to me this morning?" Melissa's face shadowed with anger. "Do you know what our little girl said? She said *'When I grow up, I'm going to work at Disneyland.'* When she grows up, Simon. Sarah isn't even going to have another *Christmas* let alone grow up. We have to deal with this. We have to talk about it …"

"Shut up!" Simon leaped towards Melissa and shoved her against the wall by the bedside table. Melissa's eyes widened above his hand which was pressed over her mouth and nose.

For the first time in Simon's life, a surge of violence rose in him, a desire to smash his clenched fist into his beautiful wife's face, to crush bone and split flesh. To *hurt* her. He squeezed her wrist hard, relishing for just a moment the knowledge that it was causing her pain, then let go, turned away from her and gripped the small table set in the window to steady himself.

"Do you know why Sleeping Beauty was called Aurora, Melissa? Did you read that bit?" He sank into a tub chair, his head cradled in his hands. "It was because she filled her parents' life with light, like the sun at dawn. The only thing is, they didn't mention what happened while she was gone from them, did they? They don't tell you what happens when the light goes out."

Melissa paused, mentally checking that she was not injured. She noted the pain in her wrist, but dismissed it as minor. It was worth it just to see some kind of emotion in her husband. She glanced at the door to Sarah's bedroom and assessed the chances of her having heard their fight.

Her voice, when she finally spoke, was small, shaken. "Because they all *slept* through it. Simon. You're *not* going to sleep through this. We are not going to just have a nice long nap while the bad bits happen. Soon Sarah will be gone and you have to start thinking about life after that. Life after Sarah. You have to start thinking about what you are going to do. What we are going to do. And right now, we have to decide how to help Sarah. She's not well, Simon. This holiday is over. I'm calling concierge. She needs to go into hospital."

Simon lifted his head from his hands. "Don't, Mel. Don't. If she goes into hospital here, she may …" he faltered, "… she may never come out. We need to get her home. I want her to be in England. Let me change the flights. It'll be okay. We can get her back home."

Melissa looked at Simon, her eyes narrowing. "Fine. Change the flights. Get a car. But I'm going downstairs to talk to the concierge about her removal to hospital if necessary. Check her temperature again. If it spikes any more, she goes to *Lagny-sur-Marne*. Behave like a doctor, Simon. Because if you don't, I'll have the park doctor come up and take over."

Simon nodded, then stood and walked towards Sarah's room. "I'll check on her and then I'll call the airline. Do you, er … do you want me to look at that wrist?"

"It's fine." Melissa snapped and walked out of the room.

* * *

"Is she asleep?"

"Yes." Simon tucked the blanket around his sleeping daughter's chin, wishing he was able to make her more comfortable in the cramped airplane seat. "What time is it?"

"About 9 p.m.. We should be home half-tennish. Dad'll probably be waiting for us already."

"Can I get you any drinks at all?" Simon and Melissa both shook their heads as a member of the cabin crew, her hat denoting her senior status, beamed at them. "There are more blankets in the overhead locker. Ring if you want any assistance. Leeds Bradford have been informed of your impending arrival, and a wheelchair will be provided to take the three of you off first. We should be coming in close to the terminal, so it is only a short walk into baggage. Security have been briefed to clear you quickly. My name is Karen and I will be your Senior Executive Flight Attendant for the evening. I'll be looking after you for the next twenty-five minutes. Are you sure you don't want any drinks - free of charge...?"

"I'll take a scotch." Simon said.

"Nuts?" The air hostess responded brightly.

"Sorry? Er ... no. Thanks."

"Ice?"

"Erm, yes, please. That would be lovely."

"Water?"

"Just give him the bloody scotch." Melissa interrupted.

"Of course, Madam." The air hostess replied tightly, her painted mouth pursing. "Anything else?"

"That's everything, thanks." Simon answered.

The girl smiled graciously at Simon. "Enjoy your flight, *Sir*." She rolled down to her next passengers, the little bottles on the trolley tinkling against each other.

"How to make friends and influence people, hmm, Melissa?" Simon unscrewed the little bottle of scotch.

"I'm sorry if I'm a little charmed-out, Simon. I happen to have a lot on my mind at the moment. Perhaps you haven't noticed."

"Don't start this again." The ice began melting instantly as Simon poured the whisky over it. "Let's just get Sarah home."

"You need to take her temperature again in ten minutes."

"I know that, Melissa."

"I'm just reminding you."

"Thank you." A hint of sarcasm.

"You're welcome." Overly brightly.

Chapter 12

There were none of the demonstrative gestures or good-humored teasing that usually peppered a Bailey/Halford homecoming. Even Porridge stood quietly in the doorway with Diana and Melissa as Simon carried Sarah, wrapped in blankets, up the stairs to her bedroom.

When Simon came back down, they filed quietly into the kitchen, taking their usual seats at the big pine table.

"Tea or wine?" Melissa leant on the island unit. Her usually glossy hair was lacklustre and purple rings shadowed her eyes.

"Wine, darling." Diana picked up her handbag and gestured towards the garden door. "Do you mind ...?"

There was a general mumble of permission from around the table as Diana, dropping all pretence, took out a packet of Silk Cut and made her way to the door.

"Oh God, that's better." She exhaled deeply, the smoke pluming out of her and into the dark garden beyond. "What do we do next, Simon? Why does she sound so short of breath?"

"Anemia. The red blood cells carry oxygen around the body. Sarah doesn't have many."

"And why are her lips so blue?" Robert interjected, his tone short.

"Cyanosis. Oxygen again."

"Is she safe upstairs?"

Melissa clunked an assortment of mismatching wine glasses onto the table, and opened a screw top bottle of red. "I've put her old baby monitor on. I'll get the other handset now." She disappeared into the hallway.

Robert reached for one of the glasses. "How long has she been like this, Simon? She seemed okay when I took you to the hospital. But now? Blue lips, wheezing. Surely she should never have gone to that dratted theme park. Why has this happened so suddenly?" Diana and Robert both stared at Simon expectantly. Simon was the doctor. He should have the answers.

"We were told that her decline would be rapid. We were also told that we could have up to three months where she was relatively healthy."

"It was too damned tiring for her. You shouldn't have taken her."

"Robert." Diana moved back to the table, having flicked her cigarette butt into the garden. "Don't."

"No, Diana. He's a doctor. He should know how to look after her. Blue lips!"

"The cyanosis has only come on over the past few hours. Granted, it looks concerning. It is ... concerning." Simon stared at the grains in the pine table, tracing them with his finger.

Melissa returned, the crackle of the baby monitor announcing her arrival. She placed the handset on the table and they all stared at the lights as they rose and fell with each of Sarah's labored breaths. "So, what do we do now?"

Three faces looked expectantly at Simon. "We call Mr. Abnam in the morning. Try and shift Porridge and I'll bed down on the floor in her room tonight. Her temperature is stable, she's responsive and she can walk. I'll check on her every half hour through the night. If her breathing worsens she may have to go on a ventilator, but I don't think it's necessary at the moment."

Diana spoke. "So she'll go back into hospital?"

"Maybe, maybe not. Given that .." Simon faltered, he pressed his lips together hard, frowning to steel himself and push the threatening tears away, "… given that it has been agreed not to proceed with any more treatment, it may be that we care for her at home. Or, she may go into Madron House."

"Already?" Melissa turned quickly to look at Simon.

"She might go on day visits. Or just stay on bad days. Either way, it's time we went to see them. I'll talk to Mr. Abnam in the morning, but I think we will be advised that we need assistance now. She's going to need pain relief, anti-nausea medicine, round the clock support …"

"How long, Simon?" Robert's voice was gruff. "How long has she got?"

A terrible silence settled over the group as each stared intently at Simon. Simon pitched forward imperceptibly, a sensation of sinking through the wooden chair and table coming over him. "Possibly only a month."

* * *

Simon did as agreed, and spoke with Mr. Abnam, Sarah's consultant. Sarah's GP, Dr. Brown, had made a house visit and Mr. Abnam, not wishing to disturb the poorly girl any more than necessary, agreed to make a remote prognosis, based on the information given to him by the two GPs.

The cyanosis had lessened, her breathing easing. Both doctors confirmed that the respiratory problems did not sound pulmonary, but were the result of anemia. Mr. Abnam agreed with the prescription for iron tablets. As Sarah had begun to complain of pain *("The sheets hurt, Daddy.")*, painkillers and anti-nausea drugs were prescribed. The Community Nursing Team were briefed and by that afternoon they had visited Sarah, with the promise that they would return once a day.

Dr. Brown examined Sarah, sitting up in her white wooden bed, propped up on pink gingham cushions and pillows.

"Right then, Sarah. I'll leave you to, er …."

"Spongebob Squarepants."

"Yes, Spongebob. Of course. One of the Community Nurses will be along to see you this afternoon. I'll come back tomorrow, before you go to look at Madron House. Okay, Sarah?"

"Why am I poorly again?" Sarah looked archly at her father and the other doctor. "I was supposed to be better. Why am I poorly again?"

Dr Brown glanced quickly at the girl's father. How much did the child know? Not a lot, it would appear. He cleared his throat. "Sometimes, when we have such a nasty illness as leukemia, it can come back again, even when we have been feeling much better."

"But it keeps coming back. It doesn't go away. They said I was better. Why am I poorly again? When am I going to get better?"

Dr. Brown looked quickly at the father. This was his territory.

"I don't know, Princess. We're trying to make you better at the moment."

"Why aren't I going into hospital?" Sarah scowled, looking steadily at each of the doctors. "Why is this time different?"

"Ah, do you know what, Sarah? Why don't we talk about this later? Dr. Brown has to get off to see all the other poorly girls and boys who are waiting for him and I think Porridge is ready for a walk, aren't you, Porridge?" Porridge, chin on paw, rolled his eyes up at Simon, looking extremely uninterested in going for a walk in the early April drizzle.

108

Sarah sighed, rolled on her side and took up the remote control for her television. "'Kay."

* * *

For Simon, Sunday brought a hangover and church. Melissa and Simon's usual evening bottle of wine had risen to two and it was not the first morning that Simon had sworn, over his effervescent vitamin drink laced with paracetamol, that they would cut back. The beneficial blurring of the senses and fogging of the mind that the alcohol brought in the evening was negated by nausea over breakfast.

"Do you want one?" Simon waved the tube of vitamins at Melissa, who stood stretching and yawning by the Rayburn.

"Hmm. Thanks. Do we have proper coffee?"

"You'll be lucky to get a Nescafe, never mind percolator stuff. You not coming to church?" Simon gestured at Melissa's dressing gown and slippers.

Immediately Melissa hardened, her eyebrow lifting. "Yes, of course, dear. I thought I'd just leave our daughter upstairs, on her own."

"You know I didn't mean that, Melissa. I thought perhaps your mum would be coming over or something."

"I think mum and dad are doing enough, don't you think?"

"I wasn't suggesting they weren't, Mel. And I presume that they will be going to St Vincent's as usual. Is it everyone back here for lunch then, like usual?"

"*No*. Sarah is too poorly for all the noise. Simon I *warned* you…"

"I know. Things aren't normal. I get it. I just thought. Well, it's Sunday. We always … never mind. I'll tell my mum and dad." Simon washed the wine glasses from the night before by hand, perversely enjoying the slight pain the scalding water caused.

Melissa drained her glass, grimacing as the undissolved powder from the bottom hit her lips. "They know. I spoke to your mum last night. Terry is coming up to say hullo around teatime, though."

"Oh." Simon dried his hands. "So, do you mind if … I'll check on Sarah first, obviously … Is it okay if I go to church?"

"Of course I don't mind, Simon." Melissa's voice was brightly false. "It's your life."

"My life. Right."

* * *

St Matthew's was packed, Palm Sunday having brought a healthy sized congregation. Simon took a palm cross from one of the boxes by the door, put a pound in the collection jug and smiled at the elderly gentleman handing out hymn books. The church was gearing up for Easter Sunday celebrations and display boards at the entrance exhibited the Sunday school's work, Crayola art depicting the rising of Christ.

Simon bit the corner of his lip, suppressing a smile. Had it been last year? No, the year before perhaps, when Sarah, well enough to be in church, had surprised both her family and the congregation with a typically loud question, mid-sermon, and so doing, unintentionally introduced a complicated theological query into a number of the St Matthew's congregation's Easter lunch conversation. *"Daddy, who rolled the stone away?"*

That was the thing with Sarah. Nothing got by her.

They would, Simon supposed, have to talk to her soon, though he could see no reason to tell her that she was nearing the end. Sarah was rapidly becoming extremely ill. Her waking moments would soon be dampened by a blanket of morphine, her lucidity compromised. There was a chance that she would never need to know what was happening to her. Why scare the child?

They were to view Madron House on Tuesday. It was a prospect that terrified Simon. The idea of visiting the home where his daughter would … the place where she …. All those sick children! The mechanical devices, the enforced good cheer, the other patients – children who all looked ill. No. He would not think about it at the moment.

Simon stood for a hymn, surprised that the service had even begun. His subconscious had performed the required responses whilst his deeper thoughts had stayed with his daughter. How on earth could he tell Sarah that she was – going? Simon steadied himself against a momentary giddiness. Where Sarah was going precisely was not a speculation Simon could allow himself. Heaven was the usual destination for an innocent child, and the most painless explanation.

For Simon, a person could not just *cease* to be. How could they? How could a vibrant, buzzing energy just simply disappear? It was not physically possible. If you bounced a rubber ball on the floor, the kinetic energy continued in some form, never entirely dissipating – or so the physicists said. Surely a person's psyche left its mark on the world, the amassed energy of life continuing to reverberate for some time after death?

Any further thoughts on the sordid details of *disposal* repulsed him. Simon's view of death had changed little from the feelings of the seven-year old boy who had held onto the body of a stinking terrapin. He continued to struggle with the concept of a corpse, a cadaver – the 'empty overcoat'. Even in medical school, he had still considered the donors to be people, and had given them the respect they deserved during post-mortems, unlike some of his more raucous classmates.

He knew what a dead body looked like; knew what they felt like; had driven a scalpel into cold, deceased flesh. It was true that they appeared – empty. Devoid. But where had the person gone? They had to go somewhere.

Sarah's body was not a thought that he had dared approach. The possibility that his daughter would be put in a box in the dark, in the ground, was unthinkable. That she would be going to heaven was as far as Simon's mind had allowed him to travel on the road to acceptance. A misty, distant land, bathed in white light and populated with – Simon did not know. He ripped himself back to the here and now, the joyous chords from the organ stirring the congregation, their voices swelling as they went into the last triumphant verse of the Palm Sunday hymn:

"Ride on! Ride on in majesty!
In lowly pomp ride on to die;
bow thy meek head to mortal pain,
then take, O God, thy power, and reign!"

The congregants around Simon gasped and stepped out of the way muttering first in confused irritation and then in concern as the man who had stood amongst them a few seconds ago slid heavily to the floor in a dead faint, his hymn book thumping onto the pew in front.

Chapter 13

"It's alright. He's coming round."

Simon squinted as he looked up at the myriad of concerned faces. *Oh bugger.* "I'm okay. Sorry. I'm okay. I'll just get up. No, really, I'm okay. Sorry. Terribly sorry. Please don't make a fuss."

Simon allowed someone to heave him up from the wooden floor, wincing with a mixture of pain and embarrassment. His hangover washed back over him and he hoped fervently that he didn't smell of second hand merlot.

"Come on, Simon. Let's get you over to the vicarage." Familiar high cut cheekbones and an elegant hairstyle came into focus and Simon groaned with relief as Mrs. Hughes smiled at him. "Gentlemen, if you could just accompany us, just in case. Can you walk yet, Simon? Do you need a moment?"

"No, no – I'm fine. Sorry, ergh ..." Simon gingerly touched his head – he must have bashed it on the way down. "Sorry, everyone. Awfully sorry."

"Do stop saying sorry, Simon. Thank you. Coming through ... thank you."

The blast of air as they left the temporarily paused service was most welcome, sharpening Simon's senses somewhat and calming his swimming head.

"I think we'll be fine now, gentlemen. Thank you so much for your help." Mrs. Hughes dismissed the men who had accompanied them out with the briskness of a woman used to dealing with The Brighouse West Scout Brigade. "Do you want to sit on a tombstone, or do you think you can make it across the road?"

"I'm fine, honestly. Sorry. I should just go home."

"Absolutely not. You doctors make the worst patients. You've cracked your head on the pew and we'd better make sure it's all working up there before you go home. Come on. You can see the progress the girls have made."

Simon groped around his memory, sure that the 'the girls' should make sense. It didn't.

They made their way slowly back to the vicarage, Simon feeling slightly better as they progressed. Mrs. Hughes held onto his arm firmly. Not, Simon mused, that there was much hope of the tiny framed Mrs. Hughes being much help should he decide to keel over again, but the support felt good.

"Watch out for dogs," Mrs. Hughes advised redundantly, their arrival celebrated by a cacophony of yipping and barking. They fought their way through the motley gang of animals and Mrs. Hughes settled Simon in a chair at the kitchen table. "Now, Simon, brandy or whisky?"

"Ergh, you're kidding? It's only 11.30 a.m. isn't it?"

"I thought you were supposed to give people a tot when they'd fainted. Anyway, as I shall be driving you home – don't look at me like that, Simon, you can't drive when you've had a banged head – as I shall be driving you home, you may as well have a drink. Brandy, or whisky?"

"Brandy would be lovely. A small one."

Simon was grateful to be treated like a small boy, albeit one that was allowed hard liquor. In fact, there could be no better person in the world to take care of him right now. Mrs. Hughes (who did actually have a first name – Muriel - but was always referred to as Mrs. Hughes by her husband Duncan and therefore by everybody else) had a gentle, yet firm, personality. Old fashioned and posh, but with the 'common touch', Mrs. Hughes was loved by everyone. Her formidable energy was bundled into one tiny, well dressed and well spoken package. She poured it into charity work, her animals, cleaning the church, running the parish opera society and a million other duties, which she took on without complaint and exceedingly good grace. In short, she was a pocket rocket.

Mrs. Hughes poured his drink and winked as she tipped a thimbleful-sized amount into a glass for herself. "It would be rude not to." She beamed and taking out a chopping board began to peel a pile of potatoes with astonishing speed. "So, Simon. How are you feeling? And I'm not just talking about your bruised head and hurt pride. We heard about Sarah. Duncan, as you know, sits on the school Board of Governors. No names were mentioned, but it came up that a child was being withdrawn. Obviously, we put two and two together. How are you holding up?"

Simon took a sip of the brandy. He noted the lady's lack of platitudes. She had not said *'I'm sorry'*. It was refreshing. Most people effused. All apologized. It was exhausting, forgiving people for something that they had most certainly not done. "Well, in fact, Mrs. Hughes, I don't think I am holding up. Melissa doesn't think I am. I thought I was, but apparently I'm 'not dealing with things'. Perhaps I'm not. I don't think I can. My mind starts to work on it, but then as soon as I start thinking about the future," Simon paused, taking a deep breath, "about certain aspects of the future, it pops back out. Like a gear shift that won't stay in place."

"You can't force it. We all have our own way of handling these things. You might talk to Duncan. He's rather good at these conversations you know. It's his job. He will be able to help you."

"Unless he can find a cure for cancer, Mrs. Hughes, I'm not sure that he can help." Simon spoke softly, staring into his brandy.

Mrs. Hughes regarded Simon steadily, taking her time. She was not a woman who was afraid of silences. In her long reign as Vicar's Wife at St Matthew's, she had consoled innumerable grieving parishioners. "No, Simon. He can't find a cure for cancer. No one is going to. Not in time for Sarah, I'm afraid. But he can help you with your grief. Help you find a way through. Help you find a life after Sarah."

"*Life after Sarah.* That's not the first time I've heard that. Right now, at this very second, I can't conceive a 'life after Sarah'. Sarah is my life. I didn't realize until it was too late. Nothing else matters. Not work, not friends, not even Melissa. I go to work to put food on the table for Sarah. I clean the car on a Saturday so that we look respectable and presentable – for Sarah. I used to do these things for Melissa, but now I'm not sure. It's all for Sarah."

"What about you, Simon. What do you do for you?" Mrs. Hughes scooped a cat off a kitchen chair and sat down.

"I don't know. I suppose work was for me. Though studying to get there, that was for mum and dad. I play a bit of golf, but I never really enjoyed it, to be honest." He gave her a wry smile. "You know, I don't think I've ever told anyone that. I suppose I just thought that was what a moderately well off family man was supposed to do on a Saturday afternoon. That, and Melissa wanted us to join. Church. That's for me. Melissa and I always seem to just miss each other with faith. First, when Sarah got ill initially, I lost faith, while Melissa became quite manically devout. Now, I still believe, but Melissa doesn't seem interested. She appeared quite cross with me for coming today, actually. I think she thinks I should be by Sarah's bedside. It's not that I don't want to be, but ...," his face contorted and he swallowed hard, trying to get the words out

118

before the tears blocked them, "there's nothing I can do. I wish I could make her better, I wish I had a prescription. If I could just open my desk drawer and write her a magic note. *Take this to the pharmacy, it'll take a few days to clear up ...* but I can't." In that instant he lost the battle to compose his features. Tears stained his cheeks and dripped off his chin onto the table below. "I can't fix this. She's broken and I can't fix her."

A renewed chorus of canine ecstasy signaled Duncan's return. He entered the kitchen with a retinue of dogs wagging their tails behind him. Duncan's voice was light and teasing. "How is the talk of the town? Has he come round yet?" Then he caught sight of Simon's tear-stained face. "Oh, Simon. A terrible thing. This is a very lonely time for you. I want you to know that we are here for you if you ever want to talk, day or night." The vicar took a scruffy jumper off the back of a chair and put it on over his ecumenical shirt and collar. He topped up Simon's brandy, ignoring the feeble protestations. "Stay for lunch."

Simon wiped his tears with the back of his hand, feeling less embarrassed than comforted to be treated like a school boy. "I can't. Melissa wouldn't ... I have to get back."

"You've had a bang on the head, Simon." Mrs. Hughes got up and indicated her large oven. "It's chicken casserole. I always make far too much. We should be keeping an eye on you for an hour or so

119

anyway and I've already said that I will drive you home. Why don't you let me call Melissa? I'm sure she'll understand."

"I'm not sure about that. She isn't very ... we're not getting on very well at the moment."

Duncan stroked a large ginger cat that had jumped into his lap. "That's not surprising, Simon. These are difficult times. Any relationship would be under strain. Mrs. Hughes and I were only bellowing at each this morning and we are not going through what you are going through."

Simon looked up from his brandy. The second shot had had the calming effect that Mrs. Hughes had intended; the pain in his head was fading. "You and Mrs. Hughes bellowing?" He raised an eyebrow in incredulity.

"Yes, Simon. Bellowing. I believe there was a smattering of name-calling as well." Duncan caught the eye of his wife, who gave a tight smile, though her eyes twinkled. "It is a common assumption that members of certain professions are faultless. Vicars get cross too, you know. And we dislike people. We even swear – yes, swear from time to time. I seem to remember hammering my thumb recently and using a panoply of curses. Rather loudly. Of course..." The vicar broke off, appraising the man before him, "doctors aren't infallible either, I imagine."

"Everyone blames me." Simon mumbled into his glass.

"No. Melissa, perhaps. But she too is grieving, and she is wrong. The only person who really blames you is yourself. And you've had a bang on the head." Duncan chuckled, Mrs. Hughes' tinkly laughter joining in. Simon looked up, surprised by their mirth. He had got so used to hushed whispers and groveling platitudes that for a moment their giggles horrified him. "I forgot to thank you for livening up the service." Duncan added. "They were much more alert for the second half." Simon surprised himself as his shoulders began to shake. The dogs barked as the three laughed.

* * *

"Thanks, Dad."

Simon waved his father off from the door. The evening was still bright, the April sun only just going down. He jogged back up the stairs to check on Sarah who was asleep, settled and satisfied having finished a Harry Potter chapter with her grandfather.

Downstairs, Melissa was at the kitchen table, half hidden by a mountain of floristry oasis, boxes of roses and ribbons.

Melissa had bought the floristry business four years ago – two years before Sarah first became ill. Long since departed from her girlhood job at the department store in Leeds, she had become bored with the life of a housewife and once Sarah was happily settled in school, she looked for a business she could take on.

Floristry was the perfect answer. She was able to flex her creative muscles, her artistic nature immediately putting her at the top of her night-school class. Once she had taught herself how to hand tie bouquets and create elegant table decorations, she found a run down little property down a ginnel on Commercial Street and set about turning it into the most fashionable flower shop in town.

Melissa was shrewd. She employed staff with far better experience than her and paid and treated them well. Within two years *'Fluff & Nonsense'* was the preferred supplier for all the local hotels, restaurants and wedding co-ordinators.

When Sarah fell ill, she sold half of the business to her senior member of staff. Lorraine was a working mother like Melissa and they shared the workload amicably. This week, Lorraine was visiting her mother in Scotland, so preparations for one of their smaller weddings fell on Melissa.

"How you getting on?"

"Ten pomanders down, fourteen to go. I won't be finished until at least 2 a.m., but at least they'll be fresh for the wedding breakfast tomorrow. The bouquets are done. These are just the table decorations. How are you feeling?" Melissa snipped a white rose from its stem and pushed the flower into a ball of oasis.

"Fine. It was just too much wine, no breakfast and not enough sleep. Do you want some help?"

"No offence, Simon, but your track record with floristry isn't great. Remember the wonky pomander trees you did that Christmas? I'm okay. Thanks for the offer. Do you really think that's a good idea?" Melissa paused, dangling the pomander from its white ribbon before her. "I know we've been drinking a bit too much wine recently, but don't you think whisky is a bit of a slippery slope?"

Simon rummaged through the freezer, looking for ice. "I really think it's time we did a supermarket shop. There's nothing in the house. No tea, coffee. Do we have ice?"

"Did you hear me? Don't you think whisky is a rather dangerous path to travel at 7 p.m. on a Sunday evening? You've already done a bottle of wine this afternoon." Melissa stabbed a sprig of gypsofilia into the oasis.

"No." Simon kept his back to Melissa. "Bugger it, I'll have it neat. I'm off to watch Top Gear in the sitting room. You sure you're alright with all that?" He gestured with the bottle at the mound of roses.

"I'm fine."

Simon tucked the whisky bottle beneath his arm, a tumbler in one hand, opening the door to the hallway with his other. "Right. See you in a bit, then."

He clicked the telly on in the small sitting room. It was cozy and smart with blue pinstripe sofas, white walls and 'shabby chic' white painted furniture. A large model schooner stood in the windowsill and a long cracked-leather footstool served as a coffee table, stacked with GP newspapers and *'Homes and Gardens'*. He sloshed a large whisky into the tumbler and fiddled with the remote, searching for the motoring program he wanted to watch.

He ran his tongue over the canyons and craters of his sore inner cheek, now too painful to chew. A large amount of the damage had been done that afternoon whilst his father was there. Terry had enquired as to whether Sarah could see some of her friends, a bit of a change from watching cartoons and playing scrabble with her family. Simon had seen no reason why not.

"Trust me, I've tried." Melissa had cradled her tea-mug and rolled her eyes.

"What do you mean?" Simon had looked puzzled.

Melissa sighed. "All of Sarah's friends suddenly have astonishingly busy social lives. Despite the fact that Izzy Hartwell has been coming here every Wednesday afternoon for months, she apparently now does gymnastics. Francesca does ballet. Harriet has a maths tutorial. Sundays are apparently out too."

"Are you saying you think they're lying, eh?" Terry, Simon's father had bristled, color rising from his neck.

"I don't think it's the kids, Terry. I don't think the parents want to be … I don't think they like being so close to illness. It scares them." Melissa leaned back in her chair. "I don't blame them really. They know their children will ask them questions, make them explain things they don't want to explain yet. They don't want their children to realize how vulnerable they are."

"Load of ruddy wimps!" Terry banged the table, making Porridge look up sleepily from his basket, where he was taking a rare break from guarding Sarah. "How would they like it if she were their child? Don't they think about that?"

"It's exactly that, Dad." Simon had bitten the inside of his cheek hard. "They think *'What if she were our child?'*. They don't want to be made to think it. They don't want to see it. They don't want their children close to it. Bad luck."

The remembered conversation superimposed itself over the television program. Simon knocked back a large swig of whisky. It was cheap and the burn as it went down and the sting against his sore inner cheek satisfied Simon's slight tendency to masochism. *Bastards.* All those patronizing smiles at the school gates, the promises of *'anything we can do'*, the endless, incessant apologies *'I'm so sorry, Simon. If there's anything we can do…' Actually, there is. You can let your daughter come over and play for a couple of hours. What's that? Oh, I see. You don't want your precious little brat to see my daughter's weird tufty hair. You don't think she should see the drip stand next to Sarah's bed. Yes, I see. I see alright.*

Simon poured another inch of whisky into his glass. The three men bickering over cars on the television were merely background noise to his thoughts. Unable to concentrate, he began flicking through his CD collection which was now, he thought sadly, becoming redundant, like the much-loved LPs that sat gathering dust in the loft. Where was the joy in an MP3 download, he wondered, draining his glass. What about the tactile feel of a record? The cover art, the disc art? As much of his memories were sunk into the snarling tusked and winged skull on the front of a Motorhead album as in the lyrics or (Melissa would say *shouts*) of Lemmy.

He turned the television off and fumbled with the CD player drawer, eventually managing to slip a disk into the correct place. The opening chords of Eric Clapton's album 'Unplugged' blared out and Simon sent a pile of rejected CDs skittering across the floor as he lunged to turn the volume down. The door opened.

"Simon. For God's sake, turn it down. Look at you. You're a disgrace." Melissa's head in the door. *Bit blurry.*

"Sorry. I didn't realize it was that loud."

"I'm off to bed."

"You've finished already? That was quick."

"It's half twelve, Simon. And yes, I worked quickly. Night." Melissa disappeared.

"G'night."

Simon leaned back against the leather footstool, holding the bottle up and surveying the damage. *Whoops. Mostly gone. Might as well finish it.*

A recognizable riff came over the speakers, Simon beginning to sing before he realized what the track was.

> *"Would you know my name*
> *If I saw you in heaven?*
> *Will it be the same*
> *If I saw you in heaven?*
> *I must be strong, and carry on*
> *Cause I know I don't belong*
> *Here in heaven…"*

Simon sang on, his baritone loud and off key. He giggled a bit as he kicked over the stack of CDs again. Who was it that said, "*You're not drunk if you can lie down without holding on*"? Simon grinned to himself as the room tilted slightly.

He didn't hear the door opening to the sitting room and jumped when he felt a little hand on his shoulder. His senses sharpening quickly, he leaped towards the stereo to turn it down. "Princess – what are you doing out of bed? Was it too loud? Sorry. I'll turn it down."

Sarah shook her head and settled herself on the edge of the leather footstool. She was barefoot and wearing only a nightie. Her frailty and tufty hair gave her the look of a very old woman, which was exacerbated by the shrewd look she gave the empty bottle of Teachers whisky.

"It's, okay, Daddy. I just wanted to talk to you."

"Sweetheart, it's very late. Aren't you cold? Come on," Simon staggered to his feet, "Lets get you up to bed."

"I've been in bed all day. I want to talk."

Simon stopped at the door and regarded the seated Sarah carefully. His seven-year old daughter spoke with a calm authority, a maturity that had been increasingly presenting itself since Disneyland. Sarah had always been articulate, observant – animated but mature. But recently … there was something else. It was as if she had slowed down, she had more time to think.

Simon moved back into the room, shutting the sitting room door and turning up the gas fire. He tripped slightly, recovered quickly and took a travel rug from the arm of the sofa to wrap around Sarah, sobering up with the speed only a parent can muster.

"What did you want to talk about?"

Sarah stood up, then hopped onto the squashy sofa and tucked her feet under her blanket. She held her father's gaze firmly.

"I'm dying aren't I?"

Chapter 14

Sarah tucked the lambs wool blanket under her toes, wiggling her feet and curling up into the sofa. The house had taken on the strange atmosphere that, in her experience, houses did, when only the grown-ups were up. The lights in the kitchen were off, the usual vibrancy of the large family room zapped. The little sitting room in which she rarely sat felt different in the night. The lamps made the room more solemn than in the daytime.

Daddy was drunk, she mused. It wasn't a particularly shocking revelation, though she did find it a bit sad. Mummy and Daddy often got what they called 'tiddly' at Christmas. And in the summer there were plenty of garden parties where the grown-ups talked too loudly and did silly things like ride the children's bikes. At her last birthday party there had been a number of trampoline-based accidents involving the grown-ups. Uncle James had fallen asleep in the bouncy castle. This kind of being drunk was slightly different though, she could tell. The yummy smelling jugs of brown stuff with fruit and cucumber - cucumber! Grown-ups were weird - that were passed around barbeques were fun, harmless. The empty whisky bottle beside her daddy was dirty somehow. Like drunk people on telly.

Daddy looked tired. His hair was longer than normal and his face was all furry. Scratchy actually. She wished he'd shave.

129

"Daddy?"

He sank into the sofa next to her and she thought he looked old. Older. He spoke slowly and his voice sounded thick. "What on earth has made you say that, Princess?"

Sarah picked at a speck of lint on the blanket. "It's okay, Daddy. You can say. I won't cry." She looked up at her daddy and noticed the rims of his eyes were reddening. "I'm not getting better am I, Daddy? You all think I'm going to die." She winced as a pain shot through her thigh bone. Leukemia sucked.

He still didn't answer. "Daddy." A little more insistent this time.

"I – we – you are very poorly." Her father shifted his weight, a hand covering his eyes. "There is a chance. No. It doesn't seem that you are going to get better. No."

Sarah had the same feeling that you get when you go over a bump in the road. Like her tummy went up and down. Normally she loved that feeling. Knew the spots in the roads they travelled regularly where they would get the sensation and encouraged her mum to drive faster, faster.

This time it wasn't a nice feeling.

"Am I going to get worse?" She picked at the lint diligently. Trying to separate the little ball from the fibers of wool. She wished her nails were longer.

"Yes."

"What?"

"Yes, Sarah. You're going to get more poorly." Her father took a sharp little intake of breath.

"Don't cry, Daddy."

"Oh, Sarah!" Her daddy's shoulders started to shake up and down, though he kept his hand over his face. Sarah wriggled up the sofa to him, wincing as a seam of upholstery scratched against her hypersensitive skin. She put her arm up to cuddle him, but his back remained to her. She patted him on the back, helplessly.

"What's going to happen to me?" The lint was free from its fibrous net now. Sarah flicked it away, found another and started working on it. "Am I going to die?"

Her father took a deep breath, followed by some other long inhalations. His shoulders steadied slightly and he turned to look at her. "We all die, Sarah." He tucked a stray hair behind her ear, his fingers feeling slightly rough against her delicate skin.

She frowned at him and gave a little nod. "We all die when we're old. Like Harry's granddad. He died last week. He was old. Harry missed PE. I'm not going to be old, am I? I'm not going to be a grown-up."

Sarah's daddy's voice went squeaky. "No, you're not going to be a grown-up."

Sarah's tummy flipped again. "Do you want a tissue, Daddy?" Sarah unraveled herself from the blanket and got up. "Do you think we could have your special hot chocolate? I'll brush my teeth after."

Sarah watched, fascinated, as her father's features contorted into a number of facial expressions that she had never seen before. He looked like he was in pain. Or like he was trying to smile at the same time as being in pain. Or having a poo. Actually, that was quite disgusting, Sarah thought, and pushed the image to the back her mind.

Daddy sniffed deeply, snot making a disgusting gurgling sound in the back of his throat. "Come here." He sniffed again, his voice cracking a little bit. "Let's go get hot chocolate. I don't think we need to worry about teeth tonight." He picked her up, a little unsteady. Sarah held on tight as he put the blanket back round her shoulders. She buried her head in his neck, breathing in the comforting, salty smell of his skin, his aftershave - so familiar - and another scent, tangy, alcoholic.

Sarah sat on the island unit in the kitchen, the blanket wrapped round her, her bare feet sticking out the end. She loved making hot chocolate with Daddy. Mummy didn't do it right, didn't break up extra bits of chocolate from the treats cupboard. She didn't do it in a pan, stirring until all the lumps of Dairy Milk or Galaxy had melted.

"Have we got squirty cream?"

"Not sure, Princess. But if we do, we're having it. Do you want to grate chocolate for the top?"

"Uh-huh." Sarah spun awkwardly on the counter, and carefully ran the bar of chocolate along the blades of the grater, watching her fingers as she had been taught. "Daddy?"

"Yes, Princess."

"How old am I going to be? How much older am I going to get, I mean?"

Sarah watched her Daddy as he stopped. His knuckles went white as his grip tightened on the pan he was stirring. He put the chocolate powder down and came to her, frowning, though not like when he was cross. His forehead was frowny, but his eyes were kind. He put his hands on either side of her hips, as a tear rolled down his cheek.

"You are very, very poorly, Sarah. We've tried everything we can to make you better, but those baddie blood cells we talk about have just been too strong for us. As you know, you have been getting more poorly recently and that is going to continue. The special hospital place we are going to on Tuesday ..."

"Mad House."

"Madron House, yes. Madron is a special kind of hospital for girls and boys, like you, who aren't going to get any better. At first, we might just go there during the day, or if you are feeling particularly unwell. After a while, you might decide that you want to stay there more, particularly as they can give you medicines that will make you more comfortable."

"How long will I be there?" Sarah felt the tummy going over a bump sensation again. This time she felt tears welling up. "When am I going to die?"

"We don't know, darling. I can't answer that." Sarah watched her daddy chewing his lip, something he did when he didn't want to tell her something.

"What happens when I die? Will it hurt?" Tears had started flowing now and Sarah wiped them roughly from her face with the flat palm of her hand. Her daddy did the same, his face creasing again, his voice going funny.

"No, treasure. It won't hurt. You will probably be fast asleep and won't know anything about it. Mummy and Daddy will be there, cuddling you and you will just slip away."

"To heaven?"

"Yes, to heaven."

Sarah nuzzled into Simon, who held her tight in her arms. It hurt a bit, but it didn't matter. "But, Daddy. Who will live with me in heaven?"

Sarah felt the arms around her slacken slightly. Her father's breathing seemed to stop for a moment. He moved back from her slowly, his face in hers, his breath tainted with the whisky stuff he had been drinking.

"God, Sarah. You will live with God."

"But I don't know God."

134

There was a pause. "Of course you do, darling. God is with you all the time. He knows you. He made you."

"But I don't know him. I don't know what he's like." Sarah started to sob now. She didn't want to go somewhere alone. She didn't even like going to the loo in restaurants alone. She was scared. She knew she wasn't a little, little girl anymore, but she still needed her Mummy and Daddy. Or her Grandpa Aitch. Or Grandma Diana. She had to have someone. She started to howl now. She couldn't help it. She'd had enough of being brave little Sarah. She was going to die and she was going to go to heaven and she wouldn't know anybody there. It wasn't fair.

"Great Grandma and Grandpa will be there – and Mummy's grandparents. They were lovely. They will take care of you. And then there is Mummy's dog from when she was little. And Grandpa Robert had a pussy cat called Winston – he'll look after you…"

"I don't KNOW them." Sarah hyperventilated, struggling to get the words out. "And I can't be looked after by a stupid cat. I need a grown-up. I need you and Mummy. I'm scared. I don't want to go on my own…"

Sarah felt herself being lifted off the counter top. She wrapped her legs round her father as he squeezed her. She could feel his tears dripping onto her neck and ears; he bit the shoulder of her nightie as he mumbled into her shoulder. Beside them the milk hissed as it boiled over, the bubbles surging up, uncontrolled, out of the pan.

"I'll go with you. I'll go with you. It'll be alright. Oh God, it'll be alright. I'll go to heaven with you."

Chapter 15

"You stupid, *stupid* bastard."

Another roll of ribbon hissed past Simon's head, followed by a carnation and a box of nameplace cards. He dodged the missiles, ducking beneath the florist shop counter. Two or three blocks of oasis crashed down upon him, projected with surprising power despite their light weight.

"What was I supposed to do? Wake you up?"

"*Yes*," howled Melissa. "No. *Yes*. You should have brought her up to bed. We could have talked to her together. I could have changed the subject. We could have worked it out. But you..." Another carnation whizzed past, "... you, stupid, selfish, drunken *bastard* ..." A rose followed the same trajectory "... decided to get pissed up and have the most important conversation we will ever have with our daughter *on your own and shit-faced*."

"I didn't mean for it to happen. She *asked*..."

"And not *only*," Melissa's face, incandescent with rage, appeared above where he crouched, "not only, did you decide to *tell our daughter she was going to die*, you also told her that you were going to *die with her*."

"I didn't!" Simon wailed, cringing in case Melissa decided to bring anything heavier down upon his head. "I didn't mean it like that. I was upset, confused. I ..."

"You were *drunk*! You'd downed an entire bottle of whisky and a bottle of wine and you let Sarah see you like that. You are a dirty, hopeless alcoholic and I *never* want to see you again."

Melissa disappeared again. Simon waited a few moments to see if more missiles would be forthcoming. The airspace above him seeming clear, he stood up cautiously.

"Being drunk one night doesn't make somebody an alcoholic, Melissa."

"A whole bottle of whisky, Simon."

"Bad, yes. But a one-off. We've both been drinking too much. I don't think it's unknown exactly, given the circumstances."

"You told her you were going to kill yourself." Melissa sat down on a plastic office chair near the back area of the little shop.

"No. I didn't. I think I told her…"

"You think." Melissa spat. "You don't even remember."

Simon sighed and leaned on the countertop. "I do remember. I said that I would go with her. She was scared and I was scared and it just sort of came out. I didn't think …"

"No, you most certainly did not *think*, Simon. There hasn't been an awful lot of thinking going on in that head of yours for sometime. I'm sorry, Simon, but I don't want you back in the house. You'll have to go and stay with your parents. I can't have a loose cannon, a drunk, in the house at this time. You're a liability."

Simon stood up straight, his hands flat on the counter. "I'm not a

138

drunk. You can't throw me out, Melissa. How bloody selfish is that? Do you think that's what Sarah wants now? Don't you think that's going to hurt Sarah a lot more than it hurts me?"

"We're shut." A startled woman shut the florist's door hastily as Melissa leaped up. She flipped the sign over. "I'm not trying to hurt anyone. I'm trying to protect my baby."

"Oh no you're not, Melissa. You're hell bent on blaming me for all this. It's just an excuse to cause me pain, and in so doing you're going to cause Sarah pain. Just when she needs us to be more together than ever."

"How dare you suggest that I don't have the best interests of my child at heart? You, you who decided to tell our daughter that you would *die with her*. I've got to tell you, Simon, Mum and Dad were really knocked back when they heard that one. It was bad enough babysitting her this morning and discovering that she knew she was going to die, but you really *iced the fucking biscuit* when you told her that she'd have some *company*."

"What on earth did she say to them?"

"Being our daughter, she breezily announced that given that she was going to die soon, she was going to eat as many sweets as she liked and she was officially putting an end to teeth brushing. She also demanded that we get cracking with the last Harry Potter book because *she wants to know what happens before her and Daddy go to heaven*."

Melissa paced the room, her hands behind her head. "I know you are hurting, Simon. I know that you find conflict difficult. I know that you love your daughter, but can you really, really tell me that you are in a healthy frame of mind at the moment?"

"Are you?"

"I'm keeping it together."

"Generally, so am I. No. Don't start shouting. Last night was stupid. And unfortunate. I didn't know she was going to come downstairs. She hasn't done that for years. And it was difficult. She asked really, difficult questions. I can cope with her ..." Simon steeled himself yet again, the words still difficult to form, " ... Sarah going... not being there, I might just recover from. One day. But Sarah being alone and scared somewhere? I can't handle that, Melissa. I cannot cope with the knowledge that she might be scared."

"She's dying – not going to boarding school."

"Don't be so fucking flippant." Simon gripped onto the counter top again, this time to quell his rage. "I'm a Christian. I believe in heaven. I don't know exactly what happens there, but I do know that Sarah is going onto another place without me. And I know that Sarah is scared about going to that other place. Alone. It's the most natural thing in the world for me to want to go with her."

"Want to? So you *are* saying that you are suicidal? Because you do realize that this isn't 'The Faraway Tree', don't you? There's no magic tree to get you up there and a special slide when you want to come back down. What makes you even think that heaven exists? Grow up, Simon. It's all a fairy tale. It's just a bedtime story we tell ourselves to make us feel better about death."

Simon looked at his wife with wonder. His wife? She was a stranger. Sure, she looked the same, almost. Anger and revulsion had besmirched her countenance. Her classic good looks were now tarnished. And yet he had coped with her hatred, understood her disgust. Had pitied her even, understanding her anger to be a part of the agony that she too was experiencing. He felt her pain in each barbed comment, comparing her to a wounded animal, unable to show her anguish in any other way than biting and attacking.

But the vicious denial of an afterlife? How could she possibly deny him – deny *herself* - faith in an afterlife, the safe place that their daughter would go onto, *the place where they would see her again*? Refutation was obscene. Unforgivable. To have lost the simple faith that Sarah was to continue being loved, to continue being …

"Do you know what, Melissa?" Simon stood taller now and Melissa instinctively stepped back. "I have coped with your rejection. I have dealt with your misplaced anger and scorn. I've soaked up your hatred and I've even felt sorry for you whilst I've done it. But I am not going to allow you to stand there and refute the very basics of the religion that we have both taught our daughter and which right now is the only thing keeping me from falling apart. Sarah will be going to the God that we have both worshipped and you will *never* suggest otherwise in my presence again. Once Sarah goes into Madron House, yes, I'll move out, if that's what you wish. But while Sarah is at home, I'm not going anywhere. And you need to know this: I will do anything, *anything* to make my daughter safe and happy. And there's not a damned thing you can do to stop me."

* * *

Simon carried Sarah out of the back of the car and set her in the wheelchair provided by the community nurses, then tucked a blanket round her legs. Madron House, named after the patron saint of pain relief, was a purpose built, colorful building, with a wavy roof and glass walls.

He wheeled Sarah towards the building, Melissa walking a few paces behind. The atmosphere between them was taut, but both were doing everything in their power to hide the friction from Sarah.

The threesome made their way from the small car park, past well kept flowerbeds, towards the entrance. A modern fountain on their left gurgled over a bed of smooth pebbles. Simon paused, as fond of water features as he knew his daughter was.

"Daddy, all the stones have writing on."

Simon felt his heart thud downwards into his stomach, like an elevator plummeting down a lift shaft. Each pebble was named.

"Oh. Right let's get going shall we?"

"No, Daddy, I want to see what they say – they're names. And numbers."

"Yes, they must be the names of all the people who live here."

Melissa caught up, visibly blanching at the water feature.

"I think they might be the boys and girls who have died, Daddy. Look, they have dates on."

Silence. What could they say?

"I'd like one of those pinkish ones when you do mine. The grey ones are boring. Ooh look, a cat."

Simon and Melissa caught each other's eyes, relief mixing with concern. Despite the friction, twelve years of marriage brings an ability to communicate without words. Sarah had always been an optimist. She was always bright and determined, but her attitude toward her impending demise seemed too casual, even for the indomitable Sarah Bailey.

"Are you okay?" Melissa asked Simon as she pressed the buzzer.

"Yup. You?"

"Yup."

A woman with an astonishing shock of frazzled ginger hair, quite the most orange Simon had ever seen, opened the door with a grin. "Hello!" She greeted them enthusiastically, her positive energy infectious. "You must be the Baileys. We've been looking forward to meeting you. Come in, come in." She ushered them into the building, beaming at Sarah as she was wheeled in.

143

The entrance hall was large and bright, carpeted in royal blue. In one corner an arrangement of beanbags surrounded a sunken fishpond covered with a mesh. This too had a small fountain in the middle, the gurgling water creating a soothing sound. Against this, a sound system played quiet music. *Enya*, thought Simon.

A couple of women, both wearing colorful flowing skirts, stood laughing and nursing big mugs of tea by a large pine desk. A baby, around 10 months old, speed crawled through the area, chased by a laughing girl of about nineteen and another older lady.

"Oscar's off again, is he?" the ginger woman called. The women by the desk put down her tea and ran, laughing, after the baby. The ginger-haired lady turned back to the Baileys, grinning broadly. "That's Oscar. He's a little rascal. He corners at about thirty miles per hour. Lucky his mum's so young; she's about the only one that can catch him. I'm Rhonda, by the way. I'm the Administrations Director and Palliative Care Consultant, but you don't need to know any of those boring bits. Rhonda will do fine."

"Hi, Rhonda," Melissa and Simon replied obediently, almost in union. There was something about Rhonda. One of those women you wouldn't want to cross, but who made you feel entirely safe when she was being nice to you. Simon felt like a schoolboy for the second time that week. He felt relief mixed with only mild irritation. Someone else was in charge.

"I see you've discovered our fish pond, Sarah." Rhonda followed

144

Sarah's gaze. Why don't we go and have a look? Would you like that?"

"Sure," Sarah replied. "How come it's inside?"

"Because we all like to look at fish. There's something very relaxing about them. But we don't always want to be outside in the horrid rain, do we? So we decided to have a fishpond indoors. Why not? We can do anything we like, can't we, Sarah?"

"Yes." Sarah responded with gusto. The proposal of a life without rules instantly appealing to the sharp seven year old.

Rhonda smiled at Simon and took over guiding Sarah's wheelchair. The action added to the impression that Rhonda was firmly in charge. "As you know, Madron House, or the Mad House as we like to call it …"

"That's what I call it!" Sarah butted in.

"You are going to fit right in here, aren't you? The Mad House was purpose built when the lease ended on our scruffy old place. So we got to build exactly what we wanted. All the kids gave their ideas, the mums and dads chipped in with their thoughts and this is what we got. Everything is designed to be fun and stimulating, but homely. We try to keep away from anything remotely 'hospitally'. Most of our guests have had quite enough of hospitals, so we like to make this more comfortable. But with more fun stuff. Hey, Sarah, if you decide you'd like to be one of our family, we'll get you your own fish, which you can name. How about that?"

"Coool ..."

"Thought you'd like that." Rhonda grinned conspiratorially at Simon. "Do you want to do the grand tour?

They set off down a wide corridor, following the same royal blue carpet. Rhonda continued to push Sarah, pointing things out as they went. "None of our staff wear uniforms. We encourage everyone to wear what they are comfortable in, even if that happens to be a rabbit costume! Believe me, it happens. Our staff are chosen not only for their clinical skills, but also for their irrepressible sense of fun. We like grown-ups who haven't quite grown up yet."

They turned left into another spacious room, domed by a glass roof that ensured the room was flooded with light. It appeared to be a large art studio, the walls lined with racks of plastic boxes, with labels such as 'Play dough', 'Paper clips,' and 'Shredded paper'. "This is our messy room." Rhonda waved at a family in one corner. "It's kind of our art studio, but sometimes, when you just want to get down and dirty, this is where you come."

The family in the corner waved back at Rhonda. A little girl, aged about two, Simon guessed, was seated in just a nappy on a large plastic mat on the floor. She squealed and giggled as her parents, apparently enjoying themselves just as much, squirted shaving foam all over her, great peaks forming a hat on her head. The tube leading from her nose to a gas tank nearby didn't seem to bother her at all. Simon could imagine the sensation of the mountains of shaving foam on bare skin and found himself chuckling along with the rest of the people in the room.

"That's Kayleigh. Kayleigh has been with us since February. Her mum and dad are staying in one of our family flats at the moment, so they can be with her as much of the time as possible. They live over an hour away, so it's a bit of a long trek for them."

"What's she got?" Sarah asked, characteristically loudly.

"Sarah!" Melissa shushed her.

"No, no – there is no stigma here in The Mad House. We respect each other's privacy but we don't shy away from the facts. Kayleigh has medullary thyroid cancer, Sarah. Like your illness, it's very complicated. Kayleigh loves getting messy." Rhonda turned to Kayleigh's mother. "We should make her up some jelly, Debbie. Does she have a favourite flavour? I'll get some in at Cash and Carry. That's one we haven't done before isn't it?"

Debbie, Kayleigh's mother nodded. "Tastes better when she gets it in her mouth," she said, laughing.

"Sensory stimulation is very important for our children. And we don't care about having to get a mop and bucket or a hoover out here. The children can do all the things that they could have never done at their family home. We say 'family home' because this is a home too. Shall we see what else there is, Sarah?"

The group said goodbye to the ecstatic Kayleigh and her parents, and followed Rhonda back into the corridor.

147

They ducked their heads into another generous-sized room, the drums, keyboards and xylophones scattered around, immediately denoting its purpose.

"This is the Noisy Room – or music room if you like. Sometimes you just get the urge to bash a drum, don't you? This is the place for that. It's sound-proofed and we have a great Hi-Fi system, so the children can play any music they fancy as well. Shall we go on?"

Simon took over pushing Sarah down the corridor, taking her silence for approval. They turned a corner, and admired a charming garden on their left side. "Our garden. Not very nice weather today of course, but lovely in summer. We quite often have picnics. The pool you see there is a heated outdoor paddling pool. It actually goes up to an adults mid-thigh, so we have some great times splashing about when it's sunny."

"What about if you can't walk?" Sarah sounded slightly down. "My legs are all wobbly at the moment."

"You don't need to walk to splash about, do you, Mum?" Rhonda had a knack, Simon noticed, of drawing people into conversations, including everyone.

"Ah, well, I suppose not."

"No. You don't." Rhonda was brisk. "You can sit at the edge and splash, you can go in with one of our physios helping you, or better still, your parents can get in. You'd like that wouldn't you, Mum and Dad?" Rhonda twinkled. "I'm sure we can get dad in his Speedos.

Alternatively he might like to do the BBQ. We rely on the dads to do our BBQs in summer. Very popular, they are. Right. I think you might like this room, Sarah, from what I hear…"

They walked into another room, which stuck out into the garden area. A range of comfy chairs and beanbags ran along one side of the room, the other housed a number of large cages and hutches.

"Rabbits!" exclaimed Sarah.

"And guinea pigs, chinchillas … We've even got a pole-cat, but I wouldn't stroke him."

"Wow!"

"Just like sometimes we fancy making a mess or a noise, sometimes we want to be quiet and we find it's even nicer being quiet when you have something to stroke. Actually, we have a lot of animals here. A couple of the nurses have dogs who are normally here when they are on shift and Fur-ball is our family cat. I haven't seen her this morning actually, she may be on shift underneath the bird table. I'd better check on that. We also allow animals to visit.I believe you have a dog, Sarah."

"Yeah – Podge. He's called Porridge really. He can come and stay with me?"

"Well, not stay. But he can certainly come and visit you. Porridge is part of your family; it's only fair that he knows where you are spending your time, isn't it?"

Simon was impressed. Seriously impressed. His immediate

thoughts had been on grounds of hygiene – how can you have cats and dogs in a hospice for crying out loud? But, as Rhonda said, this was more like a family home. What did it matter? The place looked impeccably clean. Simon understood the therapeutic qualities of animals. And for Sarah to be able to see Porridge? It was the most comforting thing he had heard in months. Porridge would be able to say goodbye.

Another lady put her head around the door. Simon recognised her as one of the women who had chased the baby. "Hi Rhonda. Is this Sarah by any chance?"

Sarah nodded and grinned at her. Totally relaxed, Simon noticed.

"I'm Fiona – I'm one of the nurses. I heard you were coming. Do you like animals?"

"Does she?" Melissa laughed, the sound startling Simon. It had been sometime since she had laughed. "She practically has fur."

"Except on my head." Sarah reminded everyone with a grin, though she had chosen a butchered Ben 10 pillowcase as a headscarf that day.

"Pah! We don't set much store by hair here. We had a head painting competition the other month. Would you like to stay and play with some of the animals with me, Sarah? We can get the bunnies out and let them have a good run around on the floor. You can join me down here on the beanbags if you like." Fiona opened a cage, pulling a beautiful soft brown, lop-eared bunny out. "Then we might find some chocolate ice-cream in the kitchen if you fancy it."

"Okay!"

Rhonda stepped in then, as if on cue. "Mum and Dad, we can go and have a boring old cup of tea. Would that be alright, Sarah?"

"Yup!"

Fiona gently placed the bunny in Sarah's lap. Simon and Melissa followed Ronda out of the room, leaving Sarah cooing in delight and admiration.

* * *

"I understand, from our telephone conversation last week, Simon, that Sarah does not know the entire truth about what is happening to her?"

Rhonda fiddled with a pencil, a clipboard on her knee, holding her notes. They had moved to her office. Like every other room, it was informal, though it had the requisite desk and filing cabinets. The tea was served in huge mugs, and Rhonda explained that all the family members with children in the hospice received their own cups with their name on.

"That's changed." Melissa interjected, her tone sharpening. "Sarah has now been told that she is going to die. Rather clumsily, I'm afraid. She asked my husband. She's been told that …er, she's been told that she's going to heaven." Simon received a look.

151

"Actually, we prefer the children to know. Most of them work it out on their own. We forget how perceptive young people are, even the very tiny ones. Many of them have lived with illness all their lives. They understand a lot of medical terminology and they pick up on the difference in conversation when treatment ceases. You'd be surprised how many actually ask. How is Sarah taking it?"

"Incredibly. Strangely. It's unreal. She doesn't seem worried at all, she's so matter of fact." Melissa glanced at Simon again.

"She did cry initially. But I gave her something to help her sleep and by the next morning she was just carrying on as usual. The only difference is that she's keyed into the fact that it doesn't matter if her teeth rot. Surely that's not healthy?"

Rhonda laughed. "I think Sarah is a character. You can tell her she should brush her teeth because she doesn't want to be smelly. But yes and no, to answer your question. Children have amazing self-preserving methods at their subconscious disposal. Little minds have an amazing power to shield themselves from situations that could cause them emotional damage. They can file away fear quite efficiently. Like a little filing cabinet in the back of the head. In children who have been abused for instance, they are quite capable of losing short-term memory and forgetting altogether. It allows them to carry on, to grow up. Problems arise when they get older and their filing cabinet is full – the drawers don't shut properly and the pain from the past catches up with them. With Sarah, of course, there will be no growing up." Rhonda looked up at the parents, her face kind but authorative. "I will apologize only once for my black and white way of dealing with this. I'm afraid we are here because Sarah is going to die. I appreciate that at this moment you are struggling terribly with this concept, but mincing our words and using fancy language to get around the truth will not help you in the end. We have an excellent counseling support system here for parents, but we will talk about that later." She tapped the pencil on the edge of the clipboard. "Sarah is not going to grow up. If she is burying any fear then we will watch her very carefully to ensure that that is not doing her any emotional damage but, quite simply, it may be best for her. She probably doesn't completely understand the concept of death. Children are usually told that they are going to heaven. As the day-to-day illness gets worse, most days are consumed with controlling pain and other symptoms. As you have seen, we spend all the rest of the time keeping the children happy and occupied. Some never mention that they are going to die. Others, like Sarah, are quite blasé."

"Sarah thinks that she …" Melissa trailed off. "Sarah didn't talk to me. She had the conversation with her father. I don't think she quite understands that she won't be seeing him again." Melissa held Simon's gaze, her cheek twitching involuntarily.

"Our psychologist will work closely with Sarah and ensure that any understanding she has is healthy for her and is what makes her

153

happy. Frankly, we don't mind white lies here at Madron. The most important thing is that the child has the easiest, happiest time from the time they come here, to when they die."

Melissa cleared her throat, awkwardly. "I don't think you quite understand. My husband," she said, managing to make the word drip with disgust, "has told my daughter that he will be going with her."

Rhonda shrugged. "If she thinks that her parents can somehow stay with her, it might be a good thing. You can talk to her psychologist, but it sounds like Sarah is in a pretty healthy place with this."

Simon stared steadily at the floor, feeling, rather than seeing Melissa's eyes on him. An enormous weight lifted from his shoulders at Rhonda's words. Maybe they could work this out.

Rhonda's tone brightened as she continued. "I should imagine that Sarah has moved onto ice cream by now. If you would like me to show you round the rest of The Mad House, we can talk more about the day to day running of the place and I'll answer any questions you have. Ready?"

Simon's shoulders visibly dropped. Melissa was going to let it go. Maybe.

Chapter 16

Simon's senior partner, Howard, rose as Simon entered his office.

"Simon! How are you? Come in. Come in. *Terrible* time for you. *Terrible*. Did Wendy get you a cup of tea? No? Sit down. Do."

Howard gestured towards the small chair by the side of his desk, normally taken by patients, and seated himself in his enormous leather wing chair. Simon sat on a molded plastic chair by the antique walnut desk. It was uncomfortable and low, and left Simon feeling a little like a child who was about to be disciplined.

"Let me just start by telling you how sorry we all are. If there...."

Here we go, thought Simon. *The anything-we-can-do spiel.*

"If there is anything we can do, you know where we are."

I wonder what would actually happen if I called in all these favors, Simon pondered. *If I rang Howard tomorrow morning and said, could you just wash the car because I've been up all night holding a bowl for Sarah to vomit into and frankly I'm too shattered to do it myself.*

"I can't imagine what you're currently going through and I know I speak for all the staff ..."

Or I could ring him up and say yes, actually, I would like your wife, whom I've only met twice, to come round and clean the bathroom. That would be enormously helpful.

"Simon. Simon?"

Oh shit. "Sorry, Howard. Bit stressed. You know. Concentration not my strong point at the moment."

Howard cleared his throat. "Aha. Well. As I said, if there is anything we can do. So, you're thinking of coming back, I hear. Is that wise? Given your self confessed level of concentration? Not that I want to dissuade you, you understand ..."

"No, no. Of course not. I think work-wise I'm fine, Howard. I'd like to get back at it. I feel bad about being absent from the surgery for so long. No, really, I do. I understand the difficulty with budgets and locums, and I think it would be good for me to deal with patients again and keep busy. After all, I'm going to have to carry on after ... ah, after, you know."

"Yes, yes. Of course." Howard looked flustered, Simon noticed.

Perversely, Simon was beginning to enjoy this. It was not often one had the upper hand with Howard. "I thought perhaps I might be able to work slightly shorter hours. Well, half my hours, actually. I need to go and be with Sarah a lot and then I have to be careful of stress. I wouldn't want to be breaking down at work. Patients don't need a GP in tears, do they?" Simon treated Howard to a winning smile. He knew full well the idea of a GP in tears would send Howard, the old fashioned, stiff upper lipped bastion of the establishment into paroxysms of terror.

"No, Christ, no. Er, whatever you feel is best for you, Simon. As I said, anything we can do to help. When were you thinking of coming back?"

"Sarah is starting at the hospice during the daytime. They can entertain her, keep her mind busy and at the same time provide the palliative care she needs better than we can. In the evenings she can come home and the Community Nurses come round to administer morphine through her canula. Stupid, huh? I'm a doctor and I'm not allowed to do it myself." Simon sighed. His irritation at being forced to have nurses come to his house to administer drugs that he could *prescribe* but they could *not*, was immense. "Dependent on how quickly she starts to decline, she may go in full-time by the end of April, in two weeks or so, in fact. If I could maybe do morning surgery a couple of days a week for the next two weeks, then do mornings five days a week once Sarah is at The Mad House full-time …."

"I'm sorry, the what?"

"Madron House. Madron. Sorry."

"Right. Yes, of course. Bryony from Human Resources will work it all out. I'll have her call you with the details. Glad to see that you're holding up, Simon. Good man. Good man." Howard stood and opened his door, a clear indication that it was time for Simon to leave. "And Simon. If there is anything we …"

" … can do. Yup. Thanks. I'll let you know."

* * *

The town was grid-locked as Simon tried to make his way back from the surgery in the early afternoon traffic. Joining what he knew was at least a three mile tailback, he turned up the radio, resigned to a long wait.

"On which U2 album is the first song a live version of 'Helter Skelter'?" Ken Bruce's melodious voice filled the car.

"'Rattle and Hum'." Simon waved a young woman driving a juggernaut of a car through. One tiny child in the back, he noted.

" 'Rattle and Hum', Ken."

"Correct! In which year did Alice Cooper have a number one hit with 'Schools Out'?"

The jaguar crawled forward a few feet, the lights ahead turning red after only seconds on green. *"Come on.* You could have gone then. 1973."

"That was 1972."

"Close." Simon craned his neck, trying to see the cause of some commotion ahead. His attention was diverted from the music quiz by a crowd on the pavement and a vivid flash of red gave him a sudden wave of déjà vu, though the bright color was incongruous against the grey, soot-stained buildings of Brighouse. The lights changed again and Simon inched forward.

The gathering, he could see now, was for some kind of large Asian wedding. Hindu, he realized, as he took in the smiling bride.

She wore a deep red sari, and he could see the complicated henna patterns decorating her hands and arms. Her groom stood tall by her side, radiating pride and happiness. A number of cars honked their horns as they went past.

A red sari, Simon ruminated.

The bride laughed and her gaze briefly caught Simon's. A jolt passed through him as he looked into her brown eyes, and memories of a recent dream stirred in his mind. He looked away quickly, feeling somehow voyeuristic.

Sati. *The ancient practice of self-immolation.* That was the dream. That night, the night they had been told about Sarah. It came back to him in snippets. A red sari. A funeral pyre. A woman – no, *Melissa* speaking to him. He looked back at the wedding party, who were beginning to disperse, the bride and groom being directed to a waiting car. *The beginning of their lives together*, Simon thought. Where would that life take them? Perhaps they would grow old together, dying peacefully in their sleep after a long and simple life. Perhaps great happiness would befall them. Or perhaps great sadness. They looked so healthy, so happy. It seemed impossible to think tragedy could ever tarnish their gilded existence.

A honk from behind Simon interrupted his thoughts and he pushed forward in the queue, narrowly missing the lights. A group of pedestrians, using the temporary lights as a natural crossing point, began to move across the road. A well-dressed woman, pushing a pram, passed in front of his car and Simon recognized her as someone he and Melissa knew well. He waved in greeting and catching her eye gave her a quick smile. She looked at him and he saw her eyes widen with a flicker of shock as she recognized him. Or was it alarm? She looked away and he pipped his horn, but she turned slightly away, put her head down and pushed on, seemingly oblivious to Simon's tooted greeting. Simon watched her scurry up the street, her previous pace now quickened.

Simon turned up the radio in an attempt to quell his irritation.

"In the 2001 film, 'Donnie Darko', which song featured on the sound track, originally by Tears for Fears and covered by Gary Jules?"

"'Mad World'," said Simon, quietly.

Chapter 17

"I saw Gina Thomas today." Simon perched on the edge of the sofa in the conservatory, idly flicking through television programs.

"Oh yes?" Melissa added a mound of chopped carrots to a pot on the stove.

"You haven't had any kind of row with her, have you?"

"No, haven't spoken to her for a while. I rang her a few weeks ago, after the ... after we heard. Not heard anything since."

"She blanked me."

Melissa wiped her hands on a tea towel and ran the chopping board under the tap. "She what?"

"She *blanked* me. I was on Commercial Street, sitting behind those bloody traffic lights and I saw her pushing Grace in a pushchair. I know she saw me – we made eye contact. But she just hurried off. She blanked me." Simon switched the television off with an accompanying *tut*. "Forty eight channels and not a single thing to watch."

"People are embarrassed, Simon. They don't know what to say."

"People? We've known Gina for over ten years. She's one of our best friends, for God's sake. Which reminds me – where are Tom and Louisa? I note Friday night suppers seem to be off."

"They didn't want to disturb us. They presumed we would be busy with Sarah, which we are." Melissa heaved a full bag of rubbish

161

from out of the bin. "Could you help?"

Simon joined her at the counter, then took over and tied the bag. "Louisa used to come round for coffee with you all the time. Tom hasn't pestered me about playing golf once. And what happened to Dave? Presumably he's still single and bored. A few months ago he was never off our doorstep. It's like all our friends have fallen off the edge of the earth." Simon picked up the bin bag, carrying it towards the back door. "It's like we've got the plague."

"We make people feel uncomfortable, Simon." Melissa shrugged.

"Don't you care? Don't you miss our friends? Aren't you …"? Simon paused, " … aren't you lonely?"

"No."

Simon unlatched the back stable door and deposited the bin bag in the wheelie bin outside, then came back in and chose a bottle of white wine from the wine cooler in the conservatory. "Want one?"

"'One' being the key word in that sentence, Simon."

"Give me a break, Melissa. We've been sharing a bottle of wine most nights for twelve years. Could you pass me that corkscrew, please?"

"True. But I'm not working my way through the drinks cabinet afterwards."

Simon swore as he stabbed his thumb with the corkscrew, the plastic seal refusing to come off easily. "I've had a night cap a few times. I am drinking too much. I know that. I'm not in some form of denial and I'm fully aware that it is not good for me. However, I'm not going to accept your snide insinuations that I have some kind of a drinking problem. I'm fully aware that I'm drinking too much. Considering what I'm – sorry, what we're - going through at the moment, I think it's fair enough."

"Give it here." Melissa deftly removed the plastic and cork and poured wine into two glasses. "I'm not arguing. I'm too tired. Look, Sarah goes in for the full weekend on Friday afternoon, yes?"

"Yeah. I was thinking I'd spend the day with her there on Friday and then we might give her a bit of space on Saturday. What do you think?"

"That's what Rhonda wants us to do. Suits me. I've got another wedding to do on Saturday. I thought you might go up to the Golf Club, seeing as you're so lonely."

Simon sighed heavily. "I have no idea how you just managed to add loneliness to my long list of shortcomings, but you did it. Well done. And yes, I think I might just do that. Right now I have a date with Sarah and Harry Potter. Come on, Porridge." Simon topped up his wine glass, ignoring Melissa's arched eyebrows and set off for upstairs, Porridge padding along beside him.

* * *

The gravel crunched expensively and reassuringly as the Jaguar rolled down the long drive to Huddersfield Golf Course. The regal stone wall of Fixby Hall, the former country seat in which the club was housed, came into view on the final bend.

Simon nosed his car into a space between a Porsche and a Mercedes, noting with displeasure, but no surprise, the packed car park. The sun had decided to make an early appearance, chasing away the April clouds and providing a perfect golfing day. The air was bright, crisp and warm.

He curled a lip in the direction of an ostentatious Bentley. It belonged to a local builder famed for his Spanish-style villa, built on the hills above Halifax. The monstrosity was complete with indoor swimming pool, marble fountains and gate house. How the man had obtained planning permission was a frequent cause of speculation, though the gossipers always came to the same whispered conclusion. Kevin Jagger, perma-tanned and bejeweled, fulfilled his stereotype of tasteless bullying millionaire with indecent accuracy. The normally placid Simon hated few people, perhaps none, but following an astonishing tirade at a clubhouse dinner, in which Kevin and his vacuous and overweight wife Paula had lambasted him for his failure to provide private health insurance for Sarah, he felt a certain justice in his abhorrence.

He waved his key fob at the Jaguar, feeling a quiet sense of satisfaction at the sound of the chirrup it made on locking. A figure standing by a recently arrived Audi waved at him and Simon squinted his eyes against the low spring sunlight, attempting to make out the silhouette.

"Simon! Perfect timing – fancy nine holes?" A small-framed man with spectacles and a generous smile stepped towards him. "Are you meeting with anyone else?"

Simon gave a nowadays rare but genuine grin. "Pavit! This truly is good timing. Are you here alone?" Simon thrust out his hand and greeted his friend warmly. "Shall I get my clubs out? You weren't expecting to play with anyone else?"

Pavit opened his boot and hauled a set of clubs out of the back. "No, I came on the off chance. Thought I'd have a beer and maybe a bite of lunch and a quick round if I got lucky. It is excellent news that I have banged into you, Simon. Are you hungry or shall we skip the lunchtime rush and take advantage of the quieter green?"

"Pavit, you've seen me play. I think we'd better make use of the temporary let-up. We could have lunch after, though – my treat."

"This sounds like an excellent plan."

The two men walked companionably round the side of the house, dragging their golf club bags. The green stretched out before them, various parties heading back in for lunch. They booked an immediate tee-time, pocketed their game-cards and trundled down a gentle hill towards the tee-off.

"Simon, I heard about your little girl. This must be a dreadfully hard time for you. I can't imagine."

165

No apology, Simon noted with gratitude as he pushed a plastic tee into the ground, one from a set given to him by Sarah. "It is difficult, yes. Shall I tee-off, given that I am the immeasurably poorer player?"

"I'm sure we have a similar handicap, don't we?"

"We do not, Pavit, and you jolly well know it. I shall spend much of the next hour repairing the course. Right then. Stand back." Simon swung at the ball, hitting, despite his modesty, a perfectly respectable shot. "Beginner's luck. I was sorry to hear that you missed out on the consultancy, Pavit. I don't spend much time at the hospital anymore – well, only as a punter, so to speak. I don't really keep up with the news, but I was up in Medical Staffing arguing about my out-of-hours clinic rota and I heard Ferguson got it. Seemed a rough deal for you, to be honest."

Pavit swung his club, sending the ball in a perfect arc over the green towards the hole. "I didn't really expect it. Ophthalmic surgery is as political as politics. Ferguson had been playing a long game. How the man ever gets any sleep, I will never know. He seems to be attending or throwing a dinner party or cocktail 'do' every night. To be honest, it's not my scene. I like my golf. I like a quiet life. Shreya was not too happy, though."

They heaved their bags onto their shoulders and started to walk towards where their balls lay in the distance. Simon was quietly taken aback to see how close he'd got to the hole. He generally just aimed for the green. "I'm not surprised. It's time you got the

166

consultancy. I hear you are very talented."

Pavit snorted. "Surgeons are not just rewarded for their clinical skills. You have to network, entertain. Shreya doesn't understand this. It might be true that I spend a little too much time on the golf course, but Shreya's determination to remain so, well, Asian, has meant that I have lost a lot of brownie points."

"You're not suggesting racism?" Simon paused, stopping to look at his friend. West Yorkshire was heavily populated with those of all faiths and ethnic backgrounds. The hospitals were completely integrated, doctors from all over the world being promoted without reference to race. Not to say that the area was not inherently racist – tensions simmered and seethed all over the West Yorkshire towns, well-documented riots and BNP electorates were regular newspaper items. But the hospital? From Simon's experience, racism in the hospital was unheard of. Doctors earned respect through their work, not their color or creed.

Pavit shook his head. "No. Not entirely. The problem is that one has to fill a certain social quota. Charity galas, concerts, hospital benefits. Shreya is not comfortable with it. As you know, she prefers *shalwar kameez* or sari, she doesn't drink, and she doesn't enjoy gossiping with the wives. I'm not blaming her, but things may have run smoother if she had been happy to play the role of Consultant's Wife."

"All sounds a bit *'Holby City'* or *'ER'*."

167

"It *is* all a bit 'Holby City', though they wouldn't want you to know that. There's your ball there," Pavit pointed.

Simon self-consciously placed himself in the position he'd been taught by the resident golf pro. Melissa had given him lessons as a Christmas present one year. Buoyed with confidence from his last shot, he whirled the club round at high speed, only to completely miss the ball. He grinned at Pavit. "I *thought* that last shot was a fluke. Here we go again …" This time he struck the ball and also the ground and a large chunk of the course flew into the air. "Ah, the first of my many divots. And a shot of about three meters. That's more like my usual standard."

Pavit chuckled and, after locating his ball, performed a perfect swing. The ball soared through the air in elegant flight. "If you spent as much time here as I do, you would improve."

"I know. I might start to. Sarah went into her hospice last night. I'm going to have some free time …" He stopped awkwardly. "Actually, Pavit, it's funny I banged into you today. I was meaning to ask you. You're Hindu, yes?"

"I'm a good Hindu boy, yes." Pavit winked and heaved his golf bag back onto his shoulders.

"I was wondering if you could tell me about Sati. Or is it Suti?" Simon shouldered his own load, wondering not for the first time why he bothered with so many clubs when he only ever used two. Many had been presents from Melissa, specially hand carved,

168

monogrammed, and weighted specifically for him. It was a pity, he mused, that Melissa hadn't realized in twelve years of golfing presents that he didn't particularly like golf.

"Sati? Sati or Suti – you can use both terms. Well it doesn't really happen anymore, you know. It's illegal for one thing. I think occasionally there is a story from a backwater in India of some poor woman flinging herself onto a funeral pyre, but it is very much frowned upon by modern Indians. Why do you ask?"

Simon's thoughts went back to his dream and to the young couple at the centre of the wedding party. Why *did* he ask? The scene had been obstinately stuck in a corner of his mind ever since then. The idea of following someone you love into the afterlife had become embedded somehow in his semi-conscience. A nagging *'what if'* - a persistent *'perhaps'*.

"I read a novel recently. It only touched on the subject. Sparked an interest, that's all." Simon hacked again at his ball, dislodging it further along the green, along with yet more clods of earth.

Pavit treaded in the divots. "Well, as you know, Sati is the term generally used to describe the practice of wives self-immolating at the death of their husbands. The name comes from the goddess Sati who couldn't bear her own father's humiliation of her husband Shiva. It is considered an example of perfect wifely loyalty." Pavit chuckled again. "I can't imagine my wife flinging herself to her death in defense of me."

They walked on towards Pavit's perfectly placed ball. "Sati was reborn to become the consort of Shiva once again. Her name was given as 'Parvati', which is a common Hindu name now. Henceforth, 'Sati' became the term or title for a woman showing exceptional devotion to their husband. Sati means 'righteous'. Ah! Close!" Pavit took a long putt and the two men watched the ball roll seamlessly forward, coming to a halt inches before the hole. "I might get a birdie."

"Good shot." Simon moved off towards his ball, no way near as close now. "So Sati is the term for a wife being burnt on her husband's funeral pyre, or for the wife herself?"

"Originally, it became a title for the woman, and it wasn't necessarily linked with the funeral pyre. Another story, for instance, was that Savitri was named Sati for her selfless act for her husband. Her husband died and the Lord of Death, Yama, came to take his soul. She begged Yama to take her life instead, which he could not do. In defiance and grief she followed Yama and her dead husband for many miles on their journey to the underworld. Yama was impressed, or irritated, I do not know. He offered Savitri an alternative - anything, in fact, apart from her husband's life. Savitri asked for children from her dead husband. Of course, in order for this wish to be granted, he had to be given life. So Savitri got her husband back. Fairytales, Simon." Pavit shrugged. "You know, you turn your body a little too much. That's it. A bit more, and drop your

170

shoulders. There now. Better."

Simon took his shot, which was a vast improvement over his previous attempt. "Thanks. Perhaps you should give up reattaching retinas and become a golf-pro. So Sati isn't strictly to do with suicide?"

Pavit tapped his ball expertly into the hole and lifted the flag to retrieve it. "Do you have a pen?" He took his game-card out. "The custom of burning a widow on the funeral pyre of her husband is more cultural than religious. Frankly, there are plenty of stories of widows being forced onto the pyre, without consent. Particularly in wealthy families, where the heirs did not wish to see the man's fortune go directly to the wife."

Pavit scribbled

"Ostensibly it was about the prestige of the woman's wish to avoid living the ghastly life of a Hindu widow. It became common in wealthy warrior dynasties. The Rajputs, for instance. The family of any woman performing Sati would gain huge respect and the woman would receive honors, almost like a saint. But it didn't happen in most of India. Only in small communities. The Mughals tried to ban it. The British, along with Indian reformers, managed to put a stop to it in the early 1800's."

Simon attempted a long putt, missing the hole by quite a few meters. "Damn it. So it doesn't happen anymore?"

"There aren't any exact figures. Before it was banned there were

171

records of a few hundred a year. Officially, the practice has been completely stamped out, though there are occasional incidents. In the 80s a young wife, a teenager, demanded to commit voluntary Sati. The villagers supported and praised her, taking part in the ceremony. Disgusting. So backward. Interestingly, a woman a few years ago – 1999 perhaps, jumped hysterically onto her husband's funeral pyre and burnt to death. The incident however, was declared suicide and not Sati, as the woman was not compelled, forced or praised for committing the act. Nearly there now, Simon. This one should be – ah. Next time."

"Sorry, Pavit. Are you losing the will to live? Pardon the expression."

Pavit laughed. "No, not at all. I'm enjoying the sunshine and the company. And it's quite interesting talking about this kind of thing for a change. Did you know that Sati is not solely a Hindu act? The ancient Egyptians, the Goths and the Scythians, who invaded India, all practiced some form of immolation, where living family members would accompany those who had died into the afterlife. Egyptian pharaohs took wives, cats, even their servants, with them. You'd be rather disappointed to find that in the small print of your job description, wouldn't you?

"Can't see myself jumping onto Howard's pyre, put it that way. So it was always women dying for men – never the other way round?"

"Well, I don't believe a Sati exactly *leaps* onto her husband's pyre. She walks to the burning ground in a procession and mounts the pyre before it is lit. She sits cross-legged, upright, cradling her husband's head on her lap. But to answer your question, yes, usually, it was wives becoming sati for their husbands. In all but a handful of cases, I believe, though rarely, very, very rarely, husbands would follow their wives. True love indeed. More frequent were grieving mothers becoming Sati on their son's pyres. *Well done.*" Pavit retrieved Simon's ball from the hole, in which it finally lay. "Write it up and we'll move on, shall we?"

Pavit strolled onwards, completely unaware of the fire he had stoked.

* * *

They lunched on prawn cocktails and *coq au vin*. The delightfully 'retro' menu was both comforting and satisfying. Conversation moved onto more jovial affairs, gossip from the golfing community, news from the medical world. Both declined pudding and were deciding whether to take coffee in the lounge or at the table, when Simon hissed a warning to Pavit.

"Shit. Don't look now. It's Jagger."

Pavit groaned and visibly shrank down in his chair. "Is he heading in this direction?"

173

"No, I don't think so. I think he's going to the bar. Deplorable man. Dreadful bully. There was a time when a club like this wouldn't have had him." Simon immediately felt his color rise, his snobbery embarrassing him. There was a time, he reminded himself, when a club like this wouldn't have had *him*. Or his dining partner.

"No, I agree. I can't stand him. Had a run in with him last week actually. Did I tell you I won that raffle?"

"No." Simon smiled up at the waiter and indicated that they would take coffee in the lounge. "Shall we?"

Simon signed the bill, indicating that it should go on his account, and the two men stood up.

Pavit continued. "Yes, I won a giant Easter egg. The size of a small car."

"I'll bet the kids were pleased."

"They were. There's still half left. You could sail to the Isle of Wight in it. Anyway, Jagger and that awful wife of his were there and he insisted on …"

"*Bailey!* And the *other* doctor. Well we are blessed with medical knowledge today. If anyone fancies having a heart attack, now's the time to do it!" An all too familiar voice boomed across the room from by the bar.

Both men stopped, not turning but not moving forwards either. This was ridiculous, thought Simon. Like kids in a playground. He sighed and turned to face the man. "Kevin, nice to see you. Hope you're well. Sorry, I think our coffee's just been taken through to the lounge … catch up again soon, eh?"

"Not a problem, Simon, not a problem. Good to see you too. Not seen you about for a long time. Still I suppose you're busy with your little one, especially seeing as she's in cattle-class. You'll have your hands full keeping an eye on the doctors who are supposed to be treating her. You're with a lucky man there, Simon. I was just talking to our Jim here …" He gestured at a sycophantic looking youth behind the bar, " … and we was saying, bit unfair your winning that egg last week, Pavit. What with you being Muslim and all."

"Bye, Kevin." Simon gave what he hoped was a winning smile, grabbed Pavit by the arm, and marched him into the next room.

Chapter 18

Porridge was whining and scraping at the back door when Simon let himself in at the rear entrance to his house. The Labrador shot past him and into the garden, relieving himself noisily against the wooden shed.

"That was much needed, Porridge. Have you had your legs plaited, lad?" Simon bent down and buried his face in the dog's fur. Porridge, having dealt with his more immediate bladder concerns, now greeted his dad enthusiastically. "Where's mum then, eh? Haven't you had a walk?"

Man and dog strolled into the silent kitchen. Porridge headed straight for his empty bowl, looked pointedly at it and then back at Simon, who glanced at the clock. "Only three-thirty, boy. Please don't look at me like that." Simon rolled his eyes. "Come on then, give us that bowl and we'll do a fresh one."

He refilled Porridge's bowl and checked the answer machine. There was one message from Lorraine, Melissa's partner at the florists - something to do with ribbons. Simon scribbled a note onto a Post-it.

He opened the fridge, contemplated a beer and decided it was too early. He turned the TV on in the conservatory and flicked through the channels. Sport, no. Carry On Matron, no. 50 Best Looking Booties in Pop, no. He settled finally for the last half of 'Live and Let

Die' and changed his mind about the beer. With a deep sigh, he sank into the squashy sofa with Porridge at his feet. He stared at the TV for a while, but despite his usual love of all things Bond, Roger Moore failed to hold his attention. Finishing his beer and grabbing another from the fridge, he started opening cupboards, deciding what to make Sarah for tea and then remembered that Sarah was not there.

He checked the time again – four-thirty now, and wondered where Melissa was. He knew she'd had a wedding that day, but usually the hard work was in the morning and they were finished and away for twelve. The venue usually took care of the leftover floral arrangements, no doubt recycling them for their non-wedding events or gala dinners. It wasn't like Mel not to have checked in with him. And what about Porridge? She usually took him with her if she went out in the afternoon.

A prickle of concern registered but was quickly cast aside. Simon decided to call Madron House and check on Sarah for the evening. The nurses were in the habit of answering the main desk telephone if they happened to be passing, and he was pleased to get Fiona on the line. Sarah was tucked in for the night. The nausea that had plagued her the previous night was under control, and they were hoping she would have a good night. They let him speak to her briefly, though she was sleepy and tipsy on morphine.

There was, it seemed, a likelihood that Sarah would stay at the hospice permanently. She was increasingly unable to come down

177

stairs and there was an escalated need for nursing care. There had, much to Sarah's distress, been a couple of bed-wetting incidents. She was also becoming less able to take solid food. A decision was to be made on Monday, but it looked likely that Sarah had moved on.

Simon felt calmer with that realization than he would have thought. The past week had been one of the hardest yet. Sarah's illness was a constant dark presence haunting the household. He had come to recognize that she was more comfortable in the hospice. Since she slept throughout most of the day, she often woke in the night. At Madron there was always someone there with whom she could chat. A person who could read to her, soothe her. During the day she wasn't confined to watching yet more TV. She could interact with other children, play, paint. There had been a little theatre performance only recently. The troop had even visited the rooms of those children well enough to watch, but too poorly to leave their beds.

Still, the silence grated. Five-thirty. Three Budweisers. Where was Mel? He pulled his mobile out, checking to see if he had missed any messages. None. He reached into the fridge for another beer and then stopped, frowning as he noticed a folded piece of violet coloured paper propped against the last beer at the back of the fridge.

Simon opened his beer, seeing no rush to read what was clearly going to either hurt or infuriate him. He shoved a small slice of lemon in the top and sucked the rim of the bottle quickly as the beer foamed up. He walked over to the shabby sofa in the conservatory, chewing the inside of his cheek, and unfolded the paper.

Simon -

If you have found this (as I know you will), then you will have drunk nearly all the beer.

As you know, Sarah will not be coming out of Madron House. Therefore, as per our conversation at the florist's, I want you out of the house. I am staying at my parents and would like you to be gone by Tuesday. As you do not start work again until next Thursday, this should give you time to find digs or whatever.

I'm sorry that it has come to this. I would have thought that I would need you more than ever during this time. But I find that I am the stronger one and that you, rather than providing strength, are merely pulling me down.

You know when you are the designated driver at a party? You hate that moment, don't you, Simon, when everyone has just started to get drunk. You always get grumpy and want to leave. You say it is like we are at different parties – the jokes aren't funny to you and the conversation doesn't flow naturally. That's what living with you is like for me at the moment. Even if you are not unconscious with booze, you are not all there ... It's like I'm living on my own anyway. You're either tipsy or hung over and I don't know where I fit in. I don't think it would even matter if you weren't drinking, to be honest. I just don't know what you are thinking anymore.

I don't want Sarah to know anything about any of this. We can still go to the hospice together and we must put on a show. Frankly, I think it's been a show for a long time, hasn't it, Simon? We'll keep going until the end. After that, I'd like us to move forward with a divorce. A new start might help you. I know it will help me.

I've left Porridge there. I haven't decided what I think should be done about him. I felt that you would probably appreciate the company tonight. I hope you got back before he had an accident. If he did, there's

180

some special spray under the sink.

I'm sorry to do this, Simon. I just think that we have come to a fork in our lives and that you have chosen a different path to the one that I am on. Perhaps we will remain friends. I'd like that.

I hope your mum and dad don't hate me.

Still yours, though as a friend,

Mel xxx

The thing that irritated Simon the most, he thought miserably, were the kisses at the end. Why did women do that? And what did three mean? Simon looked down at Porridge, who gazed up at him, totally unaware of the fissure in his life that widened by the minute. His Labrador eyes were watery and loving and at the side of his mouth his black lips curled into a totally unknowing smile.

"Come on, Porridge. Let's go to the pub."

* * *

The Whippet and Wastrel, Simon's local pub, was relatively

busy. Relative that is, to the other three pubs in the village, all of which had shut or were on the verge of shutting, following the smoking ban. Thankfully, The Whippet accepted dogs, providing bowls of water and a dog-loving clientèle who were more than happy to share their pork scratchings. As a consequence, Porridge was a big fan of the pub.

Strains of Gloria Gaynor's 'Survivor' blasted out as Simon opened the pub door. The complete destruction of the vocal part indicated that Saturday's karaoke was in full swing. Simon smiled, receiving a warm reception from the motley group of drinkers at one end of the bar. They comprised the usual assortment of pub regulars: the men with large noses and larger guts, accompanied by women clutching half pints of lager. Porridge got the louder welcome, the younger girls coming over to pat the genial Labrador and the pub's other canine residents padding over for a little friendly bottom sniffing.

" 'Usual, Simon?" The wiry landlord gestured with a pint glass.

"Please, Steve."

Simon fielded a number of generic *'how are you's* and *'what you been up to's*, paid for his pint and made his usual feeble request that Porridge should not be fed, knowing full well that he would be roundly ignored.

The Gloria Gaynor attempt came to a finish, the applause scant, and the karaoke master called up another name to the stage. The lilting opening chords of Roger Miller's 'King of the Road' made the crowd cheer.

The evening sped by in a blur of 'just one more pints', dreadful singing and worse jokes. Porridge lay underneath a table, satiated and flatulent. His owner sat on a bar stool nearby, tipsy but compos mentis.

"Fancy a whisky, Simon?" Steve, the landlord took a bottle of expensive scotch down from a private, high shelf behind the bar. The pub had emptied, all but for a group of lads playing pool and a couple having a whispered argument at one of the tables. "My treat. It's good stuff this. Brought it back from the Isle of Arran."

Simon nodded. "And then I'd better let you lock up. Do you want a hand with anything?"

"No, don't be daft. I'll do the glasses in the morning. Get some of that down you." Steve poured a generous measure of whisky into a tumbler. "How's your little girl doing, Simon?"

"Not well." Simon suddenly found it easier to discuss, now his tongue had been lubricated by an evening's drinking. "To be honest with you, Steve, she's nearing the end. Probably only weeks now. It's funny. You'd think the fear of them dying would be the worst part, but after a while it hurts even more to see them in pain. I can't bear to see her live and I can't bear to let her go." He stared at his glass but saw nothing. "There's no respite and I can't ever see any in the future. I shall always be broken."

183

"My God. I'm so sorry, mate. I had no idea it had got so bad."

Simon shrugged. "Melissa left me."

"What? Jesus. When? That's bad timing isn't it?"

"Today. This evening. Before I came in. Left a note. Twelve years of marriage, apparently disposable by *note*. Or is it a *notelet*? Melissa is forever sending people 'notelets'. Haven't the foggiest what one is. Perhaps I have been dispatched by notelet. Good whisky, Steve. Any chance of a lager – fancy one? I'm buying."

"Of course, Mate. I'll get 'em though. No. Put your money away. So what are you going to do?"

Simon looked over at Porridge who gave a little groan in his sleep. "Don't know. She says she wants me 'out of the house'. By Tuesday. Don't know anyone with a spare flat do you? Thanks."

Steve took a deep swig of his own beer. "As a matter of fact, I do. You're standing underneath it. I've got a manager's flat upstairs, below my own. Had that ditzy barmaid and her boyfriend staying up there, but they've moved in with her mum to save on rent. You're more than welcome to have it. Lord knows, I can't think of a better tenant, but I don't think you'll like it. Bloody dump to be honest. It's clean, but you know what young bar-staff are like. It's been painted every colour from tangerine to dark purple. And it's noisy. You can hear everything from downstairs."

"How much?"

"Three hundred and seventy a month. Three hundred bond. Gas

and 'lecky all in."

Simon ran his finger round the top of his beer glass. "I might be interested. Would Porridge be okay?"

Both men looked at Porridge, who, as if on cue, farted loudly. Steve grinned. "Normally, I'd say no. But I know you're going to be clean and, as long as you don't have an aversion to vacuum cleaners, the smelly old mutt can stay. But you'll have to make sure his business is picked up in the beer garden, and I don't want him barking. You want it then?"

Simon took a deep breath, then exhaled, feeling completely empty. "Why not?"

Chapter 19

Melissa sliced through the water, as sleek and streamlined as a barracuda. She kept her face in the water, her eyes wide open, watching guidelines that marked the tiles beneath her.

She performed a neat tumble-turn in the deep end and began a return lap, noting in slight irritation that a number of rubber-capped old ladies had gathered for a natter at the shallow end. The pool, a facility of the expensive private members gym, of which she was a member, was always quiet. In the afternoon, though, the elderly clientèle swam slowly, blocking the lanes and standing against the pool walls. It meant that Melissa was unable to swim with the speed and aggression with which she preferred.

Melissa loved the water. All her energy, all her anger, could be channeled into the physical act of swimming. She loved the way she could contort her face as she pushed herself to her physical limit, but nobody could see her pain. Loved the way her heart raced and her muscles ached, yet there was no sweat, no puffy red face, no damp patches, no jiggly bits, no embarrassment. Her exertion was clean, controllable, and most of all, private.

Today the chlorinated water was particularly welcome, cleansing her not only of her excess energy and anger, but also of the feeling that something about her was dirty. Now, as she executed a perfect front crawl, she began to feel a little more like herself. Cleaner. More in control.

Melissa hadn't felt much in control recently. Sarah's rapid decline had forced them to make decisions for which she hadn't been prepared. This wasn't how it was supposed to happen.

She'd planned to be ready, to have conditioned herself to a point when she was prepared to accept Sarah's final days. But the prognosis had changed so quickly, the disease had taken hold again so unexpectedly, so viciously, that Melissa was left floundering, unable to cope with being flung back into the whirlwind of medical decisions, practical decisions, emotional decisions ….

Emotional decisions! *Hah!* Simon had taken that one from her. They hadn't even planned how they were going to tell Sarah that she was going to die. She'd tried to, but nothing seemed good enough. It was never the right time. She tried speaking to Simon, but he just wouldn't talk about it. She tried desperately to get him to talk, both to hear how he was feeling and to use him as a sounding board. She needed more than anything to open up and tell the only other person in the world who could completely understand how she felt. But he wouldn't talk. He'd walk off, turn the telly up or rattle his newspaper in irritation. More recently, he'd slope off to the sitting room, bottle and tumbler in hand.

Then she had learned that he, that *Simon*, Simon who refused to discuss the situation, who blocked her *every* attempt to bring the subject up, had leaped in and told their daughter that she was dying.

That changed everything. She had been trying to contain a dangerously simmering rage for a long time. His callous act brought it to a boil, so that it erupted over the surface of her usually staid demeanor.

Melissa came to the end of another length and noted with further exasperation that the pool was filling with slow swimmers. She climbed out, took her towel and made her way to the steam room. A blast of eucalyptus scented steam hit her as she opened the door and she settled into a corner of the room, pleased that she had it to herself.

Simon would hate the steam room, she thought, and then frowned, irritated with herself. She had told Simon she wanted a divorce. Now she had to stop this habit of thinking of him all the time.

Except she couldn't help it. He had been the most important person in her life for so long. The old cliché that he was part of her felt entirely apt. Wherever she was, the supermarket, the library, a sodding steam room, her thoughts always settled onto what Simon would think, what Simon was doing, how Simon would react.

But he never, it would appear, thought of her. Oh sure, he used to. He used to bring little treats home for her, used to ring her during the day with funny little stories or just to see how she was. Many was the time he'd called her at the florists at 7 a.m. in the morning when she'd gone in early to prepare for a wedding, just to check that she was okay. Just to say hello.

But all that changed when Sarah got ill.

It wasn't that Melissa didn't understand. She of all people could comprehend the all-consuming terror that filled Simon's every waking moment. The immeasurable stress caused by having to continue to live whilst their daughter's life came to an end. But for Melissa, Sarah had not been the only person in her life. It was always Simon, Sarah, and her. They had been a team. A trio. She divided her love equally between her daughter and her husband.

The past few months had shown her something truly painful. He did not feel the same way as she did. He did not distribute his love between 'his girls' equally. It hurt terribly. She was angry.

She wondered if she should call him. The note had been childish. Overly dramatic. She couldn't quite say why she had done it. Leaving it in the fridge was snide and silly. It's just that she wanted him to know how hurt she was. She wanted him to hurt too.

Clearly he hadn't been hurt. She'd tried to call but there had been no answer. In the pub, no doubt. Just another aspect of Simon's life which didn't include her. She'd tried to accompany him to their local, but her cut glass accent had stood out. She felt uncomfortable and alien amongst the regulars.

Melissa dabbed at her sweating nose with the towel, glad that there was nobody present to witness this melting of her normally perfect façade. The truth was, Melissa thought miserably, she had lost Simon a long time ago. Perhaps the moment Sarah was born. Because there was no doubt in Melissa's mind, that the problem was Simon's. He simply didn't have the room or capability to love both of them. And so he had chosen Sarah.

She took a deep breath, feeling the eucalyptus cleanse her lungs. Perhaps she should call Simon. See if he was alright. They could go for a Chinese – that one on the high street he liked and she didn't. She imagined them sitting at the table, him ordering duck and her trying to remember the name of the chewy pork thing she liked. Just thinking about seeing him smile across the table at her felt right. Yes, perhaps she should call and make it up. She stood up and let herself out of the steam room, just as a pair of laughing women around her age came in. Giving them a strained smile, she made her way back to her locker, weaving past a number of naked elderly bottoms, pockmarked with cellulite.

Melissa took a warm dry towel from the pile by the door and peeled off her swimming suit, then stood frozen, suddenly filled with self-loathing. Was she jealous of her own child? She supposed she must be, a little. What a dreadful person that must make her. To be envious of a dying child. She felt nothing but love and protective instinct towards Sarah, but her husband's heart lay with his daughter and not with her. She was jealous.

And she felt so alone. So alone. Here she was, attempting to deal with the worst thing that could ever happen, and her husband refused to talk to her. If he was there, he was drunk, or hung-over and monosyllabic. He wouldn't talk about the future, wouldn't acknowledge the present. Somehow she had to present a solid, responsible image to the world. Be a mother, be a grown up. She couldn't care less that their friends didn't talk to them anymore. She didn't need them. She needed her husband. And she had lost him.

It was as if Simon had nothing left to say. It was as if, as his daughter died, a part of Simon died with her.

Melissa patted herself dry and hopped on one leg as she pulled Juicy Couture tracksuit bottoms on, wondering, not for the first time, why chlorinated water seemed stickier than normal water. Before the leukemia, Simon always took talcum powder when they went swimming, and Sarah loved to puff the clouds of talc onto her body, giggling as her father patted it down, soaking up the moisture and making dressing easier. Even then, she mused, she had been separate from them. Always on the outside looking in. The whispered jokes, the father-daughter trips to the park, the bedtime story that she particularly wanted her daddy to read. Never mummy. Always daddy.

And now, whilst pulling away from Melissa, whilst refusing to discuss how they would handle the hardest conversation that they would ever have in their life, he'd gone ahead and told Sarah she was dying. Not just that. He'd decided to tell her that he would 'go with her to heaven'. My God. That had been a shock. Her parents had been disappointed in him, angry at his immaturity and lack of judgment, but they didn't share the horror that Melissa felt. Because Melissa realized that Simon could do it. Why not? Because what else did Simon have if he didn't have Sarah?

She slammed her locker door harder than she had meant to, drawing enquiring looks from the other members in their various states of undress. One woman, obese and completely naked, stood calmly in the centre of the locker room, filing her nails. How could people do that, wondered Melissa? How could they display themselves like that? Looking away from the woman, Melissa tied her damp hair back into a tight little bun and smudged a little clear gloss onto her lips.

"Go with her to heaven". What the hell had he meant? Did he mean that he'd die with her? Or that he'd ensure they died together? Melissa frowned as she dabbed mascara onto her eyelashes. Surely he wouldn't hurt her, but Melissa knew how much he loved his daughter. Enough to end her suffering? Melissa narrowed a newly painted eye. *Was Simon a risk to Sarah?*

Melissa shrugged her swimming bag over her shoulder and pushed her way out of the locker room, dumping her towels in the laundry bin on her way out. *No. Not a Chinese. Maybe she should go over and find him at the pub ... no.*

She threw her bag onto the back seat of her Range Rover and slid into the driver's seat. Resting her head on the leather steering wheel, she shut her eyes, willing herself not to cry. Dinner with Simon was just a daydream, an indulgent fantasy of what could never be. The truth was Simon had made his choice clear over the past few months. There was only room for one of 'his girls' in his life – and that girl wasn't Melissa.

Chapter 20

Simon flicked a lump of dog turd into the wheelie bin and returned the shovel to the garden shed, resolving to take Porridge for a good long walk after he had seen his parents that afternoon.

Back in the house, he scooped instant coffee into a mug and settled himself at the pine table with the weekend newspapers. He supposed he had better call Melissa. There had been four missed calls on his mobile when he checked it that morning. He had already spoken to Madron House and Sarah was comfortable and well – or as well as she could be - so Melissa's call could not be urgent. *Perhaps she'd left something out of her notelet*, thought Simon grimly. He picked up the phone and punched in the familiar number.

She answered on the third ring. "Yes, what is it?"

"Oh God, Melissa. Is this really how it's going to be from now on? You end our marriage by leaving a note in the fridge. Apparently you want us to stay 'friends', but you answer your phone like that. Could we just grow up and be sensible about all of this for a minute please?"

"I was perfectly ready to be sensible last night, when I phoned you to check that you were okay. Oh, and when I rang again at 9 p.m. and then 10 p.m. and again at 11 p.m.. I suppose you were propping up the bar in The Whippet, were you?"

"Melissa, as we no longer live together, I can't really see why this is your business. But yes, on hearing – no, sorry, *reading* - that my marriage was over, on top of the fact that my little girl is dying and even, yes even that the custody of my *dog* was going to be up for discussion, I decided, on a whim, to go to the pub and get utterly *wankered*. I'm sorry if I wasn't in to take your call. Our lives, as you so dramatically put it, have taken separate paths. My path, joyously, happens to have a pub on the corner. Now. How can I help you?"

There was a long silence. "So you're okay with this?"

Simon paced up and down the garden, needing to quell the adrenalin pumping around his body. "No, Melissa. I am not 'okay' with being ousted from my own house during the worst weeks of my life. However, you have apparently made a decision, and as much as you lambaste me for being weak, you may remember from our twelve years together that I am remarkably staunch when it comes to taking things on the chin, so to speak."

"There's no need to be so angry. I'm hurting too, Simon and ..."

"Don't try to play the victim in this, Melissa." Simon snarled. "It's your split. Your decision. You don't get to be hurt."

Melissa's voice when she spoke again was quiet. Childlike. "What have your parents said?"

Simon let out a bitter-sounding snigger. "Oh, I've been saving that conversation for when I see them this afternoon. Seeing as it's going to tear my mother apart, I thought it would be more thoughtful to discuss it in person. I'll be sure to say you said 'hi'."

195

"Simon don't ..."

"Goodbye, Melissa." Simon hit the red button on the digital phone, wishing he had an old fashioned phone that he could slam down with theatrical vigor.

* * *

As his parents' front door opened, Simon was hit with the familiar scent of home, along with the fug of semi-tropical heat in which his mother insisted on keeping the house. Barbara had been a determined and vocal detractor of central heating, claiming for years that it caused everything from eczema to cystitis. Her beliefs changed dramatically when, after decades of being able to see her own breath in the morning, she had finally been talked into having central heating installed. It was an epiphany - her Damascus moment. The thermostat had been stubbornly turned to maximum ever since. It was no wonder her ferns and potted palms thrived.

Barbara cooed as she opened the door, her delight at seeing her only son obvious. "Simon! How lovely to see you, pet. Get *down*, Porridge. No Melissa? How's Sarah? Oh God – is everything alright?" Her features rearranged themselves quickly into a vista of panic.

"It's okay, Mum. Sarah's fine. Well, not fine. You know. It isn't *that*. Porridge, if you jump up *once* more you're going in the car."

"Well, come in, lovey. Would you like a cup of tea? I've just put the kettle on. Your Dad's at the allotment but I'm expecting him back for lunch. Can I make you a sandwich? I've got beef …"

Porridge's small but serviceable vocabulary included 'beef' and his ears pricked.

"I'd love a sandwich, thanks. Have you got horseradish? Great. So how long until Dad's back?"

Barbara edged past Porridge, working her way into the small kitchen, and took a loaf out of her bread bin. The same bread bin, Simon noted with nostalgic contentment, that he had bought her for Christmas sometime in the seventies.

"I can't imagine Dad will be more than ten minutes. Though it's a busy time for him at the moment. He's having trouble with his lettuces. He thinks someone is pilfering his compost as well. There's been a big hoo-ha. They're having a meeting. *Stop looking at me like that, Porridge. I'll give you a bit at the end.* How's Sarah?" Barbara flicked a strand of beef fat towards the Labrador, who dispatched it in under a second.

Simon exhaled slowly. "She's probably in The Mad House for the duration now."

"The what?"

"Sorry – Madron House. They call it The Mad House. I suppose it's a bit of an unfortunate connotation, but actually it is a magic, slightly mad place. I thought I'd find it really hard to see her go into

197

the hospice, but in some ways, I'm glad. The nurses are great. Her room is pink, with beanbags. They've even given her a goldfish in a bowl." He raked his fingers through his hair, leaving it standing in tufts, which his mother smoothed for him. "She's slowed down now, Mum. She's not the little girl she was. I think a part of her has gone already. She sleeps most of the time. When are you coming to see her?"

Barbara cut the stack of sandwiches into triangles with unnecessary force, tutting as one flew off the side of the plate. "This week. We were sorry that you weren't doing Sunday lunch today. I know that you and Melissa have a lot on, but it seems more important than ever, that we, you know – stay strong. Stay together. I haven't heard from Robert and Diana for at least a week, I don't think I've gone for more than a week without speaking to Diana in ten years. Do you want a packet of Wotsits?"

Simon nodded and took the plate of sandwiches over to the oilcloth covered kitchen table. He took plates and napkins from a drawer, enjoying the fact that nothing in the room had changed for over thirty years. There was a comfort in returning home and recognizing every corner, every picture. Every piece of cutlery - the chipped bone handle of the butter knife and the stain on one of the napkins - all were expected, their histories known, their stories part of his very fabric.

There was a ruckus at the front door and Terry entered the

hallway. "I *knew* he were taking my compost, Barbara. I practically caught the bugger at it. Simon, is that you? Saw your car outside. Where's my favorite daughter-in-law"? Terry appeared in the kitchen doorway, muddy boots in hand, his gardening jacket as familiar and loaded with past history to Simon as the school photos cluttering the staircase walls. "Aye now, Porridge. Get down, there's a good dog. Get *down*, Porridge. Simon. Good to see you, lad. No Melissa?"

Simon waited a beat, hoping that his mother would launch into her usual tirade regarding muddy jackets scraping across the wall, but none was forthcoming. "No. No Melissa. Mum's made beef sandwiches, Dad. You'd better come and have some before Porridge and I do them all."

There was a brief but uncomfortable silence. Terry took his jacket off and hung it in a cupboard under the stairs. "Is everything okay, Simon? Only we haven't been able to get hold of Robert and Diana and there hasn't been a Sunday lunch for weeks. We were going to suggest that we did it today, only we struggle to get more than four round this table … There hasn't been an argument has there?" Terry sat down and took a sandwich, tearing a piece off and feeding it into the mouth of the awaiting Labrador.

"Terrance!" Barbara tutted.

"Oh, give it a break, woman." Terry's voice was gruff.

Simon looked up in astonishment. The choreographed dance his parents usually played seemed suddenly out of step. There were

199

clearly defined boundaries to their daily petty bickering, and his father's retort, whilst minor, was harsher than the normal game rules allowed. Tension prickled the air.

"She left me." There really was very little else to say. One cannot polish a turd, thought Simon grimly.

"Oh no. I knew it!" Barbara's voice jumped three octaves. "I told you, Terry. I told you, didn't I?" Barbara began to sob quietly into her tea towel.

"It can all be sorted out. Tell me what happened." Terry's voice was grim. It was the same tone, Simon recalled, that his father had used on the few occasions that he had been in trouble as a lad. Smashing a greenhouse window, graffiti in the school toilets. The failed attempt to steal a porn magazine (as part of a gang) from the local corner shop. His father would deal with whatever problem Simon had caused, protecting his son as best he could, standing his corner, resolving any situation before soundly thrashing him.

"Nothing happened, Dad. She just left."

"People don't just leave!" Barbara wailed. "Something must have happened. You must have had a row. Oh, what did you say to her, Simon?"

Simon gnawed the inside of his cheek. This was exactly the reaction he had expected. Both of his parents adored Melissa, seeing her as a glowing example of wife and mother, the perfect daughter-in-law. So proud of Simon and Melissa's charmed middle-class existence, they both upheld Melissa as the fairy princess who held it all together. The tasteful décor, the charming and thoughtful gifts, the perfect Sunday lunches. All Melissa. All the magical flourishes that only Melissa could achieve. She was the one that sprinkled fairy dust on the family's perfect, shiny life. Simon's medical career paled into insignificance against his wife's social touches, thought Simon bitterly and somewhat unfairly. "I didn't say anything. Neither did Melissa, as it happens. She left a note."

Terry slipped another lump of sandwich to Porridge, ignoring his wife's protestations. "Well, what did the note say? She must have given a reason. People don't just walk away from marriages without good reason. There isn't somebody else involved is there? You've not had an affair have you?"

"*No*, Dad. I'd like to make clear, right now, that I am the victim in this, okay? I don't want everyone walking around declaring me the monster. All I want is for us to stay together and work through this time. All I really give a toss about right now is my daughter. If Melissa wants to go, then fine."

"So *she's* having an affair?" Barbara joined them at the table.

"*No*. There are no third parties involved. Melissa has decided to stay at her parents, and apparently she wants me out of our house by Tuesday. So, just to make sure everyone is clear on this, I am about to lose my daughter, I have lost my wife and I am about to lose my home. Oh yes, and she's announced that 'she doesn't know what to do about Porridge yet', so I may well be about to lose my dog as well. Yet somehow, somehow the blame is being placed firmly in my lap." Simon quietened himself, realizing with a shock that he had been shouting. Porridge placed his nose in his crotch, by way of comforting him. Simon ran his hands through the dog's fur. "Sorry. I shouldn't have shouted. I'm sorry. It's just – I knew that you'd react like this. Like the unraveling of my life somehow ruins yours. And that any damage to your life is therefore my fault. I'm sorry. I'm just – I'm just tired of being in the wrong all the time." There was a pause.

"Do you want to stay the night?" Barbara asked, shattering the silence and surprising everybody by dropping a whole sandwich on the floor for an equally surprised but delighted, Porridge.

"I'd like that, Mum. If it's okay. I don't want to put you out."

Terry stood up and flicked the kettle on. "No problem at all, lad. Don't worry. We'll get this all sorted out."

Barbara smiled as if nothing had happened, and got up to do the dishes. "Your dad will sort it, Simon. I've got Angel Delight left over from yesterday. It's butterscotch. Grab a bowl from the cupboard and I'll get you some."

"Thanks, Mum." Simon forced a smile, whilst wondering if his mother truly believed that the fragments of his life could be glued back together with Angel Delight.

He woke early to the sound of Porridge snoring on the rug beside him. Simon had slept deeply, sinking into the womblike reassurance of his childhood bed. The old duvet cover, blue with red and yellow triangles, was thin, cheap. The mattress was uneven. Yet he knew the contours, knew the smell of the pillows and feel of the sheets. For nine blissful hours he had been ten years old again. Safe in his bed and in the knowledge that no matter what happened, his dad would sort it all out.

Clattering noises and the smell of burning bacon lured him out of his sanctuary. Porridge was already nosing the bottom of the bedroom door in delight. Simon slipped on the dressing gown from the back of the door. It was the same red toweling affair that had hung on the door since he was a teenager, and it hadn't grown alongside him. The sleeves ended just below his elbows. His bottom was adequately covered, though his thighs were not.

He stuck his head around the kitchen door. "Can I help?"

"Oh Simon!" Barbara exclaimed, patting her chest dramatically, "You scared the life out of me. I was going to bring you breakfast in bed." She nodded towards a tray on which she had put a glass of orange juice, and a plate of bacon with very greasy eggs. A single crocus peered out of a tiny vase.

"Oh, Mum. You shouldn't have. Listen, why don't you sit down and let me make the tea. I'll eat this down here with you. It's a long time since we had some time alone, isn't it?"

"Well if you're sure, but I can bring it up if you like …"

"Mum, sit down." Simon pulled out a chair for Barbara and took over tea making.

Barbara sat down obediently. She looked as if she wanted to hold her tongue, but lost the battle in the end. "Tell me, Simon. Have you really not had any row with Melissa? I just don't understand it. You always seemed so happy. Apart from, well, you know. But you seemed like the perfect couple. I've always been so proud of you. All my friend's children are divorcing all over the place – that's if they even bother getting married in the first place. And then there was you and Melissa. Unbreakable."

Simon poured Porridge's kibbles into a bowl from an emergency stash Barbara kept under the sink. He poured milk into a little jug, knowing his mother would disapprove of tipping it straight from the bottle into a mug. "Do you want some toast, Mum? No?" He picked up his breakfast and settled himself at the table, beginning his eggs with some trepidation. His mother had never been able to fry eggs. "Melissa and I have been rowing for some time. Not about anything in particular. More – everything, really. We're under a lot of stress, as you know. Perhaps it's not fair to say that Melissa is taking it out on me. Maybe I am difficult to live with, I don't know. But for reasons known only to herself, she's decided she doesn't want me anymore."

"Do you think she's playing games?"

"What do you mean?"

Barbara stirred her tea thoughtfully. "Do you remember when you'd just left Med School? It was a couple of years before you got married. You were still living together in your Grandma's old house in Leeds. Didn't she flounce off then?"

"Hmm." Simon's eyes fell on a framed photo on the dresser. It was of Simon and Melissa, wild-eyed, happy. Tipsy. It had been taken on the day he had gained his first position as a General Practitioner. They had gone to the local Italian to celebrate. Well lubricated on *Prosecco* and stuffed with *calzone*, they'd gone home and played strip *Trivial Pursuit*, whilst working their way through a bottle of *Amaretto*. It had seemed more grown-up than a nightclub at the time. When had they last played like that? How long was it since they played a board game that hadn't been brought out in honor of Sarah? When had it all become *so grown-up*?

"I seem to remember that she came back pretty quickly when you went to see her. Are you sure she isn't just testing you?"

Simon regarded his mother, surprised at the sudden insight into the female mind. "I don't know why she's doing it. Perhaps you're right. Perhaps she wants me to storm into Robert and Diana's, pick her up and carry her home in a fireman's lift. I don't know. But it doesn't really matter, because I'm too tired to do it. I'm too tired to play games and I'm too tired carry her."

"But what about Sarah? You have to be strong for Sarah, love."

"That's just it. I am being strong for Sarah. I don't have room to be strong for anyone else. Right now it's taking every ounce of emotional energy I have to be a father. I can't be a chest-beating alpha male husband as well. Does that make me weak? Maybe it does. But right now, my little girl is scared and ill, and nobody is going to take my focus away from that."

"Your father and I went through rough patches, you know. When I had the miscarriages. After you, I mean. I always imagined I'd have a house full of little ones, but it wasn't meant to be. Two or three years it went on for. I'd think I was expecting and then, well."

"I didn't know – sorry." Simon pushed his eggs around his plate, awkwardly. He'd never questioned why he was an only child. It had never occurred to him to ask. He felt embarrassed by the insight into his mother's most private history. As an adult and a father, it had occurred to him more than once that perhaps his parents were not the simple, boring souls he had presumed them to be. There had been no documented horrors in their lives. No tragedies, no dark secrets. There had been no giggling as they smoked an illicit joint after dinner. No frantic tumbles in the woods. No hastily regained composure when interrupted *in flagrante* by their son. Or had there? Hazy thoughts rippled the surface of his memory, recollections of jumping into his parent's bed, the sheets hot and musky, his father distant and cold. How arrogant we are, Simon mused, to think that our parent's lives pivot on the axis of our own.

"How were you to know?" Barbara interrupted his thoughts. "You were only a little boy. I don't think Terry and I said a civil word to each other for a whole six-month period. Of course we tried to keep it from you. Just a young lad you were, in your sweet little cardigans."

"I didn't realize – I mean, you always seem to be so, together. You bicker a bit but I thought that was a joke, a sort of game you play."

"Oh, it is. He likes a bit of gentle nagging, does your father. Makes him feel loved. But no marriage is all sugar and cream, Simon. I would have thought that you realized that by now. There have been times when I would have happily choked your father on his own bloody parsnips. That said, I'm sure there are times when he would have murdered me. He was pretty cross when he found out I'd had a bit of a fling with old Brian Telford."

"Brian? *You*? Mum!" Simon put his knife and fork down, shock coursing through his body. He caught sight of his ludicrously attired arm and for just a moment felt like the fourteen-year old boy that had received the dressing gown one Christmas. "Mum – I don't believe it."

"Oh, don't make a fuss, Simon. It was a couple of tipsy kisses and tickles a long time ago. Your father forgave me, though he was bloody cross at the time. Only fair. What I'm trying to say – do take that outraged look off your face, Simon – what I'm trying to say is that marriages go through bad patches. You pull through. Stick together. If divorce wasn't so ruddy easy these days there would be a lot of much happier people around. With happier children."

"Staying together for the children doesn't really apply in my case." Simon pushed his eggs away, ignoring the hurt look from his mother. He was angry. He knew he was being petulant and he didn't care. A fissure had formed in the previously solid foundations of his life. The formerly familiar walls of the kitchen seemed to mock him. What had they witnessed that he had not?

Barbara pursed her lips in motherly disapproval. "Life is never straight forward, son. God knows you've been served some curved balls in your time, and no one is as sorry as Dad and I to see what you are going through. But life goes on, Simon. You have another forty years on this planet, maybe more. Don't ruin your future. I don't agree with Melissa – I'm dratted angry with her, if you must know. But you're going to need someone in the coming weeks and you'd be better off remembering your marriage vows and sticking together." Barbara got up, took the half-full plate and scraped burnt egg whites and oil into the bin. "That said, I don't like interfering. Too many mothers meddle with their son's lives. I've told you my thoughts. But whatever happens, you know we're here for you. It's your life. You'd best do with it what you will."

"Yes, Mum. It is my life."

* * *

Simon strolled down to the allotment with his father, where he made suitable noises over seedlings and tutted at correct moments regarding the Great Compost Theft. Terry didn't ask, didn't probe. He never did. Simon naturally enjoyed the quiet companionship of the older man, although today the unspoken catastrophe only simmered below the surface of amiability. Terry seemed a little distant, more reserved. Just as he had always been when Simon had done something wrong as a boy. *Only I haven't done anything wrong*, thought Simon, nodding enthusiastically over a crop of early lettuce. It was not he who had manufactured the catastrophe that boiled beneath the surface of potting shed congeniality.

Simon waved his parents goodbye and set off back home. Porridge, in disgrace for rolling on a newly sown bed, sulked muddily on the back seat.

He would go straight to Madron House, Simon decided. It was Monday afternoon and a final decision would be made as to whether Sarah was ever to return home. It was ninety percent certain that she would not. Percentages again, thought Simon grimly.

Simon did not know whether or not Melissa would be there. It was her habit to visit in the afternoons, when Lorraine, her partner at the florists, took over. They would, he supposed, have to see Rhonda together. There would be a show of unity. Not to disguise a crumbling marriage would appear disgracefully selfish under the circumstances.

Melissa had not attempted to make further contact and he had no wish to call her. For Simon, it felt almost as if she had never been. She didn't exist. As he sank into the ghastly reality of his immediate life, Melissa's part in his past and future seemed negligible. Through the words on one lilac-colored *notelet*, Melissa had become merely a woman with whom he would need to do business. Form-filling. Banks, mortgages. Signatures would be required.

There was no emotion. No bitterness, no gnashing of teeth, no desperate feelings of abandonment. They had parted. The end.

The house? Again, Simon felt anesthetized. He was dully aware that he should feel some kind of anger at Melissa's presumption to their property, but was unable to muster the necessary emotions. If anything, the loss of the house seemed a blessing. A specter of past happiness haunted the rooms, and he had no desire to sit amongst the relics of his previously perfect family, waiting for the sand to drain from the hourglass of his daughter's life.

Melissa was welcome to the beautiful, bright kitchen. To the Rayburn, to the cushion covers that had taken so ridiculously long to choose. She could keep the sleigh bed and the antique armoire and the *chi-chi* mirrors and chandeliers. She could rot in the Italian marble sunken bathtub. And mostly, most definitely, she could be the proud owner of a million Barbie dolls, plastic ponies, toy prams, Disney jigsaws, dress up clothes, play kitchens, toy tea services, tennis balls, bouncy balls, scruffy stuffed puppies, broken board games, Mr. Men books, coloring books and snapped Crayolas.

Oh yes. Melissa could have that problem – the ... disposal problem. She could be the one to sit crossed-legged on Sarah's bedroom floor and sort through the lifetime acquirements of a wealthy and slightly spoilt seven-year old. Charity shop, *bin*, charity shop, *bin* – Oh look, Sarah's hand decorated photo of the three of them at a theme park. What to do with the doll's house she had spent so many hours re-organizing – charity shop or bin? The dolls she had loved so much, despite the severe haircuts she had given them. Surely the charity shop wouldn't take them like that? *Bin*. The half-used coloring books. *Bin*. The tubs of play dough, her little fingerprints still pressed into the drying balls inside. *Bin*.

Belongings. Possessions. They tethered you to life. Simon needed to be free.

Chapter 21

"Ooh, I do like a custard cream, don't you?" Rhonda offered the plate in Simon's direction.

"I'm sorry, what? Er, no thanks." Simon waved the plate away irritably, biscuits not at the forefront of his mind. Despite Rhonda's many qualities, her constant chipper outlook and bluntly cheerful demeanor grated. Granted, the hospice manager could not play the role of constant professional mourner, but inane biscuit chatter was tiring.

Melissa, beside him on the sofa, also declined with a tight smile. The small leather settee in Rhonda's office dipped in the middle and he noticed that Melissa's thigh muscle, like his, was clenched in a determined effort to keep their legs from touching. After twelve years of marital union, their bodies had become separate, suddenly their own. They guarded their personal space jealously, the air between them crackling with hostility.

Rhonda smiled at each of them. "I hear Porridge is something of a celebrity?"

Simon gripped the arm of the sofa, levering himself a little further away from his wife as the saggy seat threatened to roll him into contact with Melissa. "He's done a tour of the hospice, yes. Generally well received. He's sleeping off his afternoon's social engagements in Sarah's room now. Thank you for allowing him in. I can't tell you how much it means to Sarah. And Porridge."

"Yes, she seemed delighted." Melissa spoke softly. "Though she seems very distant now. She's sleeping a lot."

Rhonda helped herself to another custard cream and flapped a hand in front of her mouth in the universal gesture of *hang on, I've got my mouth full.* "Yes. Sarah is a lot quieter now. You will find that she sleeps around eighty percent of the time. Talking will tire her, and whilst we are controlling her pain, I'm afraid the anti-nausea drugs don't completely stop her feeling sick. Given your daughter's exuberant personality …," Rhonda popped the last of the biscuit in her mouth and repeated her earlier performance, " … sorry, I missed lunch … given your daughter's personality, the change will seem particularly marked to you. She will have better days, but I think it is safe to say that we are now firmly in the Palliative end of her care and that the Sarah you have known will start to slip away from now on."

Melissa sat forward and took a deep slow breath in, as if steeling herself. "How long?"

Simon closed his eyes.

Rhonda dabbed at the corners of her mouth with a napkin. "A month at most. It could be two weeks. I'm afraid it is very difficult to say. Certainly you should be coming to terms with the fact that Sarah will be gone very soon. She won't be coming back to your family

213

home again. I'm very sorry to have to tell you this." Rhonda pushed a box of Thomas the Tank Engine tissues towards the couple, in a clearly well practiced move. Neither took one.

"Is she scared?" Simon's voice trembled just slightly. "Has she said anything? Does she understand?"

Rhonda put her head on one side and smiled sympathetically. "Sarah is desperately poorly. She's really too tired to be scared. As your wife will be moving into her room with her …"

"What?" Simon cut the woman off.

"Well, I presumed that you knew …" Rhonda trailed off, confused.

Melissa turned to Simon. "I'm moving into Madron House in a day or two. A camp bed can be put in Sarah's room, though as there is only room for one of us and you're going back to work, obviously it will be me."

"But I don't have to go back to work. And what about the florists? Are you just going to shut up shop? Couldn't we have talked about this? When was this decided?" Simon stood up, unable to keep up their farcical 'togetherness' act any longer.

"I spoke to Rhonda last night. You weren't here. You were staying at your parents." Melissa spoke in an accusatory tone.

"For one night. I phoned ahead and made sure Sarah was alright. I spoke to her on the phone. I couldn't come all the way back from Barnsley for an hour. Surely we should have spoken about this. I want to be with Sarah. I want to be there. You can't just push me out like this. Damn it, Melissa, she's my daughter, too."

Rhonda stood up awkwardly. "Would you two like a little privacy? I have a few things to do at the front desk and it seems that you might like to talk. Shall I …" She trailed off, apparently aware that neither Simon nor Melissa were paying the least attention to her. "Right. I'll just be through here." She slipped out of the door.

Simon rounded on Melissa. "You can't just call dibs on staying with Sarah, Melissa. We don't know when she is going to be awake and I want to be there when she is."

"You can't, you're working."

"So are you!"

"Lorraine can cover most of my shifts and we've got a student starting. Anyway, you've got Porridge."

"What? You said that wasn't decided. Besides, Porridge can come with me."

"Not all the time, he can't. He's only meant to come as a treat. He can't sleep the night here. You'll have to look after Porridge while I stay here. It's obvious that's the only solution."

"I want to do my share, Melissa. I'm only working Thursdays, Fridays and Mondays. I could sleep here at the weekends and Tuesday and Wednesday."

"What about Porridge?"

"What? Well, you'll take Porridge when I'm not here."

"My dad doesn't think it's a good idea, your being left alone with her."

"What?" Simon nearly tripped over a waste paper basket. He booted it out of the way.

Melissa looked at the disturbed bin, litter scattered around the floor and raised her eyebrows archly. "Because we don't feel that you are in a stable psychiatric state nor that, given your self-confessed suicidal feelings, you are an appropriate person to be with Sarah alone at the moment. Dad spoke to a psychiatrist friend and..."

"Appropriate fucking person?" Simon, still pacing, accidentally banged into Rhonda's desk, causing an impossibly high stack of papers to collapse, shuttering off the desk and scattering the carpet with documents. *"Psychiatrist friend?* What the *fuck* is going on here, Melissa?" Simon clutched at his hair, shaking his head in horror and disbelief. "Have you told them that you think I'm going to hurt my daughter?"

Melissa sniffed. "My father and I thought it best that the hospice be fully aware of your mental state and that precautions should be made ..."

"Mental state?" Simon howled. "I got pissed one night, Melissa. I'm not a bloody monster!" Simon kicked the bin again, finding it an inadequate release to his anger. His frustration made him want to tear curtains down and smash windows. "I - AM – SARAH'S - FATHER." Simon was shouting and crying now. "All I want to do is

216

protect her and be with her. I don't want her to die. But if she has to, I want her to not be scared. And if that meant being with her then, yes. Yes, I'd make sure we died together. Why is it so difficult for you to see that? Why is it so hard for you to understand the pain I'm feeling at the moment? You stupid, stupid, insensitive *bitch*."

The door burst open and Rhonda, wild-haired as ever, walked in briskly, accompanied by a burly man in a physiotherapy uniform. "I think that's enough now, Dr. Bailey. I'm sorry, but you will have to leave."

"You see how he is!" Melissa wailed, gesturing to the knocked over bin with its spilt litter and the documents from the desk that strewed the floor. "He's not in his right frame of mind. He's completely unbalanced. Did you hear him admit he's suicidal? He said that *he'd make sure they died together.* What does that mean? That he'll take her life as well? He's not safe. He's not well…"

Simon roared, looking around for something to throw. He found nothing within reach, so stormed out of the room, slamming the door behind him. He headed back towards Sarah's room, breaking into a jog as he heard an announcement break into the background music that played throughout the common areas. "Staff member to room nine, staff member to room nine, urgently please."

Simon reached room nine, Sarah's bedroom, and stalled for just a moment, composing himself. He made an effort to shed his anger and calm his face and body, then entered. Porridge gave a whining

217

yawn, stood up, stretched and padded over to him. He sniffed Simon quizzically, the Labrador's acute senses picking up distress instantly, then he enquired into his master's condition in the only way he knew how. He barked. Loudly.

"Shh! Porridge. *Shh!*"

Sarah opened her eyes sleepily. "Dad?"

"Yes, darling. Go back to sleep. *Shh!* Porridge." Porridge continued to bark, the noise as intrusive as gunshot in the calm sanctuary of the hospice.

The door burst open and Fiona appeared. "What a noisy dog!" She gave Simon a strange look and immediately focused on Sarah. She moved towards the dog and patted him, though Porridge, thoroughly riled, continued to bark.

"What's going on?" Sarah spoke groggily.

Rhonda and the male physiotherapist rushed into the room, causing Porridge to bark more. Rhonda's usually congenial manner had turned brusque. "Stop that dog barking this instant. Mr. Bailey, you will have to go. Take that animal with you."

"Daddy?"

"It's alright, Princess. Porridge, shut up! Go back to sleep, darling. *Porridge!*"

"Simon, just go." Melissa attached a lead to Porridge's collar. "Look what you're doing. Look at the harm you're causing. Please go."

"Daddy?" Sarah's sleepy voice was breaking now, tears clearly forthcoming. "Daddy, you are coming to heaven with me, aren't you? Daddy? You promised. Daddy?"

Without hesitation, Simon replied "I will, Sarah. I will."

The whole room glared at him in shocked silence, with the exception of Sarah who smiled in relief and closed her eyes and Porridge who was ready to go.

Simon took Porridge's lead. "I just want to be with my daughter. I just want to be with Sarah."

Melissa took the still barking Porridge's lead back and led the dog out of the door. "Just go, Simon," she said quietly. "You have to go."

Chapter 22

"Another pint, Simon?" Steve, the landlord of The Whippet, nodded at Simon's near empty glass. "Not like you've got far to crawl, is it?"

Simon shrugged and handed the glass over for refilling. He might as well have one for the road, or for the staircase as it were, since he had moved into the flat above the pub that evening. He kicked a huge cricket bag at his feet, apologized profusely to it and then realized that it wasn't his Labrador, but the holdall containing his clothes, toiletries and a photo of Sarah. Twelve years of collecting and accumulating possessions and his only real requirements fitted in the vast sports bag below. He had not even bothered to look upstairs. He needed a bed, loo, shower, hob and dog basket. He would see the flat when he was ready to go up.

Porridge had, in fact, taken up residence below the pool table, where he was fed a regular supply of bacon crisps and could avoid being stroked by every person who entered the pub. The initial excitement of being the official pub canine had worn off and he was feeling the familial discord keenly.

"There you go, mate. £2.70, please. You not got work tomorrow then?"

Simon fumbled with the stack of coins in front of him. *What was this, his sixth? Seventh?* "Yup. I'm returning to sick-notes for phantom sciatica and kids with ear infections. Can't wait."

"Must get a bit repetitive. Surprised you're not always ill, all those people bringing their germs to you. Hey, you must get pretty well paid, though, not being funny, if you know what I mean." Steve colored slightly.

"S'alright, Steve. I don't mind. Pay's not bad." Simon winced, hearing himself slur slightly.

"Why you renting that dump upstairs then, mate? Not being funny or anything, but you could afford a much better bachelor pad than that. One of those swanky studio jobbies in the mill in town would have done you. They've got a swimming pool in there, you know. Bye guys, thanks." Steve waved the last group of pool players off and took the glasses they had brought back to the bar. "I mean, upstairs is alright for the young 'uns but it's not exactly the kind of pad you're used to, is it?"

Simon put his hand down to pat Porridge, who had emerged, yawning, from the under the pool table. "They couldn't sell most of those flats you know, in the mill. They've ended up leasing it all out to the council. Place is packed with DSS and asylum seekers. Not exactly the water-side living for affluent professionals that they advertised." Simon checked himself, his snobbery both surprising and embarrassing him, as usual. "Anyway, I'm not into all that

221

minimalist, thirty-something professional loft lifestyle anyway. You have to climb a ladder to get to your bed. Speaking of bed …"

"Yeah, but even so, mate, you could probably find something better than upstairs. Don't get me wrong, I like having you round here and Porridge is a great hoover, I just wondered why you'd take such a dive on, when you could afford somewhere a bit nicer. Not being funny, like."

Simon shrugged off the question. "I just want to stay around here. That's my family home over there." He gestured out the window into the dark street. "All my memories, all our hopes. I just want to be close to Sarah. Or Sarah's home. I dunno. Can't be bothered looking for anywhere else, anyway. No point. All I need's a bed. Oh shit."

"What?"

"Bed. I forgot a duvet. Don't suppose there's anything up there is there?" Simon drained his pint and hopped off the barstool.

Steve shook his head. "Nah, sorry mate. I don't think I've got anything spare either. Only have a few bits and pieces myself, you know how it is."

Simon nodded. Steve's wife had left him two years before, which had led him to give up his job as a mechanical engineer at a prestigious international company and buy a boozer in a backwater. Judging by the rotation of his wardrobe, the man only owned two shirts and a football top. He lived on takeaways and was on first name terms with every delivery driver in town.

"That's alright, Steve. Need to take the mutt for a walk anyway. I'll pop back home. Come on, Porridge." The dog stretched and trotted over to the door. "Will you be open when I get back?"

Steve flipped off the lights on the beer pumps. "Probably not, mate. I've just about finished down here, to be honest. If you look on the key ring I gave you, there are two different keys. The bronze one will open the kitchen door in your flat – just nip up the fire escape by the kitchen bins."

"Okay, will do. I could do with walking a bit of this beer off anyway." Simon swallowed a belch. "'Scuse me. Clear head for the morning and all that. Are you not eating tonight?" Simon glanced pointlessly around, searching for Steve's usual pizza box.

"Nah. Got a Pot Noodle upstairs. Bombay Bad Boy flavor. Can't go wrong. Do you want me to stick your bag in the flat on my way past?"

"If you could." Simon kicked the bag. "Watch it, it's heavy."

"No problem, mate. Used to beer kegs, aren't I? Tell you what, I'll even put a Pot Noodle in your kitchen for you if you like. You can call it a house-warming present."

"Um ... smashing. Thanks."

* * *

223

As Simon slipped through the back gate of his property, he was surprised, considering the late hour, to see the lights still on in the conservatory. He walked as quietly as possible across the gravel courtyard that flanked the rear of the house. He made his way, somewhat unsteadily, toward the back door to the conservatory, recalling the duvet that was stashed to the side of the sofa. It had been used during the day for Sarah in recent weeks. Porridge's dog basket was also near the back door. He could slip in and out without Melissa even noticing. Simon looked up at their bedroom window and noted that the light was out. *Must be in bed already*, he thought. She was not in the habit of going to bed late.

He approached the door, idly noticing that the light in the conservatory was cold and flickering. Splashes of colored light intermittently dappled the windows. *Telly's still on. Bugger.*

Simon peered through the small gap between the conservatory blinds and the wooden doorframe, cursing Melissa for having insisted on such a tight customized and expensive fit. He could see very little beyond the strips of clear glass. Porridge trundled off to sniff his garden as Simon moved along the windows, trying to see if Melissa was still up, the half-centimeter slither of clear glass beside each blind his only viewpoint. A shape on the sofa that might be Melissa. A wine glass on the floor. A hand, trailing along the ground. An empty bottle. A smashed glass. Teddy bears. A red teddy. A teddy bear that should not be red.

"Melissa!"

Simon sprinted to the back door, fumbling with his keys as he discovered the door was locked. The key stuck slightly and he swore as his haste and alcohol intake exacerbated his clumsiness.

"Melissa!"

He finally engaged the key correctly and stumbled as he tripped into the room.

"Mel', are you okay?" Simon's sense of alarm calmed slightly as he took in the scene.

Melissa stirred on the sofa. "Sime? Don't feel very well."

Simon rolled his eyes and swore. "Jesus Christ, Melissa. I thought you were bloody dead. What are you playing at?"

Simon put his hands on his hips, realized that he resembled his own mother in that position, and folded his arms instead. Melissa lay near comatose on the sofa, next to two empty and overturned bottles of red wine on the terracotta tiles. A wine glass lay overturned, a puddle of red wine seeping across the orange tiles and soaking a previously white teddy bear in its path. "What the hell are you doing, Melissa? Look what you've done to Sarah's teddy. Mum bought her this. Jesus, Melissa, look at the state of you."

Melissa moaned unintelligibly. "Drank too much."

"Yes I can see that. *Get back, Porridge, there's glass on the floor. Good boy.* Come on, I'll have to help you upstairs. What the hell came over you? I thought I was the one who was meant to have a *drinking problem*. Jesus, Melissa, you can hardly sit up."

Simon, now thoroughly sober, tried to hoist Melissa over his shoulder, but her rag doll demeanor made her a dead weight. He managed to get her to a sitting position, taking all her weight as he dragged her off the sofa. "Whoops, steady. Right – can you walk? That's it. One step in front of the other. Here we go."

"Simon, I'm going to be …"

"Oh, Jesus, Melissa. Quick over to the sink, just hold on. Oh, for *fuck's sake*, Melissa. Oh, oh. Jesus. It's alright. You're okay. I'll never get that clean. Okay, I've got you. Don't cry. You're just a silly girl who's drunk too much. I'll hold your hair back. Hang on, I'll move the bowl – never mind."

Melissa retched again, regurgitating Chianti with astonishing power. Simon held her hair back, stroking her shoulders and muttering simple platitudes. *There, there. Better out than in. Let's get you to bed.*

They made it up the stairs, Simon grateful no more red wine was being ejected. He settled her into their bed, and took off her shoes but left her in the pinstriped dress she was wearing. He noted with astonishment a ladder in her tights.

He heaved her into the recovery position and placed a waste paper bin by the bed. Melissa muttered a thank you, then blacked out as Simon backed out of the room.

Downstairs, Simon cleaned out the sink, thoroughly disinfecting the area. He threw away the empty bottles, retrieved the broken glass and straightened the cushions on the sofa. He picked up the teddy bears, which were scattered around the sofa, a number of which were marked with black streaks of mascara. He picked up the teddy that had been stained with wine. *Ruined.*

The volume on the television rose suddenly, the late night film giving way to the usual adverts of the off-peak hour. *"We've got hundreds of girls, just waiting to chat in your area."* Simon switched it off.

The room fell silent, the house eerie, dead. The normal clutter and chaos of the family home was gone. The walls held no emotions, no vibrations, only objects. The house was an overcoat. Its soul had departed.

Porridge's nails click clacked over the tiled floor as he made his way over to his master. "We're going, boy. Come on." Simon took a tray of dog food from the larder and put it in the bin bag with the unspoilt teddy bears. He rolled up the duvet and tucked it into the dog basket, balanced a pillow on top and threw a slightly slimy and well-chewed rubber chicken on top. Awkwardly, he wedged the load under his arm, his keys in the other hand. "Come on, Porridge, we're off. I've packed Chewy The Chicken. We're going to our new home." Simon clipped the lead back onto the dog's collar and left the house, locking the door behind him.

He did not look back.

Chapter 23

The woman gabbled up another snotty tissue and dropped it on Simon's desk. The moist little ball turned Simon's stomach. Whilst blood had never bothered him and he could deal with warts, bunions and verucahs with cheerful resignation, damp tissues upset him deeply. Something about the fibers disintegrating under the weight of germ-laden mucus appalled him

He offered his waste paper basket with a tight smile.

"So, Mrs. Foster ... Mary, sorry. You've been feeling like this since your son moved to New Zealand?"

The woman snuffled an affirmative, dabbing her eyes and rolling another tissue into a damp mish-mash.

"Have you had any weight loss? How is your appetite? Are you eating more, less?" Simon scribbled on the corner of a notepad, concentric circles being his doodle of choice.

"I'm not hungry. I suppose I have lost weight. I just can't seem to be bothered eating. I can't be bothered with anything, to be honest."

"Right." Simon's circle widened. He ran out of room on the paper and began another one. "Do you find that you are still engaging in your normal level of social activity, or has that dropped off?"

The woman perked up a bit. *People do enjoy talking about themselves*, thought Simon.

"I don't want to go out." The woman began to tear corners from the tissue, causing Simon to shudder. "I used to go to Bingo every Tuesday and Thursday but now it just seems too much of a chore. I don't even go to the coffee morning at the Community Centre anymore. Everything seems such an effort."

Simon drew spokes on his circles. "And how about how others perceive you? For instance, I note that you speak slowly. Have you always spoken like this? Has anyone mentioned your speech patterns?"

The woman looked surprised. "Well, my son says I'm different on the phone. I just put it down to being tired. As I said, that's what made me come in, Doctor. I just can't seem to get up in the mornings. I've always been such an early bird but now … well, there doesn't seem much point. Oh, thank you." She put the shredded tissue into the bin, which Simon had yet again proffered.

"I think, Mrs. - Mary - that you are suffering from depression. It's not uncommon in our more mature citizens, especially those who have lost a spouse or, in your case, a son. I believe your son lived very close to you over the years, didn't he, Mary? It must have been hard for you when he got a job in New Zealand."

"Awful." Mary sniffed. "I couldn't believe he went. I know he had to do what was best for him and that – but New Zealand. I'll never afford to go there. I'll never see him again. He might as well have died."

Simon looked up sharply from his notepad. "Hardly."

"Sorry?"

"Hardly. Look, I think we should start you on a very low dosage of fluoxatine, more commonly known as Prozac. No, don't look so alarmed. We'll start on a very low amount and see if we can't help you feel a little better. Depression, Mary, is a lack of the hormone seratonin. This hormone is the chemical that balances our mood. When we don't make enough, we get depressed. This can be triggered by a traumatic event – loss of job, grief for instance, or even, in some cases, by other drugs. By administering a small amount of fluoxitine, we can begin to regulate your seratonin levels until we balance your mood again. Tell me, have you been feeling suicidal at all?"

Mary looked up at him and frowned. "No, I don't think so. I suppose it has crossed my mind. It doesn't really seem such a big thing, nothing does. There's not much to live for really. I don't feel scared by death at the moment. I don't feel anything at all. No, I've not planned to kill myself, but I've thought about dying and it doesn't seem like such a bad idea. I suppose, I have thought about just ceasing to be. Not waking up. That wouldn't be so bad…"

Simon nodded and added more spirals to the scribbles on the notepad.

"Right, well, I think that we ought to start you on a low dosage and see you monthly to keep an eye on things. They can make you

231

feel a little sick to start with. Here's an information sheet which will answer any questions but, of course, if you are really concerned about anything, come back and see me."

Mary took the information sheet that Simon had printed out for her. "But aren't these addictive? Do they turn you into a zombie?"

Simon completed the prescription and handed it over. "We will be very careful with the dosage and we can wean you off them when the time is appropriate. We won't keep you on them for any longer than a year. They might make you a little woozy and foggy for a few days – only slightly. You must keep taking them, though. There are more details on the sheet." Simon smiled and stood up, helping the woman to her feet.

"So, it's as easy as that is it, Doctor? I take these and I feel better?"

Simon opened the door. "In your case, we hope so. Sometimes counseling is necessary to deal with any underlining pain or problems, but I think in your case, Mary, we should see good results with the medication."

"Oh. Right. Thank you, Doctor."

Simon bade her farewell and closed the door. Sitting back at his desk, he completed his paperwork and buzzed reception to call his next patient: Mr. Mohammed and a varicose vein. Simon sighed. He really could not be bothered.

* * *

Simon took one bite of his chicken and bacon pre-packed sandwich and decided it was more hassle than it was worth. He intended to use his half hour lunch break to catch up on some paperwork, but first he would have to deal with Melissa.

Whilst he was pretty sure that she was safe in the position he had left her, Simon retained a dogged sense of duty towards his wife. He had, he supposed, better check that she had not choked on her own vomit, appealing though the thought was.

Also, he needed to clear up the business at Madron House. Melissa had done a thorough job painting him as a deranged maniac. Now she'd better undo the damage. He intended to see his daughter.

He took out his mobile and hit the speed dial key for Melissa.

"Yes."

Simon took a deep breath. "Hello, Melissa and how are you?"

"Fine. Shouldn't I be?" A falter – just a little one, but recognizably a chink in a piece of armor he'd been acquainted with for twelve years. *She doesn't remember.*

"No sore head? Dry mouth? Nausea – no, I suppose you don't feel sick. Got all that out of your system last night."

"Oh. It was you."

233

"Yes, of course it was *me*, Melissa. Who the hell else would be putting you to bed at midnight?" Simon stood up impatiently. He needed to pace.

"I thought perhaps I'd ..."

"No. You were certainly not in a state to do anything. In fact, if I hadn't found you, you probably would have choked on your own vomit. I won't be wearing my beige Calvin Klein jeans again, by the way."

"Oh."

"Yes, *'oh'*. I can't believe you ruined that little white teddy bear. I put it in the washing machine but no doubt it's totally ruined. A bit much having you vomiting and throwing red wine everywhere, when you've accused me of being an unbalanced drunk. What were you playing at?"

"I was watching a film. 'Reality Bites'. We watched it the first night I moved into the house in Headingly. Do you remember?"

"No." Simon lied. "And I don't see how watching a daft film from the nineties should have you projectile vomiting my best Chianti. Twelve quid a bottle, that stuff."

"I was just a bit emotional. It brought back a lot of memories. How things were ... Never mind." Melissa's voice hardened. "What were you doing there anyway? I thought you'd moved into the *pub*." Melissa injected venom into the word.

"I forgot Porridge's basket and a duvet for myself. I thought seeing Porridge had been uprooted from his home, the least I could do was provide his normal place to sleep. I thought you'd be in bed. I didn't expect to find a sozzled old drunk on the couch."

"You can talk."

"Don't start that again." Simon sat back down at his desk. "Anyway, we need to talk about all this nonsense. Obviously I need to see Sarah. I'm coming down this evening after work." There was a pause. "Melissa?"

"You can't."

"Why?"

"Well, not on your own." Melissa sighed. "You really did cause an awful lot of upset yesterday."

Simon stood up again. "I caused upset? Melissa, everything that happened yesterday was entirely your fault. The dog was upset because of you. I don't know what you've been saying to them, but you'd better *unsay* it."

"I can't. They don't feel it's safe to leave you alone with Sarah. I'm sorry, I know it may seem rather harsh …"

"Harsh?" Simon laughed mirthlessly. "So how do we sort this out? How do we get this lifted?" Simon paced again. "Because you know as well as I do, Melissa, that I pose no threat to Sarah. No man has ever loved his child more than I do. God knows, I don't want her to suffer, but as a doctor I have faith that she is being made as

235

comfortable as possible. I can't believe you are still punishing me for talking to Sarah that night."

"What does it matter if you have someone with you, then? Sarah isn't talking much anymore anyway. Dad's been reading her the Harry Potter book every day. She's quite insistent that they find out what happens."

Simon was quiet for a moment. "I want to read it to her."

"You can. Just not alone."

"This is ridiculous. I could speak to a lawyer." Simon sat down again, resuming his doodling on the notepad. "I can take you to court. You can't stop me seeing my daughter."

"We're not stopping you seeing her, Simon. You can see her whenever you want. Just not alone."

"We? What is all this 'we'? On whose authority? You and Rhonda can't just decide this. You need an authority."

Melissa sighed. "Social Services have said that …"

Simon flung his pen down and leaped up once again. "Social Services? You've got Social Services involved?"

"Calm down. You're being aggressive again. This is just not like you, Simon."

"*I can't win*, Melissa. If I'm docile, I'm not coping. If I'm angry, I'm a lunatic. If I'm crying or drinking, I'm suicidal. I can't win. What have Social Services got to do with all this?"

"Rhonda called them and …"

"'Fuck's sake."

"Rhonda called them. Currently, they don't wish to take anything further, but they have suggested that you have company when you are with Sarah, for your own protection as much as ours."

"Protection from what exactly?"

"In case you – I don't know, Simon. You just don't seem yourself. I'm worried you're going to try to … I'm worried you're going to try and help Sarah. She's in pain, you're grieving … I just, I just felt that …"

"Melissa, you can't seriously think that, can you? I took the Hippocratic oath, Melissa. God knows, it kills me to see her this ill, to see her in pain, but I'm not going to hurt her. I want her to be better."

There was a pause. "That's what I'm worried about, Simon."

Simon half laughed, shaking his head and running his hands through his hair. "Melissa. I'm not about to put a pillow over Sarah's face, if this is what you're saying. Don't get me wrong. Sometimes, when she's lying there, crying – but no. I have no intention of speeding up the process." Simon sank back into his chair once again and pulled his notepad towards him. "I take it I can call her?"

"Yes. Yes, of course. Look, Simon, I'm sorry it's all turned out like this. I just needed you to … I just needed you to be more … forget it. Call her whenever you like. I'll talk to Rhonda. Give it a

237

couple of days, okay? She's not pleased with you for causing a ruckus."

"I didn't cause a *ruckus*." Simon drew a line down the centre of a clean sheet of notepaper. "I'm so tired, Melissa." He wrote *'Stay For'* at the top of the left hand column. "We had everything. Beautiful home, wonderful family. It's like we were a triangle. You, me and Sarah. We were strong. It seems to me that Sarah's taken away and the triangle has collapsed. Like we could only love each other if Sarah was still in the triangle."

"Simon, don't do this to yourself. You're not making much sense."

"No." Simon wrote *'Go For'* at the top of the right hand column. "No, I don't suppose I am."

"I've invited your Mum and Dad round on Sunday. My parents are coming as well. I'm not going to do lunch. It doesn't … well, it doesn't seem appropriate somehow. But we'd like you to come. Come and have a chat. No rows, no shouting. Let's just talk some things through. It might help with our parents there. I'm worried about you, Simon. Everybody is. Your Mum and Dad – my parents."

"Really." Simon was deadpan. He wrote *'Melissa'* below the left hand column. "How nice of you all." He added *'Mum and Dad'* on the line below. "All I really want is to be with Sarah, Mel. If you really cared you wouldn't stop me."

238

Melissa faltered momentarily. "I'm not stopping you. I've said I'll talk to Rhonda. You can be with Sarah. It's just that I think it would be better if someone was with you at the moment, just for a few more days. You seem different, Simon. Not safe. *No, let me finish*, I know it doesn't make much sense. You want to protect Sarah, don't you? If you were concerned about my potential actions, wouldn't you do the same? Wouldn't you do anything, absolutely *anything*, within your abilities to protect Sarah?"

Simon wrote *'Sarah'* beneath the right hand column and drew a thick black line through the word *'Melissa'*. "Yes. Yes I suppose I would."

STAY FOR   GO FOR

~~Melissa~~   Sarah

Mum and Dad

239

Chapter 24

"Barbara."

"Diana."

Simon opened the front door and watched uncomfortably as the two women nodded at each other, their husbands exchanging tight smiles and handshakes. Terry tutted at his son, "Can't you have this damned dog trained, Simon? Get *down*, Porridge."

They edged uncomfortably past each other in the hallway, and filed into the kitchen, where Melissa sat at the table.

Simon shut the front door behind them, feeling once again like the disgraced schoolboy. He had no wish to be at this meeting. A summit, as Diana had called it, to discuss the recent 'events'. Never had such an innocuous word been so laden with distaste.

Melissa greeted her mother and father warmly, her mother and father-in-law less so. The family took seats at the great pine table, the Baileys taking the side served by a bench, the Halfords forming a panel along the opposite side. Melissa poured coffee. Polite thanks were issued.

"Right." Melissa pulled the last cup towards herself. "I think we all know why we are here."

"I don't." Simon muttered.

Diana raised an eyebrow. "Ostensibly, because we're worried about you, Simon."

Simon spluttered sarcastically. "You're not worried about me. You've accused me of being a danger to my child and you've had me thrown out of my home. If that's your brand of concern, Diana, then I would hate to really cross you."

Diana pursed her lips, raising an eyebrow and catching Melissa's eye. An *'I see what you mean'* look.

"Robert and I have been very concerned about you. Obviously, it was a dreadful shock to us when Sarah told us that you had gone ahead and told her she was dying."

"Hang on a second," Terry interjected. "Somebody had to tell her."

"He was drunk and he told her that he would 'go with her to heaven', Terry." Robert spoke crisply. "I don't suppose he's mentioned that little detail to you, has he?"

Barbara sighed. "Oh, Simon."

Terry took a biscuit from a tin Melissa had placed on the table. "No, I didn't know that. But I'm sure that he has his reasons. Don't you, Simon?"

The group looked expectantly at Simon.

"Oh, I see. So I'm permitted to stand up for myself? Well. I certainly appreciate that. With all the caring about me that's going around, I wasn't sure if I was going to be permitted to speak. Thank you very much. As it happens, yes, I have reasons. She's scared of being alone. Nobody she has ever known has died. Not even a pet. She doesn't want to be on her own. She's only seven."

Simon took a biscuit and defiantly fed it to Porridge.

Melissa rolled her eyes. "Simon believes in a heaven with white fluffy clouds and cherubs with harps. He takes it all literally."

"No, I don't, but in fact it doesn't really matter how I perceive heaven." Simon gnawed the inside of his cheek. "But I do find it astonishing that you don't believe what your Christian faith has taught you. You've been going to church for years, Melissa. Why did you bother? Was it some kind of social climbing strategy, Melissa?" He frowned and picked up another biscuit, rolling it between his thumb and forefinger. Then his brow lifted. "Do you know, I believe it was. It's amazing how much clearer I've been seeing things recently. What, were you going to church because you thought that was something a doctor's wife 'did'? Was it because those poncy lawyer friends of yours went? Is that what it was all about? After all, your parents have never shown much interest. Diana spends more time choosing her outfit than she does actually in prayer."

"How dare you!" Robert's voice was raised.

"Simon, lad," Terry lifted an admonitory hand, "you'll be giving Robert another heart attack at this rate, and one tragic death is quite enough to cope with at the moment." He gave his son a powerfully meaningful look. "So quiet down."

242

"No, Dad. I'm not going to quiet down. I'm not having Melissa take the piss out of my faith. Right at the moment it's *most* important to me. Yes, I believe there is an afterlife. I believe that after we leave here, we go onto another stage, another place – and that we meet again those that we once knew and loved. This is why, Melissa, I thought we got married in a church. Because we both believed in God and thought that we were sanctifying our marriage before Him. I realize now it was because you thought the acoustics would be better."

Melissa spoke a little louder. "If you're accusing me of not believing in a fairytale land where we all waft around banging into Elvis and Princess Diana, then you're right. There is no heaven. You're a bloody *doctor*, Simon. You're supposed to be a scientist. I thought you realized that a quiet display of faith was the decent and normal thing to do. Sarah gets a basis for her cultural education and we enhance our standing in the community. I didn't realize you were a fully signed up member of the bloody God Squad."

"And I only just realized what a shallow, one dimensional, self-absorbed social climber you are."

"Enough!" Terry put his hand on Simon's. "We're not sat around this table to listen to this. This isn't doing nobody any good at all. Simon, *calm down*, lad. What I want to know is exactly what you meant by 'go with her to Heaven.' Nobody is going to rubbish your

243

faith …" Terry gave Melissa a warning look, " … but I want to understand what you are trying to say, son."

"I'm not trying to say anything. I do believe in heaven. I do believe that I will meet Sarah again one day. I believe that for the time being, God will look after her – but until then she is not going to know anybody. I really can't explain it. I can cope with losing Sarah. Or rather, one day, I might be able to deal with it, but I can't deal with the idea of her being scared or lonely."

Diana spoke coldly. "The hospice says that she is reacting well to her prognosis. Melissa says that the psychologist is happy with her understanding of death. She's not scared."

"Do you really know that?" Simon turned to his mother-in-law sharply. "And even if she isn't scared now, what about the moment of death? What if she knows the moment she leaves us. What if she is scared then?"

"What are you planning on doing?" Robert's lip twitched in annoyance. "Are you going to hold her hand and shoot yourself as she dies? You're being ridiculous, Simon."

"Yes, I am being a bit ridiculous. I don't know what's come over me. My daughter's dying and I've gone all philosophical on you. Ridiculous."

"Sarcasm isn't going to help anybody, Simon." Diana reached into her bag. "Do you mind?" She took a packet of Silk Cut out and stood up, walking towards the back door. Porridge wagged his tail

244

furiously and followed her. "Just stay there, Porridge. I'm only standing in the door."

Melissa's father took the floor again. "What we all want to know, Simon, is whether you are a threat to Sarah or a threat to yourself. Melissa believes that you have been behaving oddly and I must say your manner today is quite unlike you. My friend who is a psychiatrist…"

"Here we go … " Simon rolled his eyes.

"Simon." Terry gave his son a warning look.

"My friend who is an *eminent* psychiatrist, thinks that you are displaying *'Magical Thinking'*, which is when …"

"I know what Magical Thinking is."

Barbara pushed her cup across the table. "Well I haven't got a clue what magical thinking is, but I very much doubt that my son's got it. He was asked to leave a children's birthday party when he was eight for heckling the magician. Can I have another cup of that coffee, lovey?" She pushed her cup towards Melissa. "Don't you think we're getting a bit carried away with all this? Simon's upset. Of course he's upset. We deal with things in different ways – thanks, love. No, just a sweetener, ta. Remember their wedding day? I didn't think I'd get him down the aisle."

Robert nodded as Melissa proffered the coffee jug. "There are some psychologists who believe that grief is more than a deep sadness. That it can be a temporary state of mental illness."

245

Simon snorted into his coffee. "Oh, for God's sake."

"Why isn't Melissa being accused of this, then?" Terry looked at his daughter-in-law accusingly. "Who's to say that it's Simon who is acting uncharacteristically? Melissa's chucked him out of his own bloody home. She's tried to have 'im banned from the hospice. Not exactly usual, is it?"

"I'm not talking about topping myself to go and live on a cloud with Sarah, am I?" Melissa stood up, taking the empty jug to refill. "Simon has been behaving strangely for months."

Simon's father, Terry, leant forward. "But you're not exactly yourself either, are you, my love? Throwing a grieving father out of his own house? Banning him from seeing his own daughter? Laughing about his faith when you know it's what is keeping him going? All this ..." he gestured round the table, "this cold, business-like summit. This is all your doing. Not my son's."

There was a silence, broken only by Diana banging the stable door shut. She returned to the table. "Simon's been drinking. My daughter had to ask him to leave. Did you know he hurt her? Physically? In Disneyland?"

Terry paused and looked at Simon steadily, who in turn, stared miserably at his mug of tea. "No, I didn't know that." His was voice laden with disappointment.

"And did you know," Diana sat back down at the table, "that he violently lost his temper at the hospice, kicking furniture and scattering papers around the Manager's office?"

Terry retained eye contact with Simon. "No, I didn't know that."

"It wasn't like that!" Simon threw his hands in the air.

"And then," Diana leant forward, her forefinger stabbing the table, "he caused a commotion in Sarah's bedroom, causing my granddaughter and apparently some of the other guests a great deal of distress."

"It wasn't like that." Simon spoke quietly, once again feeling like a child. His father's disappointment bored into him.

Diana leant back in her chair. "No, I didn't think he would have told you that. I'm sorry, Barbara. But you always have been completely blinkered when it comes to your son. I sometimes think he could stand over a dead body with a smoking gun in his hand and you'd still be protesting his innocence."

"What do you mean?" Barbara sounded shocked. "I've never said my Simon was perfect. Nobody is. I always thought that you thought the sun shined out of your daughter's arse, but then, I thought you thought the sun shined out of your own arse as well."

"How bloody dare you speak to my wife like that." Melissa's father rose from the table.

"Don't you raise your voice at Barbara!" Terry rose as well.

247

Diana sniffed. "Well, Melissa, if I'd known we'd been invited to be treated like this ..."

The voices swelled, indignant comments merging into one raucous cry. Twelve years of petty jealousies, minor slights, unspoken annoyances and previously forgivable idiosyncrasies rose like bile, insults spattering the family with emotional burns that would scar.

Simon slipped out the back door. Nobody made any effort to stop him, or perhaps they didn't even notice. Porridge, following, picked up a squeaky toy and in his haste to follow his master, swept a framed wedding photo off a low table with his tail.

It smashed.

Chapter 26

Simon wrapped a small towel around his waist. His shower had been lukewarm and feeble. The water pressure was similar to that of a dripping tap.

Dressing quickly, he flicked on the kettle in his dingy kitchen, remembered there was no milk and turned it off again.

He had just rung Sarah and had been pleased to be able to talk to her. She was weak and monosyllabic but cheerful. Melissa had *graciously* agreed that he should be allowed to speak to her whenever he wished – or rather whenever he could, given that she was so often asleep. Visits were still to be supervised.

He left the kitchen and headed through the violently orange corridor into his bedroom, which had been painted a more soothing shade of lilac. The furniture was simple - 1950s wardrobes and a basic double bed - but it was clean and provided all he needed. It might almost have been pleasant had it not been for the botched attempt at a giant Chinese character, which some artistically minded bar-hand had daubed in black gloss paint on the wall.

Shrugging on a crumpled shirt and brushing dog hairs off his suit, Simon finished dressing and went back into the kitchen where he poured dog biscuits into Porridge's bowl. Porridge looked at him mournfully.

"I'm sorry, boy. You can't come with me. Steve is going to come and get you in a bit and then you can be Chief Pub Dog. He'll take you out for a walk. Porridge, don't look at me like that. I'm trying my best. He'll take you out for a good walk and I'll be back later and then we'll go for one. Please don't look at me like that, lad."

Simon picked a tie up from the floor, where he had evidently pulled it off the night before. He winced as blood rushed into his dehydrated head. *Drank too much again last night.*

He followed Porridge into the flat's sitting room, painted a virulent purple, the shade children often use to paint witches' cloaks. Further attempts at Chinese characters graffitied the walls.

Porridge jumped resignedly onto the saggy sofa they had inherited, along with an ancient television, an assortment of half-burned candles which littered the fire hearth, and the sticky pub table and chairs that provided a dining area.

The evening before, having escaped the outraged howls of his warring family, Simon had perched on his usual barstool in The Whippet. He had pulled a scrap of paper and a pen out of his pocket and added a name to the left hand side. *Porridge.*

"Do you want the telly on, Podge? Right. *'Jeremy Kyle', 'Bob the Builder', 'Homes under the Hammer'* or something about people trying to lose twenty stone? No preference? Right. Fat people it is then. Give you something to think about."

Simon took his medical bag from the hallway. He had home visits all morning and would not be returning to the surgery until lunchtime. He took out the itinerary that the office had printed for him the day before and consulted it. *Mrs. Beardsley, aged ninety-eight, diabetic, emphysema, bad cold.* It was nearby and would allow a stop at the McDonald's drive in.

Shoving his list of visits back in the bag and shrugging his jacket on, Simon patted Porridge's big head. The Labrador looked at him with mournful eyes. He tracked his car keys down, checked the dog's water bowl and let himself out onto the shaky iron fire escape. Simon wasn't fond of heights. He grimaced as the metal groaned under his weight and the small platform leaned visibly away from the side of the house. Simon stuck his head back into the flat.

"Bye, Porridge. Have a nice day."

* * *

Simon's first patient lived in a modest bungalow on a small council estate. A community nurse opened the door. "Dr. Bailey? Come in. We're having a bit of a bad day today." The nurse grinned. *She's being a pain in the bum and nothing you or I can say is going to be good enough*, was the unspoken meaning.

Simon nodded his understanding and made his way through the tiny hallway. The house smelled strongly of discarded incontinence pads. A cheap floral air freshener attempted, and failed, to mask it.

"We're in here." The nurse showed him into the sitting room, where her charge sat before a gas fire, a crocheted blanket covering her legs. Oxygen cylinders cluttered the room, already crowded with furniture, knick-knacks and assorted cats.

"Good morning, Mrs. Beardsley. How are we today?" Simon put down his bag.

Mrs. Beardsley wheezed. "Been better." She eyed Simon suspiciously. "Where's Dr. Calvert?"

"On holiday, I'm afraid. But I assure you I'm very friendly." Simon smiled brightly, though his attempt at humor was met with stony silence. "I understand that you haven't been feeling very well."

"I haven't felt well for ten years." *No*, thought Simon ungenerously. *If you hadn't smoked sixty a day for as many years, you might feel a whole lot better.* "I hear you have a cold."

Mrs. Beardsley wheezed again and took a long pull of oxygen from the mask she held in her lap. "Can't clear me nose. Can't get any air in." She took another drag of oxygen. "Sore throat."

"Mrs. Beardsley didn't like the menthol crystals we tried, Dr. Bailey. *Did you, Mrs. Beardsley?*" The nurse addressed her comments to the old woman loudly. "Said they made her eyes sting." The nurse rolled her eyes. "She doesn't like the honey and lemon for

252

her throat and she's not keen on lozenges. We have to be careful because of her diabetes as well. I thought I'd better call you to make sure she hasn't got an infection, *because we don't want an infection, do we, Mrs. Beardsley?*" The nurse raised her voice again. "Thought we'd better check if we needed antibiotics, *didn't we, Mrs. Beardsley?*"

Mrs. Beardsley harrumphed breathily, her mouth pursing like a dog's bottom. "You people fill me so full of pills. I don't know what any of them are for anymore. Take this, take that. If you'd just leave me alone, I'm sure I'd be much better off." She sneezed messily and smacked her lips.

Simon watched the nurse's cheek muscles flicker in irritation. She spoke with the overly cheerful vigor so often employed by healthcare workers battling a dislike for their patient. "If we didn't come and keep an eye on you, Mrs. Beardsley, there could be an accident. Remember what happened with your insulin? Honestly, Dr. Bailey. Mrs. Beardsley kept forgetting to take it. She's still got stores of it dotted around the house. *Haven't you, Mrs. Beardsley?*"

Simon took out his blood pressure gauge and made his way through the occasional tables, stacks of magazines and oxygen trolleys. A large black cat eyed him steadily, clearly challenging Simon to move it from the arm of Mrs. Beardsley's chair. Undaunted, Simon lifted the cat and placed it on the floor, where it growled and stalked off, flicking its tail at Simon in a gesture which, if it had been human, would have involved a middle finger.

Mrs. Beardsley offered her arm without complaint and Simon took her blood pressure, breathing shallowly in response to the acrid ammonia smell that emanated from the armchair. Cat piss or old lady pee, Simon could not be sure.

"Very good, Mrs. Beardsley. Lovely blood pressure." Simon made a note and the nurse also updated her records. "Now, I'd like to listen to your chest, but before I do, I should wash my hands. Is there anywhere I could …?"

Mrs. Beardsley wheezed and hawked up a globule of matter into the back of her throat, which she spat into a bucket next to her. She waved her hand in the direction of the kitchen.

"The bathroom is just next to the kitchen there, Dr. Bailey." The nurse indicated one of the yellowed, nicotine-stained doors leading off the front room.

Simon grinned a thanks and, putting away his sphygmomanometer, went to wash away any cat or human urine from his hands. He felt contaminated in this stuffy little room. No wonder the woman couldn't breathe.

The bathroom, whilst clean, was crammed with possessions, just like the rest of the house. *The work of the Community Care Team, no doubt,* thought Simon. Another cat lay nonchalantly along the back of the bath, its paw dangling off the side like a tiger. A sleek tabby sat primly on top of the loo cistern. Simon slipped his jacket off, rolled up his sleeves and washed his hands, pleased to see that the nursing team had installed a bottle of anti-bacterial hand wash. A stack of blue paper hand-wash towels sat on the windowsill. He dried his hands and shrugged his jacket back on, swearing under his breath as he nudged a tower of old ice-cream tubs that had been balanced on the back of the bath. They contained ancient plastic hair rollers, half-full tubes of toothpaste and hemorrhoid creams, cracked soaps, bath pearls, old toothbrushes, lurid lipsticks and other assorted bathroom detritus, which all now tumbled into the bath, sending both cats fleeing in feline disgust.

"Everything alright?" the nurse shouted from the sitting room.

"Yes, sorry. Caught my sleeve. Not a problem. I'll sort it out." Simon called back, only catching the end of some rasped rejoinder from Mrs. Beardsley. He leaned over the bath and began piling the various items back into their containers. Nail clippers, nit combs, rusting razors and soggy packets of Disprin - all kept to one side, all stored for decades, just in case.

Simon paused, his eye caught by a small pharmaceutical box around the size of a cigarette packet. It lay on its side; the cardboard eroded with damp and age. A number of vials of insulin had escaped its confines and the little glass bullets lay scattered on the anti-slip mat in the bath.

"Are you managing in there?" The nurse's voice called from the sitting room.

"Yup, just putting everything back to rights." Simon scooped up the loose vials, tipping most of the pack of twelve back into the box. His hands shook slightly. Four remained in the palm of his hand. He looked at them. Tiny little ampoules filled with a potent hormone. Its strength, Simon knew, would have increased over the years. Insulin. A lifesaver or a life ender. Four little vials of magic. Four little vials of…

"Do you want some help, Dr. Bailey?" The nurse's voice sounded directly behind the door.

"No." Simon slipped the insulin into his jacket pocket. "I've managed." He quickly balanced the boxes and ice-cream tubs on the back of the bath where they had come from, then emerged from the bathroom, banging into the nurse, who stood right outside the door. "Sorry about that. My mother always said I'm like a bull in a china shop. I've put it all back, though I did find these, Mrs. Beardsley." Simon raised his voice for the old ladies benefit and handed the insulin box to the nurse, the remaining eight vials sliding around the bottom. "They must be from when you were self-medicating. We'd better dispose of them safely. Do you have a sharps bucket, Nurse?"

The nurse nodded, and tutting, dropped the box into a bright yellow plastic container that stood by the entrance to the kitchen. The

256

disposal shoot closed with the lid, enclosing the powerful medication within.

"Good." Simon smiled at the nurse. "Well then, Mrs. Beardsley. Shall we have a little listen?" Simon tiptoed his way back through the assault course of furniture and cats as Mrs. Beardsley hacked and rasped her irascible answer.

The glass vials tinkled faintly against each other in his pocket, the sound audible only to him.

Chapter 27

It took no more than a couple of days before he settled into the monotony of the working week, his days punctuated only by his evening visits to Sarah. He left directly from work, battling the afternoon traffic and arriving at Madron by around 6 p.m. Melissa tailored her routine, visiting in the afternoon and returning for the evening only after Simon had left, ensuring that they never met.

Simon's visits were watched over by a silent and patronizing presence. A nurse was constantly posted in the corner of the room, their vapid smiles and polite comments poor camouflage for their distrust.

Sarah was now barely Sarah. The life, the vitality, the spark of individuality had all but been extinguished. The little girl who lay in the bed was an echo. A wisp.

Simon's visits were spent in quiet contemplation and in reading the last Harry Potter book. Sarah would lie quite still, smiling slightly at comic moments, frowning at other times. From time to time, she would let out a soft hooting noise, which Simon came to understand as a cry of triumph as the child characters in the book overcame the great tribulations set before them.

As the book progressed, it also darkened. Simon flinched as he read descriptions of death or grief. Sarah, however, seemed untouched by these passages, intrigued only with the fight of good versus evil. Her own proximity to death seemed unimportant to her.

At five-to-eight, Simon would gather his things and leave, occasionally passing Melissa's 4x4 on his way out of the car park, as they handed over shifts. They did not make eye contact. It was as if 'they' had never been.

A walk with Porridge, a few beers in the pub and a kebab/pizza/curry shared with Steve at the bar, and Simon would turn into bed. Another day ticked off, another day completed.

Life had become a matter of low-level existence, the daily realities and concerns dampened as if played out behind thick glass. The people in the street scurrying about their business, the politicians on the news, the patients in his office and the punters in The Whippet all seemed detached from Simon, as if their lives were taking place on a different plane, a separate level of vibration.

* * *

"You coming then, Simon?" Steve reloaded the vodka optic behind the bar, talking to Simon over his shoulder. "Porridge, *out*. You know the rules."

Porridge slunk back out from behind the bar. He was enjoying his tenure as Pub Dog but struggled with the no-going-behind-the-bar-rule.

Simon called him to heel. "Well, I suppose I'll be here anyway, so I might as well listen to what he's got to say."

"Load of mumbo-jumbo." Derek, a staunch regular smacked his lips together and pushed his empty glass tankard towards Steve. "No such as thing as ghosts. If you could talk to dead people, Elvis would never get a moment's peace."

"Ah," said Steve, refilling the glass, "but he asks for people not to ask for famous people. It has to be someone you have a connection with for them to come forward. He's a Spiritual Medium. He says that we move on and when we do, some people with the correct channels of vibration, or summat, can continue to pick up little bits of communication. He doesn't call them ghosts. He says that the energy we create when we're alive continues. It just moves onto a different plane. The energy goes all the way around the world. So the amount of energy you create when you are still alive hangs around, in the atmosphere, like."

"What's his name again?" Simon dropped a pork scratching for Porridge. The A board outside the pub had proudly announced the forthcoming 'Evening with a Clarevoyant' (sic) for sometime, though Simon had paid little attention to it.

"Gordon something. He's good. No, honestly. You'll be eating your words." Steve addressed a group of regulars who barracked him. "Seriously. He did a reading for my mum and told her all sorts of stuff about me old dad. Stuff he could never have known. And she's no pushover, my mum. God, no." Steve shuddered slightly. "You won't be laughing after you've seen him in action. Might open some of your minds, you shallow old bastards."

Simon grinned and tuned out of the conversation as was so often his way these days. He grabbed his newspaper, letting the banter wash over him. His mind retreated into the safety of The Times' crossword puzzle. He worked on the brainteaser steadily, pricking his ear occasionally when he was offered a drink, and offering the occasional snort of derision where it was required. Thankfully, most of the regulars had now received their free medical advice, having treated Simon like a mobile GP's surgery when he had first moved in. One man had actually ripped off his sock to show Simon an angry bunion, and a normally shy and retiring lady of about fifty had brandished her bosom at him, encouraging him to have a good feel for lumps.

"Pizza or curry, Simon?" Steve interrupted Simon's thoughts.

"Not sure I can do any more curry. I'm a bit over-pizza'd as well. Do they do jacket potatoes at Mamma Mia's?"

"Erm," Steve took out a menu with a flourish, "yes. Though why anyone would want a jacket potato over a fourteen-inch donner kebab and pepperoni pizza is beyond me. *Tuna, cheese, beans, cheese and beans or coleslaw.*" Steve dropped the flyer on top of Simon's newspaper. "Is it my turn to pay?"

261

Simon took the menu. "Tuna and coleslaw for me. You ring, I'll pay."

"Fair enough."

Steve telephoned the takeaway, greeting the person on the other end like a member of his family. Simon chuckled as Steve articulated despair at his dining partner's choice of a jacket potato and ordered his own impending heart attack with extra cheese.

He took another look at his crossword and took up his pen, recalling the answer for number seven down. *Novel by Sylvia Plath (3,4,3)* - "The Bell Jar," Simon muttered, fitting it into the grid.

"So will you be coming to the clairvoyant medium thingy tomorrow night?" Steve asked, coming round from the bar and settling himself on a stool beside Simon.

"Probably. It's either that or sit in the flat watching Top Gear re-runs. Do you really believe in all that stuff then, Steve?"

"Dunno really. I mean, I think there must be something. After life, you know? My mum really isn't one for falling for hoaxes, and she believes in him completely. Also, I've had a few funny moments myself over the years. When my dad passed for instance."

"What happened?"

"I was sitting up in bed. He'd died the day before. I was just sitting there, thinking about him, wishing I'd said certain things to him, when I heard someone walk up my stairs. Clear as day. My first thought was that it was a burglar. But then I heard him. My cat was sitting at the top of the stairs, where she always sat – that bitch got my cat as well, but that's another story – and I heard him speak to her. Like he was never gone."

"What did he say?"

"Hello, Bad Puss."

"Not exactly enlightening advice from beyond the veil." Simon took a sip of beer.

"Well, no. But that's what made it so real. It's exactly what he would have said to her. I was just freaking out a bit when suddenly I was flooded with this white light. It was amazing. I just felt at peace and euphoric. I went to sleep and had the best night's sleep I've ever had. Swear down."

"Had you been drinking?" Simon grinned.

Steve grinned back. "No, surprisingly. And it wasn't no hallucinatory wotsit either. I really did hear him walk up the stairs. I was just looking around for something to clobber an intruder with. 'Ere, that were quick. Is that our tucker then?" he added as the delivery guy walked in. Simon handed him a tenner.

"So did you ever hear anything again? Thanks – shall I get plates?" Simon took his food.

"Nah." Steve replied to both questions. "That was it. Don't need a plate, mate – waste of good cardboard and polystyrene. Let's have a butcher's at yours then. At least there's mayonnaise on it. Do you want some salt?"

"I'm fine. Thanks. What time does the thing start then?" Simon took the plastic fork provided and attacked his potato.

"Seven p.m., though he probably won't actually start until half-seven. Be down here for seven if you want a seat, though. Three quid on the door and you get a hot dog and chips supper thrown in. Porridge can come for free." Steve lobbed a flaccid piece of kebab at the dog. "Here, you bottomless pit, have a bit of donner meat."

Simon watched Steve share his lamb donner meat *(hold the salad)* with a delighted Porridge. Living in the pub was bad for both his health and the dog's. Giving up on the crossword, he folded his newspaper and tucked his pen in his inside jacket pocket. The movement created a slight chinking noise.

* * *

Gordon Underwood - *International Clairvoyant based in Mythlroyd* - stood resplendent before his audience in a pink shirt, the buttons straining against his belly. Already, after only a few minutes, he was in full flow.

"He was a drinker on this side wasn't he, love? I'm not saying he was an alcoholic or anything, but he loved a drop. He's telling me to tell you to have one for him. What or who is John? John ... James ... John Smith! That's it. He liked a pint of John Smith's. Well, he's telling me to tell you that he misses his John Smith's but he doesn't

264

miss you. Oh no, dear. Don't look upset, he doesn't miss you because he's *with you*. He's by your side right now, Lovey. No, other side. Did you do some washing up this morning? He's telling me to tell you to be careful with that ring. You nearly lost it? Yes, well he was with you. Oh, and he says he likes your new hairdo. You've not had it done? He says you've had it done since he passed and he liked it. I'm sorry, love, he's stepping back now. I've somebody else coming forward. Does the letter M mean anything to anybody in this area of the pub? No, it's definitely over here. M or N …."

Simon sipped his pint at the bar. Gordon rattled off further random details and names, the pub crowd gasping and cooing each time a pellet from his scattergun pronouncements found a willing mark.

The pub was packed, with standing room only. Recently bereaved siblings, sons, fathers, mothers – people who were never previously customers in The Whippet - lined the walls. Great gangs of women in their sixties huddled around the tables, sipping half-pints of lager and lime whilst pontificating loudly about Geoffs, Bernards, Ians and Dereks.

A large group of youngsters in their very early twenties giggled over their drinks, the boys drinking strong lager, the girls nursing vodka and cokes. They rolled their eyes and whispered, the show of cool disbelief belied by their intense concentration each time a new name, letter or number was thrown into the melting pot of post-life

265

data. Their youthful cynicism seemed fragile amongst the deluge of potentially pertinent information. Could it be Gran? Was Granddad watching? Could Gordon have muddled an 'S' with an 'F'? Is there somebody out there, somebody watching over *me*?

Simon drained the last inch of his pint. Too polite to distract attention from the entertainment, and too concerned with causing offence, he was trapped until there was a break in the proceedings. Top Gear reruns were looking increasingly tempting. Gordon Underwood was a fraud.

Despite the delight of the audience, Simon was unmoved. He had come to the event with his mind open and found it now firmly closed. A little research during his lunch break had provided the necessary foundations for an educated overview of the evening. Simon always did his homework. Cold reading, the technique of high observation, analysis of body language and an understanding of probability was most definitely at play here.

"I've got an 'R' here. An 'R' for someone in this side of the room. No, more over here …" Gordon pointed specifically at a group of women in their late sixties. Simon smiled into his pint. Cold Reading 101. The most likely letter to be claimed by women in their sixties was the letter 'R'. Wikipedia was so useful.

"Robert, maybe Rodney?"

"Roger, Brenda! Wasn't your Dad's brother called Roger? The one that was in the army?" And Gordon was off. His breathless repartee bolstered by that useful military titbit.

A couple in a corner of the pub, ruthlessly milked by the fraudulent medium earlier, comforted each other, tears drying on their cheeks. *Brother and sister*, thought Simon. Even to the uninitiated, their body language and desperate searching faces had clearly marked them as grieving from the moment they had entered the pub. Quietly waiting for the act to begin, they whispered together and ordered only soft drinks. Their features were clearly those of siblings, and their tracksuits and myriad tattoos indicated their background.

Gordon did a number on them, reducing the grieving pair to crowd-pleasing tears within minutes. The 'International Medium' (Gordon felt entitled to the title, having once performed a reading for a bemused German couple by a poolside in Torremolinos) quickly identified the object of their grief. He held the entire room in captivated silence as he claimed knowledge of, and transmitted messages from, their deceased father. The crowd could barely hold back applause. When he discovered the man had "passed" from cancer, Gordon earnestly urged the young man of the pair to look after the watch his father had given him, suggesting he should fix what was broken on it, and wear it despite its not being fashionable.

This incredible moment of illumination met with more gasps and some tears throughout the crowd.

Simon viewed the proceedings with distaste. The watch. How many men pass a watch onto their sons? How many men have an old watch languishing in a drawer – the strap broken, the battery long since leeched? Even if the father himself had not passed it on, it was likely a piece of jewelry such as this would find its way into a grieving son's hands. Gordon Underwood was no link to the dead. He was a callous showman. A PT Barnum of grief.

"I've got an 'S' over here. No right here at the bar. No, love, it's not a Sam and it's most definitely over here. You, sir? I'm being told 'S'. It's definitely you."

Simon, facing the bar, had his back to the entertainment. He turned slowly. A hundred expectant faces looked at him rapturously. The slick little man nodded encouragement at Simon.

"It's an 'S', sir. Do you know an S who has passed recently? I'm not sure who I have with me, but they are quite persistent. I can't quite understand what I'm being told. This 'S' must have passed very recently. I'm being shown it flickering, coming in and out of focus … it's quite odd, Sir. You'll have to help me out, Sir. The 'S' seems pink. I get the feeling it's pink. I know this is going to seem a little odd, Sir, but go with it. I'm seeing a castle as well. A pink one. Do try to think - it's definitely for you, Sir."

"It's not me."

The crowd groaned. The man wasn't going to play the game.

"Could it be a Sandra?" an exuberant woman shouted, her cheeks reddened with copious rosé. "Sally?"

"It's not me." Simon spoke firmly. He stood, prodding Porridge with his toe.

"Sarah," the barmaid, unaware of the name of Simon's daughter, shouted excitedly. "Could that be it?"

"It's not Sarah." Simon felt himself color and panic as the lager he had drunk began to rise into his throat. He elbowed fellow drinkers out of the way, a chorus of *'Oooh'*s and *'What's with 'im?'*s accompanying his hurried departure.

He stumbled out onto the street, Porridge trotting by his side, delighted at the unscheduled walk. Simon steadied himself a moment, the nausea dissipating as quickly as it had begun.

He reached for his phone and called the hospice, his heart beating wildly in his chest. "I'm phoning to check on Sarah. Is she okay?"

"Yes, she is sleeping peacefully," he was assured.

"Could you please check?" he insisted.

"Certainly, Dr. Bailey."

Simon could hear the footsteps as whoever had answered his call strode purposefully to Sarah's room. The door opened with a click. There was a moment's silence.

"Yes, she is fast asleep, Dr. Bailey. Your wife too."

Simon breathed a huge sigh of relief. "Thank you, nurse. Thank you very much for checking for me."

"You are most welcome."

* * *

The evening was mild and it was not quite dusk. Simon and Porridge headed away from the pub and the village and walked towards the lights of the town below them.

At length Simon came to the limestone bridge that crossed the murky waters of the industrial river Calder. The flow beneath bubbled ominously, polluted foam formed on the banks. Simon perched on the edge of the wide stone bridge and let his legs dangle over the waterway. Porridge lay beside him, watching.

Chapter 28

There is a bridge in France, in the centre of a small but busy town, which spans the River Dronne. The water of the river is so clear even the least nimble eyed can watch the abundant spotted trout that nibble the weeds beneath. The tributary flows from the mountains of the *Massif Central*, its crystal clear gurgle meandering for miles before tranquilly passing under this ancient stone crossing.

It was sitting on this bridge, side by side with Simon, that Melissa, tanned, happy and brimful with youth and optimism, had told Simon that she was pregnant.

"I've got something to tell you." Melissa stretched a leg, appreciating the way her recent tan looked against the sparkling water beneath.

"You bought those boots." Simon grinned. "I know. I saw them in the wardrobe before we left home."

"No. Well, yes. I did buy them, but I think you're going to forgive me." Melissa rested her head on her husbands shoulder. "It's more important than that."

Simon put his arm around Melissa. "I didn't mind about the boots anyway, silly. We're not poor students anymore." Simon let go of Melissa and stretched luxuriantly. "I'm not sure I want to know what it is, actually. Is it, for instance, going to make me any more happy than I am right now?"

"Infinitely."

"Not possible. Right now, I'm the happiest man alive. I'm in France, I'm with a simply gorgeous woman, and I'm watching the fattest fish I've ever seen swim underneath me. I'm satiated."

"No, you're not." Melissa turned to Simon and placed her hand gently on his chin so that she guided his gaze to hers. "What would complete your life?"

Simon glanced down, watching a small trout nudge the banks of the stream. He looked back at his wife. "No – you're not...? Melissa?"

Melissa smiled. "I think you'd better get used to being called 'Daddy'."

"But how? I thought – Oh, my God, Melissa, this is wonderful! It's happened? How long? How far?" Simon placed his hand on his wife's stomach. "It's actually, finally, happened?"

Melissa put her hand over Simon's. "It's happened. There's a little Bailey in me. No medical interference necessary. Are you happy?"

"Happy?" Simon shook his head. "Melissa, there's no man on this earth who is happier than I am right now." Simon swung his legs back over the bridge wall so that he was facing the road. "I got through med school, and frankly there were times I didn't think I would. I've got a beautiful, funny, clever wife, I have an outrageously badly behaved puppy whom I love despite the fact he chewed my stethoscope to bits, and now I'm going to have a little baby girl."

"Girl! It might be a boy."

Simon grinned. "It might. But I think it's a little girl."

"What if it's a boy?" Melissa leaned against Simon. "What if we have a little Simon?"

Simon pulled Melissa closer to him, breathing in the scent of her shampoo. "Clearly a miniature Simon can only be a good thing. But I think it's a little girl."

"Why do you want a girl so much, Sime? I'd love a girl too, but I don't care if it's a boy. You've always wanted a girl. Why? Aren't men supposed to want a boy to play football with and teach pint drinking to?"

Simon chuckled. "If it's a boy and he likes football, we'll have to put him up for adoption."

Melissa whacked him playfully. "He might be gay."

"It's a she. It's a little girl." Simon pressed his hand ever so gently against Melissa's stomach. "She's a she."

"You didn't answer my question. Why so keen on a girl?"

Simon paused for a moment. "I'd be pleased with a boy. All I care about is that they're healthy, but, I dunno, I've always wanted a little girl, a little girl to teach to ride a bike. A pink bike with tassels on the handlebars. A little girl to protect - which reminds me – you

273

do realize that if it's a girl she's not allowed out with boys until she's at least thirty, don't you?"

Melissa snorted. "Poor thing. I almost hope it's a boy. Though, I'd like a little girl, too. Better clothes. And we can go shopping when she's older."

"Melissa, you'd still be shopping if you gave birth to a ferret."

"You have a point." Melissa grinned. "We'd better get a baby name book, then." She held onto Simon as she clambered back over the bridge wall to face the road. "Or are we already decided?"

"We decided ages ago, didn't we? You do realize this means you can't drink anymore? Well, the occasional glass of wine is fine. You'll be on driving duty for nine months. Excellent. We'll have to decorate the back bedroom. Do you think your mum will let us have that little antique rocking horse? You'd better stop going to the gym – though swimming is good, yes, keep swimming. How long have you known? Oh, shit, Melissa, this is amazing. We're going to be parents. I'm going to be a daddy. I'm a daddy. Wow."

Melissa laughed. "Slow down. I'm only a little bit pregnant. A few weeks. I've been feeling a bit sick. I got a test when I was in that pharmacy yesterday. I had a hell of a time explaining what I wanted. She would insist on trying to give me a pessary for thrush. I only did the test this morning, and I was waiting for the perfect moment. Do you know, it really is very difficult piddling on that little stick? I wasn't sure I'd managed it. Anyway - didn't you hear me? What about names …? Stop it Simon, I'm not an invalid!"

Simon half lifted Melissa off the wall. "Let's go get a big supper for my soon to be very big girl and my littler girl. We know the names, don't we? I thought we were decided. It's not like we haven't talked about it enough times."

Melissa and Simon hooked arms and leaned against each other. They began to walk leisurely back towards the town square and the bistros that circled it.

"Ben for a boy, Sarah for a girl." Melissa slipped a hand into Simon's back trouser pocket. "Does this mean I can't have mussels? I thought we'd go to that one on the corner with the shellfish …"

Simon stopped and turned his wife towards him, dropping a lingering kiss on her forehead. "We'll pretend you're not pregnant tonight. Champagne and mussels, to celebrate the conception of Sarah. Or Ben. Or Ben …" Simon added hurriedly as Melissa began to interrupt. "But I'm telling you it's a girl. My two girls – Melissa and Sarah."

* * *

Simon stared into the freezing, quickly flowing water of the Calder. The low evening sun caught an oil slick on the polluted water, the iridescence beautiful yet sordid.

"Don't do it!" A group of young men walked by laughing. "Don't jump!" They guffawed, patting each other on the back as they continued past, congratulating themselves on their wit.

Jumping was neither an appealing nor practical option. The bridge was low, the water shallow and Simon had no intention of getting wet. No, jumping off this bridge would be merely embarrassing. The wall served only as a place to sit and think.

Jumping off the Harpenden Viaduct, now there was an unequivocally fatal leap. The Victorian stone supports plunged seventy-eight feet to the valley below. The disused railway was now grassed over, visited only by the occasional dog walker. Porridge and Simon had crossed it a number of times. Once, with Sarah, they had taken a picnic.

Would one just step off, wondered Simon, or attempt more of a dive? How long would it take, he wondered? How many seconds of flailing in the air before the final crunch? Too long. Plenty of time to think. Plenty of time to change his mind. The sensation of falling was not one Simon wished as his last.

Porridge nudged him with his nose.

"You bored, Podge?" Simon glanced down at his dog and swung his legs back over the wall, his feet once again on *terra firma*. "I suppose we'd better make a move."

Simon and Porridge turned to walk back towards the village. Simon stopped. "Change of plan – come on boy."

Turning, Simon clipped Porridge's lead on and walked up the hill, in the opposite direction of home, towards St Matthews.

He needed a quiet place to think.

Chapter 29

Simon sat in a pew at the back of the empty church. Porridge settled himself in the aisle with a sigh. Simon took out his mobile and laid it on the oaken pew beside him. Being contactable was a high priority now.

Simon pitied Melissa, even felt a little love for her, but knew that he would never be able to once again embrace her as his wife. Perhaps it had been this way for a long time, Simon thought sadly. More recently he had loved Melissa only as Sarah's mother, not as his wife.

He wondered if he and Melissa would have had more in common if they had been less affluent. Their comfortable situation had allowed them both to have separate hobbies and independence from each other. They had drifted apart, love often only declared in material tokens, gestures they had thought meaningful at the time, but perhaps were not. The one thing they had in common was Sarah. And soon Sarah would be gone.

Melissa had apologized - she had even asked him to come home - but they both knew there was no point. No Sarah, no Team Bailey.

He had frozen her out, Melissa said. Pushed her away at the very moment she needed him close.

She was probably right, Simon realized. All the time he spent avoiding the issue, promising himself that *everything would be*

278

alright, he had been harboring a secret rage of his own. His wife had engendered a latent hatred in him that he had not known how to express, confused and terrified by his feelings as he had been. It was if he blamed Melissa, a sentiment he knew to be ridiculous. He couldn't help it. It was as if he had subconsciously thought her not mother *enough*. That if she had not been the bitch that whelped Sarah, then Sarah might not have been faulty.

It was cruel and it was medically unfounded, but that was how it was.

He hoped that Melissa would manage to make something of her life, recover from what was so clearly destroying her, as it was destroying him. But he knew that he would not be a part of that future, not when every sight of her made him feel faintly disgusted.

Even his parents felt less important now. "Life must go on, lad," his father had said on the telephone the day before. *Life must go on.* Simon had only just managed to quell his fury. The distaste he felt for his wife, he found, had also tarnished his relationship with his parents. Their worry for him, their hand-wringing parental concern, was smothering and unwanted. Simon had barely the emotional energy to get through his day, let alone the ability to articulate his despair to his parents. It was wearing having to worry about *their* worry. It was deeply selfish, he knew, but he could not help it.

Life must go on. *Must It?* thought Simon. There seemed so little left.

"I know that Labrador …" A familiar voice sounded from behind him. "That you, Simon? Or has somebody stolen Porridge?"

"Duncan – I'm sorry, were you wanting to lock up? I was just, having a think. You know. It was quiet."

"Of course. I'm delighted you're here. I had been meaning to speak to you, as it happens." Duncan, the genial vicar slid into the pew beside Simon. "You don't mind do you? I can leave you alone if you'd prefer."

"No, it's fine." Simon forced a small smile, though really he would have appreciated his previous solitude.

"I wondered how you were getting on. How is Sarah?"

Simon gave a little sigh. "Close to the end."

Duncan nodded. "I see. How are you bearing up? I haven't seen you for sometime."

"I'm alright, I suppose. How is one supposed to be? I'm going through the motions. I'm still making myself have a shave. I suppose that's something." Simon gave another tight smile. Describing grief was exhausting.

"You know, Simon, it is an unhappy part of my job that I have dealings with a lot of people who are grieving. I know it's difficult to talk about. Tiresome, actually. When my own mother died I grew quite sick of reassuring people that I was okay. I most certainly wasn't, but one felt one had a duty to put their minds at rest. Quite ridiculous."

Simon looked at his friend. His interest peaked only slightly in his lethargy. "I'm sorry. I didn't realize that your mother had died. Yes, it is rather repetitive. Though I realize that people mean well."

Duncan chuckled. "Oh, I'm not sure that they do."

Simon raised an eyebrow in surprise.

"Don't get me wrong. They *think* they do. And they most certainly don't mean any harm. No, what I find is they're normally reassuring themselves that there is nothing they can do. Grief is distressing; people seem worried it might be catching. They ask if you are alright, when of course the answer is that you are not. You say yes anyway, as they know you will, and then they feel absolved of duty. Don't blame them. You've probably done the same thing yourself."

"Did you feel angry when your mother died?" Simon watched a last ray of the evening sun as it shone through a stained glass window, creating a dapple on the stone aisle ahead. "I feel so damned angry at the moment. With everyone. Everything. Did you get over it?"

"I certainly did feel angry, though mostly with myself. Yes. I did get over it. Though it took me most of forty years. I was only sixteen when she died. It was my fault, actually. Hello, Porridge. Have you come for a stroke?"

"Your fault? I'm sure it wasn't." Simon trotted out the platitude almost without thought.

281

"Oh, it was. I had been smoking in the sitting room after a party. I didn't put the butt out properly. My father, brother and I escaped. Mother did not."

Simon's jaw dropped. "God. I mean – I'm so sorry. How awful. How bloody awful." He looked away awkwardly.

The two men sat in companionable silence. Some time passed until Simon spoke. "Do you believe in Heaven, Duncan?"

"I do."

"Fluffy clouds and pearly gates?"

"No. I very much doubt it. But I'm sure that our souls go on and that somewhere we meet our maker."

"What about our loved ones? Those who have died before us?"

"Yes, I think we see them again. Perhaps not in this physical form, but I think our souls meet again."

Simon bit his cheek in his habitual tic. "So what about hell? If heaven exists, is there a hell?"

Duncan frowned. "I certainly don't think children go to hell."

"That's not what I asked." Simon said.

"Okay." Duncan paused. "My church, strictly speaking, believes in hell as a physical place. I can't believe that. I don't think there is a flaming place below, if that is what you are asking. I suspect that those who led a truly wicked life have greatly troubled souls and that those souls suffer for their wickedness in an afterlife. More than that,

I don't know. And trust me, Simon," the kindly priest put a hand on Simon's shoulder, "I've given it a lot of thought."

Simon took a deep breath and exhaled slowly. "What about suicides? Do people who commit suicide go to heaven, Duncan? Or do they go to hell?"

Duncan took his hand off Simon's shoulder and turned to look at the younger man. Simon steadily returned his gaze.

"I think, Simon, that it might depend on the case. Generally though, suicide is considered a rather selfish act."

"Jesus committed suicide, did he not?"

Duncan looked up at the great stained glass window that stood over the altar of the church. It depicted Jesus turning water into wine at the wedding in Cana. "Jesus' death was an act of martyrdom, not suicide."

"What's the difference?"

Duncan spoke slowly. "Well, a suicide is normally an act of desperation. It's a selfish act, one in which the person is running away from something. A martyrdom is when a person allows their life to be taken for the greater good of others. One is selfish, one is selfless."

"What if you wish to die *for* somebody else? What if you have made a promise?" Simon tipped his head back, looking unseeingly at the ceiling arched high above. "Then surely you would go to heaven."

"Would that death cause more joy in the world, or more pain? What about those left behind? In the event that others are hurt, then no, Simon. I'm not sure that the death would warrant a place in heaven." Duncan bent down and stroked the Labrador that lay at his feet again. His voice was soft when he spoke again. "Should I be worried about you, Simon?"

Simon shook his head. "Don't worry about me." He stood up. "I'm just in a peculiar mood. Thanks for talking to me, Duncan. I appreciate it. Come on, Porridge, it's getting late and we're walking back."

Duncan stood as well, walking into the aisle and patting Porridge as Simon passed. "It never goes away, Simon. I'm not going to pretend that it does. But it becomes easier to cope. Day by day. You don't forget, but you do learn to get on with your life. I know it doesn't seem that way at the moment but…"

"I know. Life goes on."

* * *

Duncan stood in the doorway of the church and watched his troubled parishioner wander up the road, his shoulders hunched, his head down.

He wished that he could call Melissa, but he knew that he mustn't. Simon had chosen to speak to him, to ask him questions grounded in faith. Duncan had to respect his privacy.

Grief was a terrible thing, he mused. He turned back into the church, locking the heavy doors behind him. He had been intending to go straight home, to the shepherd's pie and wifely warmth that awaited him across the road, but he decided to make a prayer first. A prayer that God would guide Simon, protect him from himself and grant him the power to see how needed he was on earth.

He'd call in on Simon the next day. Try to talk more with him. Remind him of the pain he'd cause his parents if he ended his life. Remind him that the last thing Sarah would want would be for her father to die. He had dealt with the suicidal before – sometimes successfully, twice sadly not.

No matter what, Duncan thought sadly, ultimately, it was Simon's choice.

Chapter 30

STAY FOR   GO FOR

~~Melissa~~   Sarah

Mum and Dad   ~~Me?~~

Porridge

It was noon the day after Simon visited St Matthews. He was trying once again to finish an unpalatable Sainsbury's egg sandwich before his afternoon flurry of patients began. His Stay For/Go For list lay before him. He had added 'Me?' to the 'Go For' side, but had since crossed it out.

What *did* he want? He wanted his daughter to be happy. If not here with him, at least to be happy *somewhere*. He stared at the list. That Sarah would simply cease to be was not a possibility he could face. It was too final, too blunt. Therefore, he had to believe that she would go on to another place. The only theological option he knew of was heaven.

If he killed himself (and he noted his dampened emotions seemed unmoved by the idea of leaving the world) would he, too, go to heaven? Would he know Sarah in the afterlife?

That suicide barred one entry to heaven was a common theory, but not necessarily an accurate one. Simon had led a previously good life. He had been kind, generous - unafraid to stand up for those weaker than himself. That he should gain entry to heaven in normal circumstances seemed, to him, reasonably assured.

But if he died at his own hand? He looked at his list and thought of those he would leave behind. He would cause a great deal of pain. His parents, already grieving for their granddaughter – well, it would kill them. And Melissa? Melissa who was about to lose her daughter, her only child, a baby born after years of hope when it seemed conception would not happen.

He looked once again at the collection of photos on the wall of his office. Sarah beamed a gappy-toothed grin down on him – it was a school photo. He remembered that morning. She'd just lost that tooth before school.

Another frame held a wedding picture. The picture was taken inside the reception venue. The original plan had been to take photos outside the church, but that had been abandoned due to horrific weather. Simon smiled, admiring his bride. Melissa had looked wonderful as she had walked down the aisle, yet more wonderful still when she pulled on wellies in the church-porch to walk back to the hired car.

He thought of the Hindu bride he had seen on the steps of the Temple. It seemed impossible to believe that any tragedy could

287

befall them. It had seemed impossible on that rainy day eighteen years ago to believe any misfortune would blight *their* lives. But here they were. Separated, barely talking and with a child who would shortly die.

Beside him, his phone vibrated, dancing across the desk. He picked it up, his voice gruff. "Hello?"

"Dr. Bailey? It's Fiona at Madron House. You should come now. Sarah's slipping away."

Chapter 31

Robert, Melissa's father, put down the Harry Potter novel he had been reading to his granddaughter. The heavy tome was the final installment of the series and Sarah's visitors had been taking it in turns to read it to her.

Sarah's eyes had closed and she was sleeping, one corner of her mouth twitched up into a half smile.

Melissa slept also, her chair pulled up to the bed, her head resting by Sarah's. She held her little girl's hand in her own.

Robert closed his eyes. They had come to the end of the book.

* * *

In his office, Simon put down the phone and stared at it for a few seconds. Then he put the lid on his pen and put it back in the pot on his desk. He straightened his papers and locked his prescription pad in the drawer. He stood and drifted towards his coat stand and took his jacket, as he had done so many times before. The vials of insulin in his breast pocket jingled cheerfully against each other.

His mind had gone blank. He felt numb. Weightless. He felt himself smile in the direction of the receptionist, who watched him walk calmly out of the surgery.

It was on a sub-level of consciousness that he started the Jaguar's engine and headed out of the surgery car park, towards Madron House for the final time. The chirpy women on the radio's traffic update blended unheeded into the usual cacophony of car journey sounds.

"Looks like we've got a gas leak on High Street guys, which has been shut down for the repairs, so watch out for heavy traffic on all routes out of town."

But Simon didn't hear anything at all. As he nosed the car through the traffic towards the hospice, he was hardly aware of the act of driving. In his mind he sat on the rug of their sitting room floor, building a Lego house with Sarah, amiably arguing about who should use the last red block.

* * *

Beside his daughter and his granddaughter, inside the sleeping Robert, sixty-eight years of enjoyable cheeses, cream, and Fruit and Nut bars were doing their work. Arteriosclerosis, a final layer of built up plaque, settled in his left artery, narrowing and hardened, the remaining elasticity of the tubular muscle ceasing. Blood gushed to the damaged tunnel, slowing considerably as it forced its way through the ever-tightening gap.

* * *

All around Simon traffic honked and blared, the gridlock inescapable as 30,000 office workers attempted to escape the drudgery of the week and head back home to light barbeques before the good weather disappeared again.

The temporary lights tripped back to red, letting only three cars through. The roar of angry commuters was audible on the street through open car windows, as the temporary lighting system let only three cars through. Snatches of different radio stations competed in the air, and drivers tapped impatiently on their car roofs, their shirts sticking to their backs, dark patches appearing beneath their arms.

Sitting at the head of the queue, untroubled by the rage around him, Simon smiled. In his mind, he helped Sarah arrange plastic trees around the Lego house.

* * *

Robert's breathing slowed. The Harry Potter book slipped to his side. A nurse put her head around the door and smiled at the peaceful scene. Grandfather slept soundly in the armchair. Mum slept with her head resting on the bed. In the centre, Sarah lay quietly.

Inside Robert, somewhere around his ankle, a random platelet activated, adhering to the wall of a blood vessel before being joined by another sticky little platelet. They formed a tiny white clot, which began travelling with the blood stream, slowly making its way up through his tweed trouser-clad leg.

* * *

Pulling up into Madron House car park, Simon stopped and let his head fall back against the headrest. He closed his eyes briefly and sank back into his mind. He watched Sarah put a Lego man into the house. She smiled up at him, love and trust twinkling in her eyes.

Simon opened his eyes and turned off the engine. He got out of the car and strode towards the hospice entrance, past the fountain with its engraved pebbles. In Reception, he walked straight past the desk. "I'm here to see Sarah."

The nurse leapt up, following him along the corridor. "Dr. Bailey, your wife and father-in-law are with Sarah. We don't believe she has much longer. We rang the moment her vital signs began dropping. We're making her as comfortable as we can. Can I get you a cup of tea?" She trailed off as she noticed his expression.

Simon looked up at her, smiling. Her words barely rippled the pool of tranquility that formed a seal over his emotions.

The nurse waited, braced for abuse, anguish or questions but none were forthcoming. "Right, well – I'll take you down there."

They padded down the thickly carpeted hallway, arriving at Sarah's doorway in silence. The nurse smiled quickly at Simon, then opened the heavy door and led the way into the room.

Simon glanced at the two sleeping adults and walked over to the book, which now lay on the floor, next to Sarah's sleeping grandfather. He picked it up.

"They finished it."

"I'm sorry?" The nurse unhooked a bag from the stand.

"Nothing."

"Should I?" The nurse gestured towards Robert.

"No, don't wake him."

Melissa stirred and looked up at Simon, bleary eyed. "Hey you."

"Hey you."

They exchanged a sad smile.

The nurse interrupted. "I'll be at reception if you want anything. Just buzz."

Melissa and Simon both nodded as the nurse left.

Simon gestured towards Robert. "Your dad managed to finish it then."

Melissa looked at her father. "He's been reading non-stop for three hours. He was determined to get to the end of the book."

"What happened?"

"Harry Potter wins. He grows up, gets married."

"Oh. Sarah will like that."

A tear trickled down Melissa's face. "Yes. She will."

"Where's your mum, Mel?"

"She's on her way. She was shopping. We didn't … Where's your mum and dad?"

Simon lifted one shoulder in a shrug. "I haven't rung them yet. There doesn't seem much point – I mean, I'd like it just to be us. You know."

"Yeah. I know. My dad's…"

"He's asleep. Leave him." Simon looked at Sarah, sleeping peacefully as he had seen her sleep a thousand times before.

There was something slightly different now. Her features had arranged themselves into a mask of serenity. It was hard, looking at the little girl, to imagine she was feeling anything but quiet happiness and calm. Had Sarah been lying in her own whitewashed wooden bed with the hearts cut out of the headboard, it might have seemed as if she was sleeping after a long and exhausting day at the park.

He put his hand into his jacket pocket and closed his fingers around the four glass vials. Life saving, life ending. Simon knew what he must do.

For Simon realized that if wanted to see his daughter again, he would need to ensure his place in heaven. Hurting those who remained behind was not something that God – or Sarah - would want. He would see her again, one day. But for now he would have to wait.

The choice he thought he had had never really existed. To be a good man was the only option. A good man would never hurt those who loved him.

Simon moved to the corner of the room, lifted the one-way shutter lid of a sharps bin and let the ampoules fall from his hand into the irretrievable confines of the receptacle. He nodded to himself.

Returning to the bed, he gently moved the tube feeding morphine into the girl's hand. Tenderly moving the drip over Sarah's arm, he kicked off his shoes. Being careful not to wake or hurt her, he climbed onto the bed and wrapped himself around his sleeping daughter, his head cradled in his upper arm, his lips just grazing her ear.

Melissa held one of Sarah's hands in her own. With her other, she took Simon's.

* * *

In Robert, the tiny white mass was arriving at its destination. Like a piece of driftwood in a rain-engorged beck it stubbornly slammed against the entrance of the tunnel as it tried to pass through with the torrent. Unable to proceed, it blocked the passageway.

* * *

Simon squeezed Melissa's hand. He could feel Sarah breathing - so very shallow - and his own breath sounded thunderous in comparison.

Lying there on the bed, with his child and his wife, he felt three years of anguish and anger slip away. His mind began to clear. The respite after months of furious thought and stress, was exquisite. As he drifted, balancing on a precipice between sleep and lucidity, he began to dream.

* * *

Robert stood before Simon. His exact position seemed unclear. The normal rules of perspective were blurred, though it seemed as though he were slightly above Simon.

Sarah's grandfather, so familiar, so definitely him, was different. He was younger than Simon had ever known him. He wore old-fashioned tennis clothes, carried his racket in a much younger hand. At his feet, an enormous black and white cat wound between his tanned and youthful legs.

"Sarah!" Robert smiled towards Simon. His voice sounded younger too, the slight husk of age no longer there. "Come on darling! You're to come with me now. Don't dawdle. Winston wants to meet you, don't you puss? You're quite safe, pet. That's a good girl. Come along now. There's lots of people who can't wait to say hello. That's it, lovey." Robert's hand stretched out in encouragement, not quite at Simon, but in the direction in which he felt himself to be.

The waking dream faded to the purist white - a white that seemed to bathe him in a bright, soothing light. His own breathing slowed and Simon, exhausted, fell into a deep sleep beside his wife and child.

In his arms, Sarah was still.

~The End~

A Note from the author…

Thankfully, Simon and Melissa's story is not mine and is entirely fictional. However, there are many parents who are living this nightmare.

Whilst Madron House is also a product of my imagination, the similar children's hospices around the country do amazing work looking after children in their last days and caring for the needs of their distraught parents.

It costs between 2.5 and 6 million pounds per annum to run a hospice. Most of this money has to be found from charity.

If you have been at all moved by this tale, perhaps you would take a moment to call a hospice and make a small donation. It doesn't have to be much. Just £2 would buy a can of squirty cream for a Kayleigh. It would buy a goldfish for a Sarah. It would buy a cup of tea for a Melissa and it would buy a moment of kindness and counselling for a Simon.

C x

Child Hospices UK: (44) 0117 989 7820

Forget Me Not Hospice, West Yorkshire: (44) 01474 487570

St Martin's House, West Yorkshire: (44) 01937 844569

In the USA: http://www.hospicefoundation.org/

In Canada: http://www.hospicedirectory.org/

Made in the USA
Charleston, SC
03 June 2013